SHIFTING MAGIC

SHIFTER & MAGES, SCI-FI FANTASY, AND PARANORMAL ROMANCE

MULTIPLE AUTHORS

ACKNOWLEDGMENTS

The Shifting Magic authors came together to cross-pollinate paranormal, science fiction, and fantasy romance genres to allow our readers a new experience in supernatural other worlds. We worked tirelessly to offer creative, unique, and original works of fiction. Each author submitted their story print-ready; we trust you'll enjoy our efforts.

Please consider posting a review for Shifting Magic if you enjoyed the stories. Word-of-mouth referrals are great ways to spread the word to your family and friends and the best way for us to develop new readers. You will find information about the author at the end of each short story. We trust you will take the opportunity to register for their newsletters and follow them on social media. Thank you from the bottom of our hearts for purchasing our limited collection of works.

SHORT STORIES

Please note the steam level by one to five asterisks, one being clean/sweet and five being erotica

*** **Soul Love** by D.F. Jones, USA Today bestselling author

** **The Talent Test** by Ana Morgan

*** **He's a Rogue and My Mate** by ID Johnson

*** **Devil's Magic** by Tia Didmon, USA Today bestselling author

**** **Killian's Quest** by Maggie Adams

*** **A Twist of Magical Fate** by Brenda Trim, USA Today bestselling author

******Wild** by Margo Bond Collins, New York Times, USA Today, bestselling author

*****Dragon Awakened** by Maria Vickers

D. F. JONES

USA TODAY BESTSELLING AUTHOR

SOUL LOVE

TIME TRAVEL ROMANCE

BLURB

From USA Today bestselling author D.F. Jones comes a new time travel romance, Soul Love.

Destiny unfolds past lives with driving passion that erupts turbulent emotions.

Summer Jewel accepts a dinner invitation from a new neighbor. One thing leads to another when she inexplicably finds herself back in time and discovers the truth about her former life.

Rogan Randolph is an agent for The Order of the Invisible Effect, monitoring time and making minor adjustments in the lives of ordinary citizens of earth when one portal opens to his past, giving him a chance to right a wrong with a woman he meets from the future.

Solving past life issues results in changing time events that may create rippling effects.

CHAPTER 1

Summer Jewel left her briefcase on the bench in the mudroom and called out, "Aunt Em, are you home?"

She didn't hear a response.

Hm. I bet she's with Bob playing bingo again at the Heartsville Community Center. Good for her.

Summer entered the kitchen, opened the fridge, and poured herself a large glass of milk. She hopped on the barstool and took a chocolate chip cookie from the Cookie Monster jar.

That was when she noticed a note.

Darling, I'll be late getting in. I left you a plate of dinner in the microwave. Don't wait up. Love, Aunt Emily.

The change in Aunt Em after falling in love made Summer hopeful that maybe someday she would find love too.

She'd gone through most of her college years without a date, never fitting in with the popular cliques. After graduation, she had inherited her parents' estate, including their house, bookstore, and sizable bank account. She would've given it all back to have them in her life.

Twenty years ago, her mom and dad had chartered a plane for a romantic weekend getaway that turned disastrous. Neither the aircraft, Blackbox, nor her parents' bodies were ever recovered. At seven, she had been too young at the time to remember much about it.

Aunt Emily, her father's sister, had raised her.

A vehicle backfired outside, followed by the shrieking of grinding gears.

Summer hurried into the entertainment room and peeked through the three-inch wood blinds. A moving van had parked in front of the house across the street. Even before her parents' accident, the place had sat empty for years.

She loved the old Victorian with its steep varied, red-shingled rooflines, towers, and turrets. She adored the stained-glass windows and its gingerbread trim work.

But like her, the house didn't seem to fit in with the rest of the upscale neighborhood. Most were modern-day farmhouses varying only in the exterior paint colors.

The renovation was complete. Whoever the owners were, they kept the charming home's character, and it backed up to the wildlife preserve. Once, it had been a part of the farm sold to developers long ago.

Craning her neck, she couldn't tell if the newcomers were a family or not. She decided on snooping and went out the side door.

One moving truck. Three men. One seemed to be in charge.

Oh crap, he caught me staring. He's coming over.

Summer stopped at the mailbox and quickly tore open a piece of junk mail. Her fingers trembled as she waved. "Moving in?" Could she sound any lamer?

He threw up his hand. "Hi, I'm Erik, the designer. I have a question." He didn't wait for her reply. "Have you ever met the owners?"

"Um. No. Why? Haven't you?" How odd. It sent up a red flag.

"I hoped you might know them. We worked through an attorney who never disclosed names." He shrugged. "No harm in asking."

"I love the house. Any chance I could peek inside?" Sure, it was forward of her, but it might be the only chance to satisfy her curiosity.

Erik nodded. "I'm about to wrap the project. This is our last load of furniture. I love showing off my work." He reached into his back pocket and pulled out a business card. "I'm posting the project online if you wouldn't mind commenting on social media?" His hands went into prayer mode.

"Sure thing." Summer hated social media but took his card anyway.

She followed him up the white-painted plank steps, through the open door, and inside the foyer. Then something peculiar happened. The hair on her neck and arms rose. It felt like someone or something was waiting for her. Trying to shake off the unsettling feeling, she turned in a slow circle and said, "It's beautiful."

An elaborate crystal chandelier hung in the entry—the rich mahogany staircase set against blue-green textured walls. A baby grand piano was positioned in the living room corner to the left of a rock fireplace.

The art over the mantel looked like a Renoir. She wondered if it was an original or a reproduction. She adored the Impressionist period.

"I chose a warm beige as the throughout color," Eric said. "And updated the lighting fixtures and completely renovated the main kitchen. Three stories with the attic and a downstairs complete with a cookery and staff rooms." One of the movers dropped the end of a very expensive-looking bureau. Erik shouted, "Do not scratch the floors or furniture. It costs more than your company makes in a year." He glanced at Summer. "Feel free to look around. I must keep on track."

Yippee—exploring without supervision. She strolled through the library, next to an open-ended entertainment room leading to the kitchen—super sleek, stainless-steel appliances and a walk-in pantry bigger than her bedroom. Next to the pantry was a set of narrow steps. She glanced over her shoulder. Erik was too busy chastising the movers to notice her.

She'd read too many novels about treasures in the attic not to check it out first. She went up three flights of stairs that opened into a renovated space. She fantasized about writing a novel in the room. The walls, the woodwork, and the cozy sofa were white with gray and black accents—and she loved the black lacquer desk.

The cameo windows were installed horizontally, and the view looked directly at her house. She often kept her bedroom blinds open to allow natural lighting inside but made a mental note to close them at night.

She noticed a door on the other side of the room. Suddenly, bright rays of light shot out from the cracks in the wood. What the heck? She approached slowly and reached for the knob.

"There you are," Erik said. "Hon, this room is off-limits. Sorry."

Ugh, I hate when someone calls me hon. "What's behind the door?" She turned, and the white light had disappeared.

"That's none of your beeswax." He shooed her down the stairs. "Ask the owner if you ever meet him."

Him.

"Thanks for letting me look around, and I'm sorry if I wasn't supposed to go to the attic."

"I'm sorry, too, but I had instructions to leave the door alone. Take care."

He ushered Summer out through the front entrance.

She had an overwhelming sixth sense that the mysterious door called to her. Her heart pounded. Her mind filled with possible scenarios of what it led to, but the most logical was probably a balcony that looked over the forest.

Minutes turned into an hour, and the moving company left, followed by Erik.

Summer waited another thirty minutes before venturing back over. She glanced up at the attic window and thought she saw a figure. She rubbed her eyes and looked again. No one was there.

It would be dark soon, so she silenced her phone and tucked it into her pant pocket. She opened her new neighbor's side gate and followed the curving sidewalk into the manicured yard. It had tons of wildflowers belonging more to the English countryside than to the rolling hills of Tennessee.

She tiptoed to the house, cupped her hands, and peered through the French doors.

"Hey, what are you doing?" a deep baritone voice asked.

Summer jumped a foot in the air. *Busted.* "You scared me."

A handsome man leaned against a fence post leading to the wildlife preserve on the yard's edge. She felt a sudden urge to run her fingers through his thick, dark brown hair. He had a perfect jawline, and he must bleach his teeth. His smile nearly blinded her.

She raised one hand. "Um, I'm Summer. I live across the street, and I'm being nosy."

"I see that."

"I apologize. Your designer allowed me to look around earlier. I love your attic." Summer glanced up. The balcony theory failed. She hesitated to ask about the mysterious door seemingly leading to nowhere.

One minute he leaned against the fence, and the next, he stood in front of her. "How did you move so quickly?"

"You're a curious creature." He glanced at her mouth, and she got a funny feeling she knew him.

"Your eyes are gorgeous," she blurted. "Sorry, I have no filter."

He laughed. Oh, what a great big belly laugh. "I'm Rogan Randolph. This is my house."

"Well, it's *Better Homes and Gardens* good."

"You live in the house across the street?" He stared at her, and her knees weakened.

"Uh-huh." Suddenly tongue-tied, she crossed her arms over her chest.

"I must say adieu for the evening, but I look forward to seeing you soon." Rogan bowed.

Summer tilted her head to the side, caught his sandalwood scent, and nearly swooned. "So, you're trying to get rid of me?"

He took her by the elbow, ushered her through the gate, then said, "Good evening."

Summer stood in her yard and looked up at the attic once more.

The hair on her arms rose again. Someone was definitely watching her.

Was it Rogan?

CHAPTER 2

Rogan felt an instant spark with Summer. He caught her scent of sun-ripened raspberries. *Delicious*. Her auburn hair flowed in the warm breeze, and he was a sucker for freckles. He wanted to trace his fingers over her pale peachy skin. Her amber eyes had mesmerized him.

Stop it.

He needed to stay at arm's length. He worked for The Order of the Invisible Effect on a direct mission assigned by The Superintendent. He couldn't get tangled up with the beauty across the street. No matter how badly he wanted to.

He scaled the stairs to the attic, walked across the room, opened the portal door, and stepped into The Superintendent's office.

"He doesn't have you on his schedule, Rogan. May I help you?" Avery asked. The android possessed quantum physics that could run more outcomes on any scenario than the fastest computer software available on earth.

"I need additional information on the woman across the street."

Within seconds, Avery replied, "Ahh, Summer Jewel. The portal has chosen her."

"Why her? And, why me?"

"Why does the portal call any of us?" Avery replied.

"How should I handle our interactions? Do I allow her access now or later?" He leaned against the edge of her crystalized desk.

"We'd rather Summer find the portal without your intervention. We'll entertain a new strategy if that doesn't work. Remember, we have no control over outcomes. We're only here to prevent a paradox." Avery moved around her desk and took his hand. "Satisfy her curiosity, not your own."

"Perhaps, I'll invite her over for dinner and a bottle of wine. Allow her curiosity to open the door." He exhaled. "Earthlings have no idea how lucky they are to be utterly oblivious to the mind-bending reality they live in a supervised bubble."

"I agree." Avery frowned. "The Order of the Invisible Effect keeps the world chaos to a minimum through agents like you."

"Thanks. What does Summer like to eat?"

Avery brought up hologram images, scanning thousands of recipes. "Lasagna with meat sauce, Caesar salad, buttered toast, and chocolate cake." Avery shook her head. "Maybe use vegetables instead of meat. You're not used to eating animal products."

"Any particular restaurant?" He shrugged. "I don't want to cook, but I can fake it."

Avery spat out a card with contact information for Germano's Italian Cuisine. "They deliver."

"You're a lifesaver." Rogan kissed Avery on the cheek, and she blushed. He exited through the portal door and returned to the attic.

He strolled through each room, inspecting the furniture and decor. Erik had done excellent work on the remodel.

It'd been a hundred years since Rogan had stayed on the farm. He had no clue why The Superintendent had sold the property surrounding the mansion.

The Order had created a species of beings like humans and manipulated their DNA to travel through space—nomads of the vast expanse. Rogan was one of the millions serving without complaint, mostly.

Of late, he'd become weary. He wondered what it would feel like to settle down and have a family. He didn't ponder the question long.

Inside the main bathroom suite, he took a shower and then pulled on a pair of sweatpants. He opened the drawer that held a blend of vitamins which helped him acclimate to the earth's electromagnetic fields. He popped them into his mouth and drank water from the faucet.

He slid into bed, enjoying the cool, crisp linens and a body-conforming mattress. He leaned against the headboard, grabbed his new laptop, and turned it on. Avery had worked with him long enough to know his desired preferences.

He searched for the local news outlet, scanned it into his memory bank, and checked for Summer's social footprint. He only found her bookstore. He read her biography and studied her face.

She wasn't a classic beauty, but she was stunning.

He dozed. His last thought before falling asleep...was Summer.

The following day, he woke with renewed vigor. He washed his face, brushed his teeth, shaved, and combed his hair. He put on khaki shorts, a polo shirt, and sandals.

He jogged down the steps and met Claude, a domestic android, in the kitchen. They worked most cases together, including the last one in this house.

"What time did you arrive last night?" Rogan took a bite of freshly baked strawberry pastry. "Good. Very good."

"This morning, sir." Claude wore a black short-sleeved shirt and slacks with no socks or shoes.

"Should you put on shoes or sandals?" Rogan nearly laughed. "Besides you, any other staff?"

"No, sir, just me. I have been instructed not to materialize in front of Summer Jewel. And I prefer bare feet." His stoic demeanor relaxed, and he smiled.

"It's good to be back. It seems like yesterday we were here." Rogan sipped his coffee. "The farm is gone, but at least they saved the woods. It's under the protection of the Wildlife Preserve Society."

Rogan handed him the restaurant card. "I'm inviting Summer over for dinner tonight. Would you prefer to cook, or do you want me to call for delivery?"

"Delivery, sir. I'm tasked to the bookstore today. I'll meet Summer's employees and run diagnostics to see if we have any alerts. And, since we're close to Nashville, I thought I'd spend the night downtown. I heard from the android pool that there's great music on Broadway. I'll return tomorrow."

"Okay, but use the portal door in the attic. I want to keep your presence unknown until I know I can trust Summer. Deal?"

"Yes, sir. My rooms are downstairs. I will stay hidden when she is in the house."

"Good. It didn't take her fifteen minutes to find the portal door. I think that's a record." Rogan chuckled.

"Indeed." Claude tidied the kitchen.

He finished the pastry and coffee. "Wish me luck?"

"Sir, you don't need luck."

"Yeah, I think I do with this one," Rogan added. He checked his appearance in the hallway's full-length mirror, one of the antiques he'd acquired during his last stay in the house. The frame had been hand-molded with natural-looking branches and flounced skirting. He threaded his fingers through his hair and walked out the front door.

He had a connection to Summer.

Were there any new protocols keeping him from developing a romantic tryst?

CHAPTER 3

Summer yawned and stretched. She sat up and glanced at the alarm clock on the nightstand. *Eight o'clock. Ugh.* She'd tossed and turned all night, thinking about Rogan and the mysterious door.

She got ready for the day, then slowly headed down the stairs through the living room and into the kitchen.

The sound of Aunt Em's lyrical singing and the scent of cooking pancakes poured forth from the kitchen.

"Good morning, love. It's a glorious day." Her aunt twirled with a spatula in her hand.

"Boy, you got it bad, Auntie." She popped a K-cup into the coffee machine. "Bob's lucky to have you."

"Oh, darling. He's so sweet and thoughtful." Aunt Emily blushed. "I'm staying over at his place tonight."

Summer nearly choked on a sip of coffee. Her sixty-year-old aunt getting it on with her boyfriend wasn't something she wanted to visualize. "Um, okay. This is a big step for you, and I wish you nothing but great joy and happiness."

Aunt Em put a heaping bowl of fruit salad on the table. "Thank you, my dear. How was your day?"

Rushing to change the subject, she relayed yesterday's events.

"Rogan Randolph. What a great name. Is he handsome? Single?" Aunt Em sat at the bar and nibbled on breakfast.

"He's too pretty for me. And I didn't see a ring, but that doesn't mean much these days."

Aunt Em pursed her lips. "You are your worst critic. You're beautiful inside and out. Believe in yourself and just watch the world come to your feet."

Summer scooped blueberries into a yellow ceramic bowl trimmed with sunflowers. "I'm going to sit on the front porch this morning. Do you want to join me?

"I would, but I'm meeting Bob in an hour. We're hiking the big hill at Barfield Park."

"Take a backpack with water and snacks," Summer added. "The trail is nine miles round trip."

"I'm in much better shape since last year. And I will carry my lightweight bag." Aunt Em sighed. "I'm happy, Summer, for the first time in years...." Tears welled in her eyes. "Since Wilder passed."

Wilder and Aunt Em had been married ten years when he suffered a stroke and died. Summer barely remembered him. "We've experienced our share of heartache. I say, make hay while the sun shines." She kissed her aunt's cheek and stepped out onto the porch.

She placed her coffee cup on the side table and eased into the white rocking chair. The scent of honeysuckle and lavender perfumed the air. Not quite summer, but close. No need for a sweater. She sighed—what a nice way to spend her day off.

Her stomach clenched when Rogan opened his front door. She straightened her back.

Her pulse raced as he strolled down his driveway. Her fingers trembled when he crossed the street, heading straight for her.

"Good morning, neighbor," Rogan said with a wide grin. "I trust you're well on this fine morning."

Summer sat on her hands so he wouldn't see them shake. "It is a beautiful day. I think the high is eighty-two with not a cloud in sight." The weather seemed a safe topic of conversation.

"May I sit?" He pointed to the rocking chair next to her.

She nodded. "Would you like a cup of coffee or tea?" *And me?* Thank goodness she didn't say what was on the tip of her tongue.

"No coffee. But I would like to start over. I was a bit abrupt yesterday. I want to invite you over for dinner tonight. How does lasagna, salad, and a bottle of merlot sound?"

Lasagna was her favorite. Wine made her loopy, but it might lessen her anxiety about being alone with him. She swallowed hard. "I accept, but I insist on bringing dessert."

"Deal."

"How was your first night in the house?"

He leaned his forearms on his thighs. "Slept like a baby. I've always liked it here." His eyes drifted toward her breasts but quickly rose back to her face.

She had completely forgotten she wasn't wearing any undergarments. She crossed her arms over her chest. Could she be more embarrassed? *Wait. What did he say?* "You're familiar with the place?"

He redirected nicely. "I meant to say I like small towns. I especially like the woods behind the house. Do you ever walk the trails?"

"I love walking outdoors but haven't had the chance lately." She calmed her racing heart. "I own a bookstore in town. We've been busy. Many of my customers stick around and read in our coffee shop. We offer local author signings from time to time.

And Saturdays we have children's hour. I have great employees, so I took today off."

"You're on the square. I saw your store driving in from the airport. I must stop in for a visit soon." Rogan leaned back in the chair and rocked.

Summer's nerves had settled, and the next few minutes of conversation flowed freely. Like they had been friends forever.

"Favorite reading genre?" she asked.

"Anything with time travel, alternate universes. Do you believe there's life out there?" Rogan pointed to the sky.

Usually, she was skeptical but replied, "It's hard to imagine we're the only ones in the vastness of space and time." She paused, then interjected, "Have you ever been driving and turned left instead of right and wondered if that decision may have changed your destiny?"

He tilted his head to the side. "All the time."

"Really?" her voice rose an octave.

Aunt Em opened the front door. "Oh, I didn't know we had company." She extended her hand. "I'm Emily Jewel."

He stood and shook her hand. "Nice to meet you. I've extended Summer an invitation to dinner this evening if you want to join us?"

Aunt Em raised a brow. "I appreciate the offer, but I'm off for a hike, then staying with a friend tonight. You two have fun, though." She kissed Summer's cheek and whispered, "Hubba, Hubba."

Summer chuckled. "Don't pull a hammy. And keep your phone on."

"I know how to pace myself." Aunt Em retreated into the house and closed the door. Minutes later, she backed out of the garage and honked the horn as she left.

Silence.

More silence.

The chemistry between them was charged with an undeniable draw and intense attraction.

Rogan leaned against the loadbearing column and glanced at his watch. "I don't want to overstay my welcome. Let's say six for cocktails and seven for dinner."

Summer looked up into his handsome face. His eyes had changed from grass green to violet. She'd heard of the term Alexandria's Genesis, which originated in Egypt a thousand years ago. The myth stated that a supernatural light appeared in the sky, changing their appearance. "Your eyes, they've changed colors."

Rogan blinked, then stepped off the front stairs onto the sidewalk. "I was born with a type of heterochromia. Does it bother you?"

Summer reached for his forearm, and the touch ignited a flame of passion she had never experienced before or daresay would ever again. Her heart hammered. "No. Not at all. On the contrary, I think your eye color is spectacular."

He placed his hand over hers. "Good. I'll see you soon." He returned to his house and closed the door.

Summer plopped down in the rocking chair again. There was something strangely exciting about Rogan, except she felt he was hiding a secret. She had no proof. She just knew it.

CHAPTER 4

Rogan placed the lasagna in the warmer, the salad in the crisper, and opened a bottle of merlot. He swirled the liquid in the stemmed glass and sipped.

The wine was velvety smooth and plummy. He placed the second bottle of wine in the sleek, black wine refrigerator with a glass door. The LED light helped identify the wine selection Claude stocked before he left to spend the night in Nashville.

Rogan chose to entertain in the kitchen instead of the dining room. He thought it would create a more intimate setting. He opened the windows and sliding French doors. The solar lights in the yard would kick on around dusk.

He looked at the clock on the microwave. Summer was five minutes late. What if she changed her mind? He didn't quite understand his burgeoning feelings for her, but he liked how it made him feel.

He wore jeans and a white collared shirt rolled at the sleeve with a pair of dark brown leather slides. A knock at the door had him jittery with nervous excitement.

Rogan opened the door, and the air in his lungs backed up.

Summer was radiant.

She wore a form-fitting cream top, white linen pants, and dark red sandals with tomato red nail polish on her toes. Her hair was straight and long, parted down the middle. She didn't need makeup, but she'd added a little blush and pinkish lip gloss.

"I'm a little late. I picked up dessert at the store. Our bakery has delicious peach cobbler." She walked inside. "The lasagna smells great, and I'm starving."

Again, he felt familiar with her, like he knew her from the past—drawn to her. "I'll take the dessert. I thought we'd eat in the kitchen. Oh, I picked up dinner from a local restaurant."

"Germano's is the best place in town." She giggled. "Wait until you taste their calzones."

He poured her a glass of wine as she sat at the table.

They spoke about everything and nothing. Time passed, and an hour seamlessly slipped away.

"I thought a la carte would be easier." He placed the lasagna, salad, and bread on the counter. "I'm not good at gauging portion control."

"Forget portion control. This is my absolute favorite dish in the world. I may have to come out of these pants later." Summer raised a brow and then burst into laughter. "You should see the look on your face."

Rogan tried to control his feelings for her, but it got more complex by the second. He gulped the rest of his wine, and she matched him, so he poured more. "I can't remember the last time I had so much fun. The food, the wine, and the company."

"I was thinking the same thing. It seems too good to be true." She paused and added, "Is it?"

He swallowed. "Is what?"

"Are you, I mean, is this thing between us too good to be true? Or am I imagining it?"

He moved to sit next to her and placed his hand on the curve of her cheek. "It's hard to make sense of it, so let's not try. I want to feel the experience and not analyze every detail for once in my life."

"You do that too?"

"Every day."

Thunder rumbled, and lightning streaked across the sky. A strong wind rattled the sliding French doors. Rogan jumped up and closed them. "It wasn't supposed to storm tonight."

"In Tennessee, the weather is never predictable. One minute it's sunny and eighty-five degrees, and the next, it's raining and sixty-five." Summer helped him clear the table.

"Would you like another glass of wine, or do you prefer brandy?" he asked.

"I'll wait. I'm getting a bit tipsy even though it's not like I'm driving." She snorted.

"You snorted." He laughed so hard he couldn't stop.

"Well, be glad I didn't burp or worse." She waved her fingers. "I'm sorry. I blame the wine."

Lightning struck again. A siren went off. "What's that?" he asked.

"First weather warning. Do you have a safe place?"

"Safe place?"

"Interior room with no windows or a basement."

"Downstairs." Claude would not return tonight, so he went to the door next to the back staircase.

Summer looked up the stairs. "I'd love to see the attic again."

"Better not." He pointed to the kitchen windows. "Dark clouds are spreading low and quick across the sky."

The power went out, followed by sirens. "What's that?"

"Tornado sirens," she replied. "It means someone has spotted a twister in the area."

"We need to shelter downstairs." He went to the drawer next to the sink, grabbed a flashlight, and clicked it on. He took her hand. "Be careful."

Her proximity to him on the narrow staircase made him hyper-aware of his intense attraction. He labored to breathe. On the bottom step, the lights came on. They stood facing each other with barely an inch between them.

Rogan glanced at her mouth as Summer reached up with her arms and circled his neck. She kissed him with such passion that shock waves spread through his body, releasing a spectacular adrenaline rush. He moaned, "You taste so good."

"It's the garlic bread." She giggled and twisted her fingers in his hair, and he scooped her into his arms. She pulled back slightly and searched his face.

Thoughts swirled in his mind. Recognition registered deep in his memories, telling him he had kissed those lips before. He could no longer contain the passion that ignited such a swell of emotion.

Did he know Summer? Had he met her before?

Suddenly they tore at each other's clothing, kissing frantically, afraid to stop as if the magic unfurling between them would disappear forever. He whispered, "I want you, Summer."

"Take me, all of me, leave nothing."

Spontaneous colliding of souls. Fire and heat accelerated on a cellular level transfixing him as she showered him with her love in perfect unison, so intense as she took him. Their love blooming where time didn't exist, not at this moment. He'd gladly pay any consequences from The Order. He pushed everything out of his mind except her. She was warm, tight, and with every thrust, euphoria intoxicated him. It was maddening and marvelous. And when release finally came, they lay utterly exhausted in each other's arms.

His last thought before falling into a deep sleep—*love is never forgotten.*

CHAPTER 5

Summer woke in Rogan's arms and watched him sleep for a while. Her smile went wide, thinking of their wild lovemaking. She didn't want to wake him, but wine invariably made her mouth as dry as the Sahara.

Carefully, she slipped from underneath him, put on her clothes, and tiptoed out of the room to make her way upstairs. After opening several cabinets, she pressed a glass under the water dispenser. Hydration was the key to avoiding a hangover, so she gulped, then drank some more, and placed the empty glass in the sink.

Leaning against the counter, she bashfully glanced at the floor. She'd never experienced a one-night stand before. She prayed this new relationship would last, but if it didn't, that was okay. Rogan made her feel loved.

She started to go downstairs but eyed the steps leading to the attic.

Maybe one peek before returning to Rogan. She raced up the flight of steps in her bare feet. The hair on her arms and neck rose when she entered the attic.

The mysterious door glowed again.

Summer glanced downstairs, but her curiosity got the better of her. She opened the door, and light engulfed her. The sensation wasn't pain, but definitely not pleasant either.

Her knees hit the wood plank floor. Her hands trembled as she came to her feet. The light had propelled her back into the attic again, but it wasn't the same place. It was different—nothing except dust, spider webs, exposed beams, and odd and end pieces of furniture. The beautiful desk, sofa, and finished walls were gone.

From the horizontal windows, waning sunlight cast long shadows across the clutter. She shuffled by the old chests, and crates and peered outside.

No neighborhood—snow instead of summer. WTH?

There was a dirt driveway with several vintage cars parked out front. She heard music downstairs, something old and jazzy. She turned and caught her reflection in an old mirror. *Oh, my lord.* Her hand flew to her chest. She touched her face. The person in the mirror did not look like her at all. This woman had dark brown hair swept high on her head. A single ringlet dangled over her right shoulder. She wore an Edwardian red velvet gown that looked like it belonged on the set of *Downton Abbey.*

She tripped, making her way back to the light, but it faded and then disappeared. She flung the door open—a balcony overlooked the woods. A sinking feeling kicked as she readied herself for fight or flight.

What am I to do?

Her heart hammered in her chest.

She heard a familiar voice and maneuvered to the steps. "Rogan?"

"Nora, thank God." He took her hand. "I've looked everywhere for you. It's not safe up here. You're missing the Christmas party." His tux reminded her of Jay Gatsby.

"Who is Nora? What am I doing here? Where's my neighborhood?" she asked as hysteria took over.

He caressed her cheek with his hand and she swatted it away.

"The doctor said you may get disoriented," his voice lowered to a whisper. "Since you couldn't remember your name after the accident, I called you Nora with your permission. Do you remember details of how you got here?"

Summer took a step back. "What accident? What year is it?" Surely she was dreaming, no having a nightmare was more like it. She pinched herself. *Ouch.* Okay, that didn't work.

"Let's go downstairs. It's freezing up here. I'll take you to your room." He reached for her hand.

She jerked away. "I'm capable of walking downstairs." She followed him down one flight of steps.

Rogan opened a side door and entered a wide hallway with a red oriental runner. Enormous paintings with gilded frames hung on the walls. It looked more like a museum than the house she remembered from yesterday.

Summer glanced over the banister; the first-floor foyer was full of guests. A few seconds later, she entered an art-deco-inspired bedroom with a French Louis Majorelle bed. She took a seat in a hand-carved chair with needlepoint upholstery. "Please tell me again, how I got here?" She gazed at her reflection again in the dressing mirror. She was in someone else's body. *Come on, girl, keep it together.*

He pulled another chair next to hers. He reached out to place his hand on her knee, and she shook her head.

"A few weeks ago, you crashed a Ford Roadster. The force of the impact threw you into a ditch. By the time I found you, I didn't think you'd make it. I brought you to my home, and Claude, my valet, fetched the local doctor. You came around with smelling salts. Besides a few bruises and minor scrapes, you were unhurt except for not remembering your name or where you're from."

She trembled. "What year is it?"

He frowned. "It's 1926. Should I get the doctor? He's downstairs."

Unbelievable. 1926. "I want to go home. To my home." She slumped in the chair. A thousand different thoughts swirled in her mind, and none of them were helpful.

He took her hand and pressed it next to his lips. "Nora, I don't want you to worry or stress. The doctor said trauma could cause memory loss. I will take care of you. I love you."

"You love me?" she shouted. "You don't even know me." But then, she looked into those beautiful green eyes. He was Rogan.

But that made her wonder, *who was Rogan?* How could he look exactly the same a hundred years in the future? Was the other Rogan still sleeping in the basement?

He kissed her hand. "Do you believe in fate or destiny?"

Boy, howdy, do I believe. "I need to lie down. I don't feel well."

"I'll ask our guests to leave and I'll come back up."

"No. Don't spoil your party. Who's down there anyway?"

Rogan rattled off half a dozen names. Some of the names she recognized as the founders of Heartsville. The last one made her pulse race. Guy Jewel was her great-great-grandfather. She wanted to bolt downstairs and see if it was really him. He brought electricity to their rural community.

The librarian in her wanted to witness history in the making. But she had read H.G. Wells's *Time Machine* and didn't want to create a paradox.

The man of my dreams is a time traveler.

"I'll save you a piece of fudge." He grinned, and her heart melted. Rogan left the room and shut the door.

Summer slipped into bed, frightened beyond her capacity to think clearly. She curled into a ball and forced herself not to cry. She must find a way back home. But how?

The mysterious door had opened for her. Maybe it would again.

CHAPTER 6

Present day

Rogan rolled over and reached for Summer. He bolted upright. She was gone.

He raced upstairs and noted her purse and sandals on the kitchen's baker rack.

Heart pounding, he took the backstairs two at a time to the attic. His worst fear came to fruition. The portal door was wide open—the pulsating light churning energy then faded away.

Rogan went to his desk, opened the middle drawer, and withdrew The Order's mobile device. He punched in Claude's contact number.

After two rings, Claude answered gruffly, "Hello."

"I hate to wake you in the middle of the night, but we have a problem. Summer went through the door. I need you here while I go to Avery."

"Getting dressed, and I'll be on my way. Are you sure she didn't go home?"

"Positive. Her purse and sandals are in the kitchen." Rogan shouldn't have reacted to his physical attraction to Summer. He couldn't help himself.

"You will find Summer. You're the best agent I know."

"Thanks for the vote of confidence, but I broke protocol." He paced the attic floor.

"Already?"

"Yeah. I'll let you know once I find where Summer teleported."

"Don't despair. You'll find her. I will stay at the house."

Rogan added, "The aunt may come looking for her."

"Don't worry. I'll redirect the aunt. Worst-case scenario, I'll suspend her time clock and keep her in the basement."

"Oh god, Claude. Don't hurt Aunt Em."

Claude chuckled. "I won't hurt her, man. She'll never remember what happened after a memory wipe anyway. Go! Stop talking to me."

The device went silent. Claude cut the transmission.

After quickly dressing, Rogan closed the door to reset, opened it again, and went through the portal.

Avery glanced up. "The Superintendent is not available."

"I lost Summer. She opened the door. Can you help me find her?"

The android looked surprised. She glanced over her shoulder, then pushed away from her workstation and approached him. "I may have tampered with the mission a tiny bit."

"What do you mean?" He frowned.

She blinked a couple of times, and two hologram images materialized.

Nora Hawkins's likeness appeared. It was the first time he'd seen her in nearly a hundred years. Next to Nora was a shimmering image of Summer. "What have you done, Avery?"

"You were so distraught after Nora died. It took decades for you to smile again. So, I waited and watched. Once Nora's soul, well, her lifeforce, transferred to Summer, I knew you'd find Soul Love again. You did find her, right?"

Rogan's hand went over his eyes and dragged down his face. "We're not supposed to interfere with the natural order of things. You told me that, remember? Yes, I loved Nora, but I'm in love with Summer. Set the time portal for 1926. I must return to Heartsville and bring Summer back. We must allow destiny to unfold as it was intended."

"I only wanted to help you." Avery blinked several times, but no tears flowed down her cheeks. The android was programmed with human emotions, but she wasn't. How could Avery possibly know the calamity which awaited Summer?

He squeezed her hand. "I appreciate the gesture. I do. Get prepared for a paradox in case I run into me."

Avery nodded.

He didn't want to upset her further. He needed Avery to cover their tracks if he disappeared into the void.

Rogan remembered every detail of Nora's face. He had loved her. He closed his eyes. This event was supposed to happen.

Summer is Nora.

Avery waved her hand, and the portal materialized. "The time is set, Rogan. I wish you much success."

He kissed Avery's cheek. "Thank you." Then he went through the door's light.

Déjà vu washed over him as he entered the attic. He took a couple of minutes to ground himself, then approached the windows. It was night. Snow blanketed the farm, and he shivered.

He remembered finding Nora after her vehicle had crashed in a snow-covered ditch. She had a faint pulse when he brought her to his house. Nora had reminded him of a fictional Snow White character.

He prayed. *Please let Summer be Nora.*

Rogan removed his shoes and stealthily went down the attic stairs, through the staff door to the second floor. He inched to Nora's room and knocked gently. "Summer. Are you in there?" He rapped again, and Nora opened the door. His stomach plummeted. Unprepared for the onslaught of emotions at seeing her again.

Tears glistened on her cheeks ."Is it really you? The Rogan I made love to only hours ago?"

"Summer?"

"Yes." Her knees buckled.

Rogan swept her into his arms, closed the door, and locked it. After laying her on the bed, he opened the nightstand drawer, withdrew an embroidered cloth, and dipped it into the water basin. He squeezed out the excess water and placed it on her forehead.

Summer opened her eyes. "I don't know what I want to do more: hug or punch you. Who are you, really? How am I here in someone else's body with my consciousness?"

"May I sit on the bed with you?"

She nodded.

"I work for an intergalactic commission overseeing the advancement of humanity. Typically, I never get involved with subjects, but you and I are meant to be." He swallowed hard. "One soul may experience several lifetimes before moving on to the next phase of the soul's journey. I met Nora nearly a hundred years ago. But the thing is, you are Nora. And vice versa. I loved Nora, but I am in love with you."

"Well, that's just messed up." Summer sat up. "I'm too angry with you to respond to your declarations of love. My great-great-grandfather was here. I could've caused a paradox meeting him."

"H.G. Wells was a brilliant writer. He made valid points. Each soul has a finite number of chances to evolve. The Order uses agents like me to divert or avert chaos and calamity. Sometimes it works, other times it does not."

"Are you human? Alien?"

"I am a citizen of the universe. We share DNA characteristics and a common creator. Agents like me have undergone molecular manipulations to travel through time and space without a meltdown. You made it through the portal, which means you must possess those same characteristics. I have some supernatural abilities, but I'm not Superman. My body was designed to self-heal."

"I think you were very in love with Nora. I saw the way you looked at her."

"You are her. Don't you see that?"

"My head hurts. I tried to use the attic door and found a balcony. How do I get home?"

He inhaled and exhaled deeply. "Ah. That's the quandary. The 1926 version of me must realize his love for you before the portal opens again." He did not want to relay any information than necessary. "My past self cannot run into the present-day me."

"What happens if you do?" She frowned.

"One will live, one will die. Both cannot live in the same timeline." He took her hands and kissed her knuckles. "I ache with a fire that burns for you. Love gets messy. It can break your heart, but I would cross a thousand galaxies, again and again, to find you, Summer."

"That's pretty good." Her smile warmed. "I forgive you. So, what's the plan?"

"You must wait until I ask you to marry me."

With a raised brow, she said, "Marry you?"

"Yes, I will ask you to marry me. As soon as I say those words, you must run to the door in the attic. The portal will open. Jump into the light. I cannot remember the sequence of events, but I'm positive you return home at the stroke of midnight on New Year's." That was the day he found Nora dead on the attic floor. "I will check on you every night, but I cannot risk being seen in the daylight hours."

"Will you stay with me tonight?"

He glanced at the mantel clock. "I'll stay for an hour, but I must depart before dawn." On Christmas night, 1926, Rogan made love to Nora for the first time. They would spend the next several days in bliss. "Your Aunt Em will come looking for you."

"Oh, poor Aunt Em. I don't want to ruin her joy."

He hesitated to inform her that Aunt Em would not remember anything of Summer's departure. Many variables and possible changes in humanity's timeline were at risk. One person could cause a ripple in time. "I promise to care for Aunt Em."

CHAPTER 7

Three short raps on the bedroom door. "Miss Nora, I'm here to help you dress."

Good grief. I don't need help.

"Come in." Summer rolled out of bed and waited for one of Rogan's staff to enter.

The young woman looked at her crumpled dress. "Oh, miss, I could've helped you out of the evening gown. Let's get you into a hot tub. Breakfast will be ready soon." The servant went to the adjacent door and pushed it open.

Summer followed the woman into a pink and white bathroom with dark rose tile and diamond-paned windows. "Please forgive me, but I've forgotten your name."

"Avery, ma'am." She placed the towels on a side table. "If you wish, I can shampoo your hair."

"That sounds nice. The pins in my hair hurt. I'd like to wear it down."

Avery unbuttoned the back of the evening gown and helped Summer change into a light dressing robe.

Summer sat on a low stool and kept still so Avery could remove the pins and brush the tangles out of her hair. The woman had a light touch, and Summer rather enjoyed the pampering. When Avery finished, Summer removed her dressing robe and stepped into the iron claw porcelain tub.

The hot water soothed her achy muscles as she bathed. She closed her eyes as Avery shampooed and rinsed her hair.

"How long have you known Mr. Randolph?"

"Oh, I've known him for some time," Avery said. "He's an honest, hardworking man."

"I can't remember what happened to me."

Avery sighed. "Sometimes it's better not to know."

"Do you know anything about me?"

"I sensed you were running from something or someone. You had bruises on your wrists. The doctor said it was from the accident, but I think someone did that to you."

Thirty minutes later, Summer got out of the tub, used thick towels to dry, then twisted and tucked another one about her hair.

Avery stoked the fire in the bedroom. She guided Summer to the stool and used the towel to dry Summer's hair. She went to the art deco wardrobe and pulled out a red tartan dress with a black velvet sash. "Mr. Rogan bought you some clothes from town. I thought this dress would be festive for Christmas."

"It's gorgeous. Any pants in there?"

Avery's eyes widened. "It is a small town. I don't think they sell pants for women."

"Oh, that's okay. Where I'm from, pants are all the rage."

Avery helped her with the stockings and undergarments and then into the dress. "You are beautiful, Miss Nora."

Summer looked at her reflection. *Who are you, Nora?* It was still weird seeing Nora's body instead of her own. She'd try to make an effort to play her role until New Year's Eve.

Besides, Rogan was still the same person.

"Thank you for helping me."

Avery curtsied. "You're most welcome." She opened the door to the hallway. "I will take the back steps. You go down the main staircase."

Summer nodded and descended into the foyer.

The fireplace crackled and popped with flames. In the corner, a large evergreen tree was decorated with candy canes, string popcorn, tinsel, and real candles in clip-on holders.

Rogan sat at the baby grand piano and played "Silent Night." He stopped when he saw her.

She waved. "Please finish the song."

He sang the chorus beautifully, then stood. "I love your hair down."

"Avery did it. I still have a tinge of a headache and didn't care to wear it up."

"I don't blame you. Headaches are not fun. I can check on headache powders?"

"Oh no. I will be fine once I eat and drink coffee. You do have coffee?"

Rogan's head cocked to the side. "You have a different accent."

"Maybe it's the real me, no longer pretending to be someone else." Her answer seemed to placate him.

"Well, Claude has outdone himself with Christmas breakfast." He pushed away from the piano and offered her his arm. "I hope you don't mind, but I asked the staff to join us."

"Of course, I don't mind. I appreciate the clothes you bought me. I will pay you back, I promise."

"No need. I wanted to."

They strolled into the dining room with cherry-red painted walls, white trim, and a gorgeous chandelier. Avery, Claude, and two more employees chatted cheerfully near the twelve-seat art-deco-inspired dining table and chairs, with a matching walnut sideboard laden with food.

"I'll say grace," Rogan said.

Everyone hushed and moved to their places.

Summer lowered her head but peeked as he recited a prayer of thanksgiving.

"Please make yourself at home." Rogan held the chair for her. Then he sat at the head of the table, next to her.

She learned that the Vaughns were the other couple at the table. They ran the farm.

The time spent with all of them warmed her heart. Later, she and Rogan watched the staff open presents next to the tree, and each shared a glass of wine.

Rogan's interaction with everyone intensified her feelings for him. After their celebration, the staff was let go for the rest of the day.

Rogan joined her on the sofa in front of the fire. "Would you like anything else to drink or eat?"

"Heavens no. I'm full, but thanks for the offer."

"May I hold your hand?" he asked with an air of formality.

"Of course."

They sat in silence, except for the fire logs hissing and flickering.

"What did you find out about me?" Her head tilted to the side.

"The sheriff made a few inquiries around the surrounding counties; he couldn't find anything. Whatever you were running from, the officer working your case agreed with me. There's no reason to inform anyone of your whereabouts. You're safe, Nora."

Hearing him call her Nora would take some getting used to. She turned to him and touched the side of his face. "I'd like to express my gratitude with a kiss."

"By all means," he answered with a grin.

Their closeness made her heart flutter. She leaned in, pressed a feather-light kiss on his cheek, then moved slightly and kissed the other side. His cinnamon scent made her tremble.

The seductive dance of desire and soul melding had begun as before. "Rogan, I want you," she said with a throaty rasp. The art of light kissing was underrated. It was hot. She was playing with fire and knew it. She pressed her cheek next to his and closed her eyes.

Did he sense the connection? Cupping her face with his hands, Rogan glanced at her mouth, making her hungry for more. He hovered a second or two before brushing his lips against hers. Their chemistry was electric. "Take my hand. Your room or mine?" he asked her.

"Your room." The last thing she needed was for the present-day Rogan to catch her with this one, but if he slept with Nora, surely the one from the future already knew it and hadn't told her about it.

Summer wouldn't delve further into the time travel loop, or her head would explode. Instead, she allowed herself to feel the emotions, to live in the moment. She held his hand and went up the stairs. They proceeded down the hall on the opposite end from her room.

Rogan's room was a little bigger than hers with eighteenth-century furnishings. It had blue-green textured walls and several multi-colored rugs. The fireplace, having been stoked, made the room warm and toasty.

Her eyes went to the bed covers turned down and ready for use. She swallowed hard.

He brushed her hair off her shoulders, unbuttoned her dress, occasionally pressing delicate kisses on her neck and shoulders, then removed her undergarments. He scooped her into his arms, placed her on the bed, quickly removed his clothes, and slid beside her.

"Are you sure? It's not too late." He placed his hand tenderly on the curve of her cheek. He seemed to need validation.

Summer took his hand and placed it over her heart. "Since the moment I met you, Rogan, I have belonged to you." She needed him like she needed the air to breathe.

His hand slid up her leg, rolled down her stocking, and then proceeded to remove the other. He took extra time caressing her skin with soft kisses, tasting her, tittilating her with pleasure. She tried to hold onto the sensation, twisting the sheets with her fingers and then shuddered with an incredible climax unfurling the most sensual experience rippling throughout her body.

Rogan raised his head, his eyes almost feral as he pressed between her legs, and entered her with one powerful thrust. Neither spoke but allowed their body language to respond instead; creating the most splendid rhythm.

In the short time she had known Rogan, she had experienced real love, a love that didn't need apologies, a love that existed beyond time, a love that two shared with an instantaneous connection shouting to the cosmos: we are one.

CHAPTER 8

A rooster crowed before dawn, followed by a chorus of tweeting wild birds. Summer slowly awakened and glanced at Rogan. He snored softly, a melodious rumbling rather than sawing logs. She watched the rise and fall of his chest, then carefully slid out of bed, put on her clothes, and left his room. She padded down the hallway in her stocking feet.

Entering her accommodations, she stifled a scream. "You scared me to death."

The present-day Rogan was at the fireplace, his hand on the mantel. "I waited in the attic for hours, and once the house settled in for the night, I came here." He added, "I was concerned for you."

"Why?"

"Because you made love to him." He pointed with his thumb toward the east wing of the house.

"I made love to *you*."

He crossed his arms over his muscular chest. "I remembered falling for you."

"You fell for Nora."

"No. I fell in love the day you took over Nora's soul. Strong, confident, and curious, none of those traits were present before our souls sang. I can't tell you what happened in 1926 or what will happen in the future. We're treading on thin ice, baby."

She took a couple of steps toward him. "Rogan, you are timeless perfection." Her hands slid over his muscular biceps. "Gloriously sculpted and deprived of aging. There's a new language forming between us with every touch, unspoken yet understood. I am yours." Her hand slid to the nape of his neck, her fingers twisting in his hair as she led him to a kiss.

He moaned as he withdrew from the kiss. "There's nothing I would rather do than take you. Make you mine. But someone is coming for Nora. She's in danger."

She gasped. "Who? Why? What shall I do?"

"I cannot tell you."

"Why not? Where are you from anyway?"

"I work for The Superintendent. He formed an intergalactic mission to save your planet. Earth is less than a century from spewing humanity out of existence. I came here to work with Guy Jewel. He combined theories from Einstein and Tesla and created a working formula with an energy grid that would've lasted centuries, except a plot of the world's richest men stopped him. If I hadn't met him, I wouldn't have found you."

Summer left the warmth of the fireplace and crawled into bed. "They killed him. Aunt Em relayed the story to me years ago. I thought she embellished the details." She looked up at him. "But what brought you to me?"

"Avery."

"Avery? The sweet lady who helped me dress yesterday?"

He nodded. "She's an android."

"No kidding? An android." She turned over onto her side and yawned. "Lie with me. I'm exhausted."

Rogan reclined beside her. He took her into his arms and kissed the top of her head. "Playing with time and unfolding the sequence of events is tricky. Honestly, we could disappear forever if either of us makes a wrong move."

She placed her hands on his chest and looked into his eyes. "I need the truth. Do I die?"

"I don't know how much I should tell you about New Year's Eve." He traced the outline of her face. "It's safer for things to happen naturally."

"Where is Nora?"

"I'm not sure. I believe she's deep inside your consciousness. You're stronger than she."

"I want to know what happens to her and me."

"Timelines could change if I relay the events to come." His face softened. "I understand why you want to know the future, but I won't take the chance of losing you. Please do as I request. The moment I ask you to marry me, run to the attic, go through the door. Don't delay. Promise me."

"Promise."

Nora tried to reach the surface of her consciousness as if she wanted to warn her about something, but Summer drifted to sleep.

Rogan got out of bed, took one look at Summer in Nora's vessel, then made his way back to the attic before daylight and before he could run into anyone else in 1926. He opened the portal door and stepped into Avery's office. "Please look at the readouts. Is there anything I can do to facilitate Summer's safe return?"

"The Superintendent will speak to you now." Avery reached over and squeezed his hand.

Rogan's gut twisted as the door quietly slid open.

The Superintendent wore a fitted tweed jacket, black turtleneck, jeans, and loafers with no socks. No doubt returning from a mission in the 1960s. He pushed away from the glass-topped desk and approached Rogan with a handshake. "Good to see you again. Please sit with me."

He ushered Rogan to a white, ergonomic sofa. "I understand Avery instigated Summer's curiosity leading her into a past life experience with the soul of Nora. That android's emotional software program is more advanced and compassionate than most souls in the world today. However, what she facilitated was wrong. Sending you to present-day Heartsville to meet Summer was also wrong. What shall we do to rectify the situation?"

Rogan labored to breathe. "Please allow Summer to return."

"Ahh. I see it in your eyes, my friend. You're in love with her," the Superintendent stated. "Have you told Summer about Nora?"

"No, sir." He swallowed hard. "May I wait for her at the portal door on New Year's Eve 1926?"

"I won't stop you." The Superintendent went to the floor-to-ceiling windows that overlooked the heavens, stars, and vastness of deep space. He turned and looked at Rogan. "However, if you meet yourself during the transition, I cannot guarantee your safe return. Manipulating outcomes has unexpected consequences."

"What about Guy Jewel?"

"Choose Guy or Summer, not both."

"How does one choose?" Rogan paced about the floor. "Guy Jewel has potential, but we know the haves will not bestow the have-not's dominion over such extraordinary power."

"Then your choice is made." The Superintendent placed his hand on Rogan's shoulder. "I wish you much success." There was a finality about how he spoke as if Rogan might never see him again.

"Thank you, sir."

Rogan backed away, lost in thought. Each conscious being makes millions of choices over many lifetimes. He had possessed one infinite lifespan. He was willing to risk himself for Summer.

CHAPTER 9

New Year's Eve

Summer descended the staircase. The bottom of her flapper fringe dress brushed against her knees. She glanced at the elaborate metallic lace intermingled with delicate embroidery and intricate beading.

Her smile widened. She'd never imagined ever wearing such a flirtatious dress. It made her feel so chic. Avery had styled her hair with long ringlet curls gathered loosely, half up, half down, secured with a headscarf that matched the dress.

Avery met her inside the foyer. "You look gorgeous. Lillian Gish has nothing on you."

She immediately envisioned the silent film star who performed in *The Whales of August*.

As the staff prepared for the party, a sense of excitement sizzled in the air. Rogan had asked her to help plan the soiree with a real roaring twenties celebration, Gatsby style. She'd read about such events in the local society pages but had never attended.

They had transformed the house into a speakeasy with black and gold décor. The dining room had a full bar, specialty cocktails, and an appetizer buffet. The furniture in the main rooms had been removed and replaced with white linen-covered tables topped with candles in glass votives.

The orchestra set up against the wall opposite the French glass doors that led to the terrace. The lead singer imitated Al Jolson and performed "Always."

Rogan stepped up beside her and swept her into his arms. "Dance with me."

It seemed like a dream waltzing with him. She registered the guests arriving, but she couldn't break the magic spell. The intimacy and sway of dancing nearly brought her to tears. She loved him, this humanoid from space.

Although her heightened emotions fluctuated between joy and happiness, she knew their time together would soon end. This was not her time, not her home. She'd have to flee as soon as he offered her his hand in marriage. That was what the present-day Rogan said. She believed in him.

The evening became a blur of noisemakers, champagne, and music. Her attention solely focused on Rogan.

He introduced her great-great-grandfather, who resembled her father. Guy was such a charmer. The chatter among guests made engaging in conversation challenging. Her ears perked up at the mention of Einstein and Tesla. The two brilliant theoretical physicists made astounding discoveries to change her future world.

As midnight neared, the revelers grew louder.

Rogan draped an arm around her. "Come with me to my study."

Her stomach filled with butterflies as she followed him. She dreaded and anticipated the moment. Spending time with Rogan's younger self in 1926 had been priceless and lovely.

He closed the door and bent to one knee. He pulled a black box from his tux pocket. "I know we haven't known each other very long, but I love you. I want to spend the rest of my life with you. I want to share my world with you. Will you marry me?"

The grandfather clock struck midnight.

Panic set in, and her heart pounded as though it would leave her chest. A myriad of emotions caved in on her at once—excitement, sadness, and fear. Her throat constricted. "I'm sorry," she croaked. "I must go." She fled the study, leaving a shocked Rogan behind. She raced down the hall toward the main staircase.

Claude opened the front door. A strange man with a murderous look locked eyes with her.

She froze.

Nora screamed in her mind. *Run, Summer. Run.*

Summer pushed past people blocking the staircase and jogged up the steps.

The man chased her and screamed, "Stop, you whore of a wife."

When she reached the top step of the attic, shots rang out.

On the other side of the room, the mysterious door flew open, and within the bright light, she saw present-day Rogan. "Come to me, Summer. Keep your eyes on me."

Of course, she had to look down. Blood ribboned through the sparkling lace.

She glanced over her shoulder. The 1926 Rogan fought the dangerous man on the stairs.

Summer felt her life force spill onto the floor but doggedly forced one foot in front of the other and leaped toward Rogan. He caught her, pulling her into the brilliant light. One last turn— Nora lay lifeless on the attic floor.

"He killed her," Summer shouted over and over, tears streaming down her cheeks.

"You're okay. We're okay."

As the portal closed, the veil before her faded into the background.

She looked at present-day Rogan. With ragged breaths, she cried, "Take me home."

The next day, Summer woke inside her bedroom.

She heard Aunt Em singing "Always" and caught a whiff of bacon frying. She got up and went to the full-length mirror on her closet door.

Nora was gone.

She picked up a hairbrush from her dresser and stroked her long auburn hair. She was scared to look across the street. Afraid she would learn Rogan had never existed.

Slowly, she shuffled downstairs, through the hall toward the kitchen. Her heart broke into pieces, and then suddenly, the sunlight streamed through the windows, and her pulse raced.

Rogan read the newspaper at the white pine table. He pushed away from his chair and, in two long strides, scooped her into his arms. "You're okay. We're okay."

"Are you really here?" She kissed him all over his face. That's when she noticed a diamond engagement ring on her finger.

"You bet he is—and on his second plate of pancakes." Aunt Em took off her apron. "Are you hungry?"

"Yes, Auntie, I'm starving."

Summer would eventually speak with Rogan about the 1926 events. She wanted to know everything about his origins, but for now, it was good enough to bask in the glow of his love, and she knew without a doubt that time was precious.

The End.

I trust you enjoyed *Soul Love*. If so, please consider posting a review. Reviews and Word of Mouth referrals are the best way to reach fabulous readers like you.

Thank you!

D. F. Jones

About the Author

USA Today Bestselling Author **D. F. Jones** began her career as a broadcast consultant at the ABC Affiliate in Nashville, which led her to open
an advertising agency. Over the years, she's created many campaigns for clients but fell in love with writing fantasy fiction.

Writing takes her to a place where anything is possible, and fiction takes her to a place made of dreams.

She's happily married to the love of her life with two gorgeous sons whom she loves and adores. She loves to laugh, and her husband keeps her in stitches!

She's a fan of the Tennessee Titans and MT Blue Raiders. She also enjoys working in her flower gardens.

Whether it's angels or demons, time travel adventures, witches, wizards, or ghosts, her books are action-packed with supernatural and romantic elements.

Register for her newsletter and read a free book Follow her on social media for special giveaways, and freebies. Go to www.DFJonesAuthor.com

Also By D.F. Jones

The Witches of Hant Hollow 1

The Witches of Hant Hollow 2

The Witches of Hant Hollow 3

Shifting Magic Anthology (limited series)

Angel Watcher (A Ditch Lane Diaries short story)

Angel Watcher Audiobook

Ruby's Choice (The Dreamer) Ditch Lane Diaries book 1 (Free at most digital stores)

Anna's Way (The Healer) Ditch Lane Diaries book 2

Sandy's Story (The Soul Reader) Ditch Lane Diaries 3

Lee's Lesson (Warrior Angel) Ditch Lane Diaries 4

Ditch Lane Diaries Angel Series
(4 books)

Spinning Time (A Time Travel Romance)

ATTRA Chronicles 1 (a Spinning Time short story)

Happily Ever After, Again (Ghost Mystery)

Tis the Season: Sweet Romance Novelettes
(Free at most digital stores)

www.DFJonesAuthor.com

THE TALENT TEST

ANA MORGAN

PREFACE

Encyclopedia of History...Spellcaster Rebellion...Summary:

During the Pogrom of 2382, spellcasters faced a choice: renounce their talents or brave death. Some chose execution. Others went into hiding and published a defiant Declaration of Unity: *We hold this truth to be self-evident. All talents—mundane and magical—are equal.*

This declaration ignited a civil war that came to be known as the Spellcaster Rebellion. For years, conflict ravaged the realm. Weary leaders finally negotiated a truce that called for the construction of a wall. Until a permanent peace settlement could be reached, spellcasters would live on one side of the wall; mundanes on the other.

Eighty years have passed. The terms of the truce have been codified into law. Peace talks are stalled. The promise of the Declaration remains unfulfilled.

BLURB

One last chance to pass her magic talent test.

In a realm where magic is a requirement, Crystal Dare must prove she possesses a spellcasting talent. And she would—if she knew what it was.

Now, on the eve of her twenty-first birthday, she's run out of time. Facing expulsion, she seeks out an outlawed soul reader and discovers she does have a talent. One that could destroy everything.

Can she abandon the man whose touch electrifies them both and do what she fears most?

CHAPTER 1

Truce Rule 2(a): By noon on their 21st anniversary, each Citizen must demonstrate proficiency in at least one (1) magic talent by passing a Certified Talent test.

Crystal Dare staggered out of the Mage Street Talent Testing Station and gripped the exit handrail.

What was wrong with her? Why didn't she have a magic talent?

Her mother had been a certified shadowcaster. Her father, a celebrated vine-speller. They had conceived her late in life, but even then, their spellcasting skills were still strong.

The testing station door opened behind her. The bubbly teen who'd stood behind her in line skipped out, accompanied by her jubilant parents. They linked arms and strolled toward the street, chatting excitedly about plans for a party.

Crystal blinked back tears. Tomorrow was her twenty-first anniversary, and she didn't have anything to celebrate. She'd taken a talent test every day for the past two years and failed each one. If she couldn't prove she had a magic talent by noon tomorrow, she'd be banished.

An energy billboard flashed over a storefront across the street: *Your Talent or Your Credits Back.*

She'd seen numerous Talent Aid ads. Anxious twenty-year-olds walked in. Happy ones walked out. Not a single deficient—like her—in sight.

The color of the sign changed to sympathetic blue.

Maybe she wasn't what her parents thought—a late bloomer. Maybe she needed help. Talent Aid help.

As if affirming her thoughts, the sign turned warm yellow.

She crossed the street and peered through the office window.

Four plastileather comfort chairs floated between a free-water cooler and a cash-only candy dispenser. Two workers wearing red Talent Aid vests and matching berets busied themselves behind a customer service counter. The gap in their ages suggested a boss and a trainee.

For years, she'd believed she just needed to be patient until her talent blossomed, but time had run out. She was desperate and needed a miracle.

She stepped inside.

The older man motioned to the younger one as she approached the service counter, then he retreated into an office.

The younger man's nametag said *Burke.* He was tall and slim, with a hawkish nose under a tall forehead, wavy hair the color of roasted rillnuts, and gold-flecked irises. He greeted her with a rehearsed, "Welcome to Triple A Talent Aid. We'll find your talent."

"I hope so. I can't seem to find mine."

He crossed his hands on the counter and fidgeted with the silver moonstone ring on his index finger. "It's not easy to misplace a talent. Have you looked for it?"

Was he mocking her? She jerked her gaze up and searched his face.

No hint of apology.

Coming here was a waste of precious time. She had eighteen hours to leave the only home she'd ever known.

Choking back her fear, she spun on her boot heel and headed toward the door.

"Wait." He rushed around the counter. "I'm sorry. I saw you looking through the window, and you seemed so sad. I thought a joke would cheer you up." He caught up to her and reached for her wrist.

A white-hot spark arced off the tip of his index finger and landed on the back of her hand.

Expecting a burst of pain, she flinched. But instead of discomfort, warmth flooded her body, as if she'd stepped onto a sun-drenched beach. "Is that your talent? Soothing people?"

He grimaced. "Quite the opposite. I make things worse." He flexed his fingers, and more sparks leaped onto her arm.

An odd, yet pleasant tugging sensation rippled through her.

He glanced guardedly at his boss' office. "Please don't go. I'm sure I can help you. We'll start fresh, from the beginning."

Touched by the pleading in his voice, she allowed him to escort her back to the service counter.

He dashed around to the other side and smiled. The lopsided tilt of his lips reminded her of an eager frenpup, waiting for a treat. "Welcome to Triple A Talent Aid. How may I help you?"

"Tomorrow's my twenty-first, and I can't find my talent."

"You've come to the right place." He plucked several forms off the shelf behind him and picked up a pen. "Name?"

"Dare, Crystal."

"Address?"

"43 Enchantment Way, apartment 2B."

"Or not to be."

She stiffened. Why did he keep cracking jokes? Her life was on the line.

His forehead furrowed. "I'm sorry. I didn't mean to do that. Please forgive me." He cleared his throat and poised his pen over the customer information form again. "Relatives on this side of the Wall?"

"None living."

He marked X in a box. "Any on the mundane side?"

"None that I would know."

He checked another box and turned the form around. "Sign here." He waited while she followed his instructions. "Now, let's set up your account."

She dug her credit disc out of her hip pocket and inserted it into the slot on the countertop processor. Five seconds later, the green light on top of the processor box lit up. Her disc popped out, and she tucked it away.

"Great," he said cheerfully. "Now we can begin. I will read a list of talents starting with Level One. Tell me which ones you've tested for. Fire starting."

"Failed it."

"Fire stopping."

"Failed."

"Fruit ripening."

"Fail."

"How about rainmaking?"

"Didn't summon a drop."

"You'd be a perfect picnic partner." He flushed, then continued down the list. "Thunderbolt throwing. Wound healing. How about sea parting? Invisibility cloaking. Mind reading. Palm reading."

"All tried. All failed."

He turned the form over. "Here's one people often overlook. Voice throwing."

She shook her head.

"Color changer."

"No."

"Did you try lightening *and* darkening?" he asked. "Lavenders are trickier than basic reds and blues."

"Couldn't even conjure a black smudge on a white ball."

"Not to worry. We have lots more choices." He smoothed a second form out on the counter. "I know we'll find something."

She glanced at her timekeep, then at the *Hours of Operation* sign mounted above a potted fern tree. The Talent Aid office closed in half an hour.

failed check by every talent.

She turned the form over. Level nine talents. The ones no one wanted to have.

Garbage de-stinker.

Sludge sweetener.

Corpse disintegrator.

She couldn't do those either. Her knees threatened to buckle, and she leaned against the service counter for support.

"Let's try this." Burke rummaged under the counter and pulled out a deck of playing cards. He held up one card. The imprint of a long-toothed telebeast faced her. "What suit? Trumpets, crowns, staffs, or coins?"

She strained to see through to the other side. She already knew card reading was not her talent. A lucky guess now wouldn't guarantee she'd pass a test tomorrow.

Burke jiggled the card encouragingly.

"Trumpets," she guessed.

He pursed his lips, then fanned out the deck. "Pick a card and make it disappear."

She couldn't.

His expression turned mournful. "Have you considered that you may not have a talent? That you may be a Deficient?"

Panic buzzed her like a swarm of angry hornets. She squeezed her eyes shut and silently chanted the affirmation she'd learned in nursery school. *You have a talent, I have a talent, We all have a talent.*

When she felt steadier, she opened her eyes. "Please, you have to help me. I have no idea what life is like on the mundane side of the Wall."

Burke leaned forward and waved her in close. "There are two options that I'm not supposed to mention. There's a tester who'll issue a certificate. No questions asked."

"How much does that cost?" she asked warily.

"Last I heard, one-hundred-thousand."

She gasped. She'd inherited enough to live frugally until she passed a talent test and got her work certificate. If this first option cost one-hundred-thousand credits, the second would surely cost more.

A sob clogged her throat as she turned to go. Tomorrow, she'd be marched to the Wall and forced into a realm she knew nothing about. She'd have to find a way to survive while the Truce Force auctioned off her home, kept half of the proceeds for their so-called fees and expenses, and then took months to transfer what was left to her account.

The energy sign sputtered in the window. *kcaB stiderC ruoY.*

My credits back. She spun around and slammed her fist on the counter. "I demand a refund. You didn't find my talent."

Burke's boss rushed out of his office. "A thousand apologies, Miss"—he snatched up her ID form—"Dare, for the substandard service." He leveled his gaze at Burke. "I warned you shoddy work would not be tolerated. Collect your things and don't come back."

Her mouth fell open. Had she caused Burke to be fired?

He rubbed the back of his neck, then pulled off his beret and shrugged out of his vest. Reaching under the counter, he withdrew a bulky, camouflage go bag and dropped in a nondescript work mug. As he walked past her, she tried to catch his eye, but he avoided her gaze.

She drew a shaky breath. Her lack of talent was ruining her life—and now she'd dragged him down, too. Could today get any worse?

The boss stood stiffly until the door shut, and Burke passed by the store windows. "Once again, let me apologize, Miss Dare. He said he'd been fully trained." He set a fresh set of forms on the counter. "First thing tomorrow, we'll go through these again. We'll find your talent."

Crystal clenched her fists. It was hopeless. Going through the forms again wasn't going to fix anything. She'd tried them all. Her talent—if she had one—wasn't on the Talent Aid lists.

Suddenly, she remembered. Burke had said there were two options, and she'd cut him off before he could explain the second.

Maybe the second one didn't require an almighty ransom. Maybe she had the talent it required. Maybe, just maybe, it would save her from being force-marched into exile.

She snatched her ID form out of the boss' hand, crumpled it into the hip pocket of her jumpsuit, and bolted for the exit.

CHAPTER 2

Truce Rule 2(b): Citizens may take one (1) Talent test per day.

Truce Rule 7(a): The list of certified talents is subject to change.

Burke stopped at the corner of 5th and Mage Street and leaned against the streetlamp pole. He'd botched another undercover assignment.

His orders were to keep his mouth shut and his eyes open. Covertly record corrupt practices like overbilling, temporary talent boosting, and denied money-back guarantees. When the Rebellion amassed enough evidence, proof of Talent Aid's deceitful practices would be broadcast throughout the realm on animated flyers. No one would be able to deny that the Talent Aid Corporation—hand in hand with the Truce Force—fleeced the citizens it was supposed to help.

Like Crystal Dare. She'd shelled out a small fortune in test fees and still come up empty.

He longed to help her. She'd strode into the Aid office with her flowing mahogany hair, smoky blue eyes, and figure-hugging denim jumpsuit and...sparked him. Nothing like that had ever happened to him before.

She'd interrupted him before he could describe the second option, but now that he'd had a few moments to clear his head, he was relieved. Mind-melds were illegal, and the soul readers who performed them were outlaws.

Public servicasts compared mind-melds to terminal roulette, but that description was misleading. The number of SAMMs, suicides after mind-melds, was less than point one percent.

However, not all mind-meld outcomes were cake and sunshine. He was living proof of that. Bad talents, like his, required constant struggle. Whenever he let down his guard, he blurted something inappropriate, triggered a mishap, or caused a scene. Each encounter, every situation was different. The only constant was he made things worse.

He forced all thoughts of bad jokes, magical sparks, and Crystal Dare out of his mind. Time to face Commander Ahrens and concede that she was right. He wasn't suited to be an undercover agent. The Rebellion needed janitors, too.

"Burke, wait up!"

He looked over his shoulder, and his heart leaped into his throat.

Crystal darted recklessly into the street, right into the path of two lorries and a minicab.

Transports lurched to a halt in a squeal of brakes. She crossed the street and hurried up to him. "I have to know. What's the second option?"

Before he could answer, the melon-sized bulb in the overhead streetlamp buzzed ominously, then shattered with a loud *pop*. Shards of glass plummeted toward them like razor-sharp sleet.

He spun her out of harm's way and somehow ended up in her arms. Sparks bounced between their bodies again. This time, the sensation felt like a welcome breeze on a scorching summer day.

"Soothing in the Talent Aid office," she murmured. "Now cooling out here. How many talents do you have, Burke? Wait, don't answer that." She seized his hand, pulled him under a city bus stop shelter, and pointed at the sparks. "Are you doing this?"

"No. It has to be you. Maybe it's your talent."

"I wish." She kicked at a crack in the sidewalk. "What's yours again?"

His chest tightened. He hated his talent, always making things worse. He hated that he'd be mopping floors instead of actively overthrowing the system that forcibly separated Talents from Mundanes. Most of all, he hated having to explain his talent. "I already told you. I make things worse."

Her eyes widened. "I thought you were joking. You have a certificate in making things worse? Of all the stupid...." She shook her fists in the air. "How does making things worse protect and preserve the common good?"

"I have no idea," he hissed. "I'd rather have no talent than the one I've got, but there's nothing I can do about it. It's the one I was born with."

She set her hand on his arm.

He shrugged it off. "I didn't put 'making things worse' on the certified talent list. The damned Truce Force did."

She reached out again.

He recoiled and took a step back. "Haven't you wondered why peace talks between the Talents and Mundanes always break down? It's because Truce Forcers aren't the ones being banished. They're getting rich off people like you. You return week after week, pay for test after test. The Truce Forcers need to be thrown out and—"

"Don't you think I know it?" She cuffed his shoulder. "I'm about to be banished because of their arbitrary rules. But I don't have time to wait for the change I believe in. I need a talent right now." Her chest heaved with anger, straining the tan buttons of her jumpsuit. "Are you going to explain the second option or not?"

Breathing hard, Burke glanced at the ground, then gazed straight into her eyes. He had to try to make things better for her. However, he couldn't simply spit out 'mind-meld' and walk away. "I'll tell you, but not here. Not out in the open."

He stepped out of the shelter and scanned both sides of the bustling intersection. "There. The Shamrock Tavern. They have privacy booths."

Happy Time was in full swing in the pub. The tunes of a Celtic jig danced out of recessed speakers, creating a cheery, fill-my-glass-again atmosphere. Two servers sporting spotless waist aprons maneuvered skillfully around tables and up to high-backed booths, their compact credit processors hovering near their wrists.

Burke spotted an unoccupied booth and stood until Crystal settled on a cushioned seat. He sat facing her and toggled the privacy switch. Faint blue tracer dots swirled around the booth. The toe-tapping music muted.

Satisfied, he set his credit disc at the edge of the table.

A blond server approached, processed his disc, and opened a bar tab. "What'll it be, my friends?"

"Donneybrook ale for me," Crystal said.

"Make it two," Burke seconded.

"Excellent choice." The server swirled his hand over the table. Two full, froth-topped mugs appeared. "And because today's been a fine day," he continued, "and you are a fine-looking couple...." He swirled his hand over the table again.

A hot skillet of tato crisps topped with melted cheese appeared. A second swirl materialized three side sauces. "Enjoy."

Crystal nodded appreciatively at the retreating server, and then gingerly plucked out a golden tato slice and dipped it into the tart cream sauce. "I'll eat. You talk. What's the second option?"

Burke turned the privacy setting to high. "I know a soul-reader who unlocks magic talents."

Her eyes narrowed as she picked up her mug. "Mind-melds are illegal."

"So is not having a talent."

She set down her mug, untouched, and pursed her bow-shaped lips. "How much does it cost?"

"Allegiance to the Rebellion."

"You found the Rebellion?" She leaned forward. "How? I've been searching for months."

He drew a deep breath and looked down at his moonstone ring. "My father was a toy builder who worked magic with hand tools. The day before his twenty-first, the Truce Force revamped the certified talent list and decertified the talents that were no longer on it. His hand-tool talent was one of them. Desperate for help, he rushed to a Talent Aid office, but they couldn't find a substitute talent. He was banished the next day."

"That's outrageous. How old were you?"

Burke drew an X in the condensation coating his mug. His dad only had time to leave him two things, a teary photocast and his moonstone ring. "Too young to understand why he was sent away."

"That must have been hard for you."

"It was worse on my mom," he said bitterly. "She and my dad were planning their wedding and had set up a joint credit account. When she went to pay the rent, her credit balance was zero. The Talent Aid office had drained her account for 'Services Rendered' despite their money back guarantee. When she filed a complaint, the office locked its doors, and a Truce Force administrator stamped her case *Closed*."

He lowered his voice even though the privacy block was engaged. "Two weeks later, that Talent Aid office reopened under quote-unquote new management. Mom joined the Rebellion and has worked nonstop to expose Talent Aid corruption ever since."

"Have you heard from your dad? Or about him? Is he alive?"

"Mom's sure he's alive. She says she'd know if he weren't." Burke thumped his chest. "In here. In her heart."

Crystal pushed the skillet in front of him. "When did you join?"

"On my nineteenth."

She nodded pensively. Her long hair caressed her shoulders. "Do you think it will work for me? The mind-meld?"

Unable to promise, he dipped a tato slice into the hot radish sauce and chewed it slowly.

Shame burned the back of his throat. The soul-reader hadn't found the glimmer of a second talent inside him, not one. Making things worse was the only talent he had. 'You'd be better off being a Deficient,' the soul-reader had said.

"Did he unlock your talent?" she pressed.

Burke gulped the rest of his ale. "He confirmed it. My talent is making things worse."

Crystal reached across the table and covered his hand with hers. "You haven't made my life worse."

He gazed into her eyes and for a moment saw himself in a different light. His heart thumped in his chest. With each beat, the desire to protect her grew stronger.

"I'll take you to the soul-reader," he said. "But know this. You'll have to live with the talent he unlocks, whether you like it or not."

She emptied her mug and set it down with a decisive *thump*. "I have to do it. It's my only hope."

CHAPTER 3

Truce Rule 6(d): Talent tests are administered at Truce Force test sites.

Truce Rule 6(e): Practice tests may be taken at Talent Aid offices.

Crystal ran her fingers over and over the jagged edges of the crack in the stained plastileather tram seat. She and Burke had changed trams three times, and she didn't recognize any of the streets or graffiti-coated buildings that whizzed by.

The tram joggled around a curve, then plunged into a tunnel. The car's dim lights flickered, momentarily turning the silent, scattered passengers into menacing apparitions.

Her nerves already on edge, she shuddered.

"You all right?" Burke asked.

She nodded. "I just want it to be over. Get my certificate and know I'm safe." She laced her fingers in her lap, hoping they'd stop trembling. "Does it hurt?"

"What? The mind-meld?" He cocked his head toward one shoulder. "I wouldn't describe it as painful. More like a probing. I felt it here." He tapped several spots on the back of her head and then the center of her forehead. "And here."

A shower of tiny sparks tickled the bridge of her nose.

"What about payment?" she asked. "How do I swear allegiance to the Unity Rebellion?"

"Don't worry." He stretched out his long jean-clad legs. "I'll take care of that."

Don't worry? She squeezed her hands until her knuckles turned white. Why didn't he understand? She needed to know what to expect. "Is there some sort of ceremony? Do they prick my finger and make me sign an oath with blood?"

He shook his head. "You've watched too many shock movies."

"Then stop being evasive and tell me."

"It's simple. You show your ID, and I vouch for you."

"That's it?"

"It is when you're a day away from being banished."

She pressed her palms against her stomach and tried to will away her jitters. His explanation made sense. Her mother had often chided her for having an overactive imagination.

The tram emerged from the tunnel. The sight of daylight calmed her.

"I'm sorry I got you fired," she said.

"That's okay. I wasn't working for the paycheck."

"Of course." She swiveled sideways to face him. "You were working undercover. That's what Rebellion agents do." She lowered the pitch of her voice and mocked a familiar public servicast. "Be on the lookout. A Rebellion agent could be sitting next to you right now."

"Makes us sound scary." A grin lit up his face, then faded quickly.

This was the second time he'd smiled since they met. The off-kilter tilt of his lips that had bothered her before now seemed endearing. She impulsively touched his hair. The thick glossy strands were surprisingly soft, like velvet or silk. "I don't think you're scary."

He pulled back. "That's because you don't know me."

"I know enough to know you're helping me."

"Don't," he said sharply. "You may hate what the soul-reader tells you. Then you'll hate me."

A bright flash swept the window. Startled, she turned and looked out.

The hair on the back of her neck stood up. The bright light emanated from the peak of a lighthouse she'd seen only in news broadcasts. The tram was approaching the waterfront warehouse district. The place where runaways disappeared. A place she'd been warned never, ever to go.

Burke picked up his go bag. "We're here."

This couldn't be right. Why would the Rebellion keep its headquarters here? The warehouse district was a maze of dark alleys and dead ends, reputedly rife with illicit magic, manipulative magic. Her heart pounded. Was trusting Burke a mistake?

He unzipped his bag and pulled out a long-brimmed, midnight blue cap. "Put this on."

She withdrew until her back hit the metal sill of the tram window. Her pulse raced with fear. "Why?"

"Security cameras. Tomorrow's your twenty-first. The Truce Force doesn't need to know you're here."

Again, his explanation seemed reasonable. Her pulse slowed. "I get it. You're protecting the soul-reader."

"I'm protecting every member of the Rebellion, including you." He set the cap on her head and tugged the six-inch brim down low. Everything above her nose level went dark.

The tram slowed with an ear-piercing squeal of brakes. The doors rumbled open.

He held her back until the other riders disembarked, then led her out onto an elevated platform. Below, a steady stream of lorries lumbered on a paint-streaked thruway, each laden with goods for or from one of the hundreds of warehouses that crowded the waterfront zone.

Laborers scurried along gray-ribbon footpaths. The air reeked with the sulfurous stink of stagnant water and spent magic.

"Stairs are to your left," Burke murmured.

Their feet hit the steps in unison as they descended the wide metal staircase. They reached a landing, angled, and started down another flight. With each rung, her view grew smaller. She couldn't see Burke's face, and that filled her with foreboding.

When they finally reached the bottom, she tapped the brim of the cap. "Can I take this off now?"

"Not yet." He cupped her elbow. "This way."

They stepped quickly along a sidewalk. Transports roared past, their levitation jets blasting. An air horn blared.

She raised her chin and attempted to track the sound, but the confining duckbill brim blocked her view.

"Almost there," he insisted.

She heard an ominous *crackle*, and then nothing. No motors, no honks, no footsteps.

A cobweb fog swirled up around her. Her flesh prickled, and she cried out to Burke for help, but the fog swallowed her plea. She couldn't hear her own voice.

Oh God. She'd put her trust in someone whose talent was making things worse. He'd made sure the Truce Force cameras didn't record her face. If something bad happened, if she failed to show up at the Wall tomorrow, no one would know to search for her here.

What had she done?

CHAPTER 4

Truce Rule 2(c): Talents must be individual. Linked, co-dependent, and interactive talents are not valid.

Truce Rule 1(c): Truce Force decisions are final.

The suffocating fog vanished. Crystal stood in the mouth of a cul-de-sac between two towering warehouses. A warding barricade shimmered behind her.

Burke's hands steadied her shoulders. "Are you okay?"

Okay? No, she wasn't okay. She'd thought she was about to die. She took a step back, stripped off the duckbill cap, and slapped it against his chest. "I've never passed through a barrier that strong before. Why didn't you warn me?"

He gulped. "I didn't think it would affect you like that. I just wanted to get you safely inside."

"Am I safe?" She glared at him. "Where's the Rebellion?"

"In there." He pointed at a set of steep concrete steps cut into a head-high loading dock.

They approached the dock, climbed the steps, and walked into a cavernous space filled with rows of industrial shelves. Red preservation glows encased each filled shelf. The Rebellion was stockpiling food and supplies.

She heard a hum overhead and looked up.

A man with a trim beard, his head covered by a yellow bandana, hovered on a floating pallet stacked with cartons of squeezefruit. He locked eyes with her, then tapped a black communicator on his right shoulder.

A deafening *whoop-whoop-whoop* suddenly split the air.

Burke grabbed her hand. "Follow me!"

He towed her deep into the warehouse. They slipped through a strip curtain, rushed past more towering shelves, and raced around a corner.

Four brawny men jumped out and stopped them. Each man wore a battle-gray jumpsuit and a sidearm holster attached to a black utility belt. One clamped his big-boned hand around her arm and growled, "Just where do you think you're going?"

Her heart hammered.

Burke took a defiant step forward. Compared to the four fighters he resembled a bean pole, easily snapped in two.

A tall woman with wavy, silver-streaked hair strode up.

"Commander Ahern." The fighter holding Crystal's arm snapped to attention. "Burke allowed an intruder into—"

The commander silenced him with a chop of her hand. "You and you." She pointed at Burke and Crystal. "Come with me."

Crystal stood in front of Commander Ahern's desk while Burke summarized the talents she didn't have. Weather, horticulture—she knew the list by heart.

Floating orb lamps lit the commander's oval office with shadowless light. Straight-backed chairs sat on both sides of the desk, two in front, one behind. On long, metal shelves, wire file organizers stood like soldiers at parade rest. Oversized maps of every district in the city papered the wall behind her desk.

A side wall was crowned with a bronze plaque engraved with the Rebellion Creed:

All talents—mundane and magical—are equal.

Judging twenty-firsts is unjust.

We will abolish the Spellcaster Truce.

The Wall will fall.

Burke finished his recitation and fell silent.

Ahern paced behind her desk. "Did you offer her a refund?"

"I didn't get a chance to. Slavik ordered me to leave."

"Leave?" Ahern stopped and raised her brow.

He shuffled his feet. "His exact words were, 'Collect your things and don't come back.'"

"You were fired." The commander frowned. "Again."

"It wasn't his fault," Crystal cut in. "I demanded a refund, and the Slavik guy blamed Burke. Then he tried to talk me into coming back tomorrow to go through the same stupid lists again, but that will be too late. I need a talent tonight."

The commander ignored her and lashed out again at Burke. "So you told her you could get her a soul-reading."

Crystal clenched her fists until her nails dug into her palms. Burke didn't deserve a dressing down—any more than she deserved to be banished. "I'm sure I have a talent. Everyone does. I just need help to identify it."

She pulled her ID out of her hip pocket and slapped it down on the desk. Her two-inch hologram formed above the square wafer. "I've wanted to join the Rebellion for a long time, but I didn't know how. You don't make it easy."

She paused and prayed her ID and Burke's witness were all she needed. They were all she had, all that stood between her and deportation to the other side of the Wall.

Ahern pursed her lips. Slowly shook her head.

"She's who we're fighting for," Burke snapped. "Twenty-firsts like her. And Dad."

Crystal gasped. Was this woman—the local Rebellion commander, the person who decided who could see the soul-reader and who would be turned away—Burke's mother?

Tears filled Ahern's eyes. She looked down and stroked the slender silver band on her little finger. "I hope you were careful."

"I was, Mom," Burke said. "Privacy booth setting on high."

"Mind-melds are dangerous."

"I know." He laced his fingers around Crystal's fingers and raised their clasped hands. Firefly sparks formed an iridescent mitten. "But how often does this happen?"

His mother's eyes widened. She tapped her shoulder communicator.

A crisp voice answered, "Safe-care."

"Ahern here. I have a twenty-first who needs an emergency reading."

"Are you sure, ma'am?"

"I'm sure." Burke's mom disconnected. Then she deactivated Crystal's ID, handed it back, and walked around her desk. "Welcome to the Rebellion, Crystal Dare."

"That's it? I'm in?" Crystal sank into the nearest straight-backed chair, which was funny because she felt light enough to float away. For the first time in two long, lonely years, she wasn't alone. She'd joined forces with Burke, his mom, and every Rebellion fighter to end the Spellcaster Truce and reunite the magic and mundane realms. She couldn't wait to put on a uniform. Meet her fellow fighters. Get her first assignment. Tear down the Wall.

"Crystal, dear," Ahern said gently. "Have you had anything to eat or drink in the past hour?"

"No. It was a long tram ride."

"Good. Burke threw up all over the soul reader's shoes."

Crystal followed Burke and his mom into a bustling work center. Colorful tear-down-the-wall posters lined the walls. Jumpsuited fighters clustered on broadcast production sets. Dozens more sat along a long, curved workstation that faced a huge wall-mounted screen displaying the names of Talent Aid offices. Each name was prefaced by a red, yellow, or green light.

"All one hundred and fifty-three offices," Ahern explained. "The green light means we have proof that Talent Aid office is corrupt. Offices with yellow lights need corroboration. Reds still need to be caught."

Crystal scanned the alphabetical display. Triple A Talent Aid had a yellow light. Now that she knew Rebellion agents worked undercover...

She turned toward his mom. "If Triple A denies me a refund tomorrow morning, and I secretly record it, would that be enough corroboration?"

Ahern nodded thoughtfully. "Let's find your talent first."

They crossed to the other side of the work center and walked down a wide hallway, passing a cafeteria, relief stations, and an infirmary. The corridor narrowed and ended at a thick steel door marked *Authorized Personnel Only.*

Ahern positioned her feet on two floor markers and was quickly enveloped in scan light. A mechanical voice said, "Identity confirmed."

The entry door slid open. They walked through, and it shut behind them.

They stood in a small anteroom.

A slender woman dressed in aqua nursing scrubs stood at attention in front of a door. "Commander."

"Mercy," Ahern acknowledged. "Is the soul-reader ready?"

"I roused him, ma'am, but a mind-meld could—"

"I know Erian's frail," the commander said. "I also know he's not afraid to die." Her voice softened. "He can refuse, Mercy. Let's leave it up to him."

"Wait," Crystal said, suddenly uncertain. She couldn't go through with the mind-meld if it hurt the soul reader. No matter how desperate she was.

"It's all right." Burke's mom wrapped her arm around Crystal's back. "Erian has the right to decide what he will and won't do. Just like the rest of us." She nodded at Mercy.

The nurse opened the door and stepped aside.

Crystal had never seen anyone like the wizened man in the next room. Tufts of white hair crowned his long, narrow head. Big, cat-like eyes lacked both brow and lashes. His limbs were stunted, his chest a barrel. Cloaked in a short, burgundy velvet robe, he sat in a hover chair in front of a screen with woodland decorations. A pine scent perfumed the air.

He extended greeting hands toward the commander. His high-pitched voice quavered. "Astra, 'tis good to see you. How goes the fight?"

Burke's mom bent and kissed his cheek. "Making progress, Erian, as always."

"I am told someone needs me." He crooked his index finger at Crystal. "Step forward, child. Don't be afraid. What's your name?"

"Crystal Dare, sir." She willed herself not to quake as his gaze swept slowly over her.

"Tomorrow is your twenty-first?"

"It is, yes."

"And you say you don't possess a talent."

"Not one that's on the Truce Force lists."

"What would you like it to be?"

"Sir?"

"Your talent. If you could choose one, what would it be?"

She did have a secret wish. "Baby-cry translator."

Approval lit up his face. "I hope you are right. Kneel, please."

She complied.

The soul reader adjusted the height of his hover chair, then leaned forward and touched his forehead to hers. His skin was paper-smooth and pleasantly warm. She closed her eyes and braced for a stab of pain.

A butterfly-like flutter touched the crown of her head, then penetrated her skull. She felt a *ping* behind her eyes. A *zing* at the base of her neck. A first-to-last review of her life flashed like a highspeed chase on her closed lids and left her breathless.

Erian pulled back, and she opened her eyes.

His expression was grim. "You have a very rare talent, Crystal Dare. One that puts you in grave danger."

CHAPTER 5

Truce Rule 1(a): The Truce must be defended at all costs.

Truce Rule 1(b): All rules defend the Truce.

A chill ran down Crystal's spine. What sort of talent would put her in grave danger? High-wire-performer? Bomb-defuser?

The soul reader continued. "You are a lucky charm. For better or worse, you make other people's talent stronger."

She struggled to her feet. "You must be mistaken. I've never affected anyone's talent."

"You affected Burke's in the Talent Aid office and under the streetlamp. And then there's this." He instructed Burke to touch her forearm. Sparks cascaded between his fingers and her wrist.

"He's doing that, not me."

"Technically, you are correct," Erian said. "Burke has developed a secondary talent, but he's only able to do it because of you."

She swung her hands behind her back to stop the glittering shower. She needed a talent of her own to get a certificate, not one that was dependent on Burke. Under Truce Force rules, linked, co-dependent, and interactive talents were invalid.

"That can't be Crystal's talent if she only affects him." Burke's mom freed one of Crystal's hands and held it up. "See, Erian? Not one spark between us. Not even a glimmer."

"Because sparking is not one of your talents, Astra," the soul reader explained patiently. "Yet Crystal has had a lucky charm effect on you."

Burke's mom stiffened. "She has not."

"Before today, when was the last time you treated Burke like a son?"

The commander blanched. She stared at Burke while he stared at the floor.

The awkward silence lingered.

Erian elevated his hover chair until his face was level with Crystal's. "You must not tell anyone about your talent."

"But tomorrow's my last chance to pass a test. If I don't get a certificate, I'll be banished."

"Everyone wants a lucky charm. Especially those who would take advantage of it. Take advantage of you."

She gulped. "The Truce Force?"

"Precisely."

"If they find out, you will be imprisoned and forced to do their bidding."

"Crystal can live and work here," Burke exclaimed. "We could keep her safe."

Erian shook his head sadly. "I would like that. We all would. But she has taken innumerable tests and set up a Talent Aid account. The Truce Force knows tomorrow is her twenty-first. If she does not pass a talent test or present herself at the Wall tomorrow, they will issue an alert. Security scans will show she entered the Mage Street tram with you and exited here. They will poke and prod and eventually storm this building. Everything you have worked so hard for will be lost."

Dark spots formed in front of Crystal's eyes. If she claimed her magic talent, she'd jeopardize the Rebellion. And if the Truce Force learned about it, they'd abuse her. Exploitation or banishment—those were her choices.

Burke put his arms around her and stroked her hair.

She clung to him and sobbed. A few minutes ago, she thought she'd joined the Rebellion and gained a new family. Now she had twelve hours to pack, visit her parents' graves, and suffer the humiliation of failing one last talent test.

As soon as she was able, she pulled herself together and said, "I should go."

Erian gave her a blessing, then retreated behind the forest screen.

Mercy squeezed her hand and whispered, "Good luck."

Ahern hugged her. "I'll have someone transport you home."

Burke walked her out to the loading dock and escorted her down the steps.

A man wearing dark sunglasses and a navy Mage Courier Service uniform stood beside the passenger side of a white delivery van. He set his hand on the door handle and nodded. This was her ride.

Tears filled her eyes again, and she blinked them away before turning toward Burke. "You did warn me I might not like what the soul reader said."

Burke hung his head. "I'm sorry," he whispered. "I never meant to make your life worse."

"You didn't. For years, I thought I didn't have a talent. I believed I was worthless, a disappointment to my parents. Thanks to you, I know differently. I have a very special, very rare talent."

"One you can't claim," he exclaimed. "It isn't fair."

"Then keep fighting to make it fair. Go undercover at another Talent Aid office. Turn all one hundred and fifty-three lights green and broadcast the evidence. People will rise up because the system is corrupt."

He drew her into a second embrace and held her as if he didn't want to let go.

Sparks enveloped them from head to toe and showered her with the certainty that she'd met her soulmate.

The van driver cleared his throat.

She had to go. She rose up on her toes and kissed Burke's cheek. "I'll never forget you."

Crystal didn't sleep at all. After visiting her parents' graves, she lugged everything of value out of the house. Dishes, furniture, books, plants—she set everything on the lawn for people to take. Then she packed her father's high-handled vinespeller's tote with an assortment of clothes, her mother's tortoise-shell hairbrush, a blanket, and a poncho that could serve as a coat or a tent. Into the tote's front pocket, she tucked her father's silver letter opener, the only thing she'd found that could serve as a defensive weapon.

At eleven-thirty, she reported to the Mage Street Talent Testing Station. She felt numb on the outside, hollow on the inside.

A Truce Forcer asked for her hologram ID. Another asked what talent test she wanted to take.

Her emotions warred. She wanted so badly to declare her talent and claim the right to stay on this side of the Wall. This was her home, where the memories of her parents and her childhood resided, where she could do some good fighting against injustice.

On the other hand, Erian's warning had frightened her to the core. To live imprisoned and used by the very entity that she wanted to abolish was not an option. She did the only thing she could do under the circumstances.

She lied.

She stood her ground and pretended she was a nobody. A lowly, unworthy mundane. A Deficient.

A third Truce Forcer handed her a paper card listing her name and banishment date and marched her out a narrow back door.

The Wall loomed in front of her, a hundred feet high, fortified with energy cables. Helmeted Truce Forcers wielding stout black batons stood in two parallel lines. The ten-foot-wide gap between them led to the thick gate that would open at exactly noon. At the same time, an identical gate would swing open on the other side.

Gripping her father's tote, she trudged past the first set of Truce Forcers, her eyes downcast.

"Crystal!"

She stopped and looked up. For a moment, she thought she saw Burke standing in the crowd of deportees assembled in front of the gate.

It couldn't be. He'd had a talent certificate, a mom, and the Rebellion. He wouldn't sacrifice them for her—and she wouldn't want him to. They were too precious. But oh, how she would miss him.

Tears flooded her eyes, and she stumbled.

"Keep moving." A Truce Forcer prodded her with his baton.

"Leave her alone!"

"Burke?" She wiped her eyes and scanned the crowd again. He was there, the olive-green straps of his camo go bag draping his shoulders. Two Truce Force guards prevented him from rushing back to meet her.

Her heart raced. She didn't know whether to laugh or cry. He was here, giving up everything to be with her on the other side of the Wall.

He waved as she approached. She squeezed between the two guards, but before she could say anything, he cupped her face and crushed his lips against hers.

Sparks tickled her cheeks as she let her tote drop to the ground. She and Burke had an undeniable, magical connection. On the mundane side of the wall, it would be their secret. Their special, potent, powerful secret.

She wrapped her arms around him and kissed him back.

"Our orders are to find my dad," he murmured when they finally separated. "Then determine if there's a Mundane Rebellion force. If there is, we'll join it. If not, we'll start one."

A siren sounded. The gate opened. The Truce Forcers closed ranks behind the crowd of deportees to ensure no one tried to escape.

Burke picked up her tote and held out his other hand.

She laced her fingers between his. They were fighters on a mission. Lovers with a secret. Facing the unknown together.

The End.

ABOUT THE AUTHOR

Ana Morgan lives with her husband and three very spoiled rescue cats in a log cabin on an organic farm in north central Minnesota. Weekdays, she creates Secret Garden soup mixes. On the weekends, you'll find her out in her son's market garden or in the kitchen, baking with her grandkids.

In addition to The Talent Test, she has published two historical western romances and two sweet novelettes. Works-in-progress include a romantic suspense about a reclusive blogger determined to prove her imprisoned father is not a murderer and a time travel romance set in 1490s Brittany. She is also chronicling Crystal and Burke's adventures on the Mundane side of the Wall.

Visit her Website

Join her newsletter

Go to www.AnaMorgan.net

ALSO BY ANA MORGAN

Sweet Contemporary Novelettes

Neely's Big Idea

Tricia's Dream

Western Historical Novels

Stormy Hawkins

Mary Masters

https://www.anamorgan.net

ID Johnson

HE'S A
ROGUE
AND MY
MATE

BLURB

Tucker

When my mother insisted I run from my pack lands during an attack, I was terrified and all alone. I had no idea I'd be running right into the arms of my mate. Now, with her by my side, I know I can return to my village and claim what is rightfully mine--the title of Alpha.

Charlotte

Finding a rogue in the caves near my village was scary, but the more I got to know Tucker, the more I realized he was special. In fact, I realized he is my mate. But when he returns to his own territory, will I leave everything behind for him? Or will we have to say goodbye?

Based on She's My Beta and My Mate, He's a Rogue and My Mate is a shifter romance you won't want to put down until the very last word.

Chapter 1: The Nightmare Begins

Tucker

My lungs burn as I run through the forest, too scared to look behind me. The screams of my family echo in my mind, and no matter how far from home I travel, I know I'll never get those cries out of my psyche.

Dirt flies up out of the forest floor along with dry pinecones and leaves, and I can't help but think about the death and destruction I'm leaving behind.

My parents... my friends... everyone in my village.... Will anyone else make it out alive?

I can't let my mind go there right now, though, or else my feet will falter. I have to think about what my mother told me to do.

"Run, Tucker. Run as far as you can, as fast as you can, and don't ever look back!"

I had shifted and taken off, seeing the terror in her eyes. I didn't understand why she couldn't come with me or why my father wasn't alongside us, but I knew his responsibilities as Alpha meant that he couldn't leave the pack.

Even if it meant he would die fighting to defend the village.

I dodge around a large bush, and a thorn tugs at my fur, pulling out a large hunk. I know I should probably stop and collect the gray hair and get rid of it so that I can't be so easily followed, but I don't want to stop because I have no idea if I'm being chased or how close behind me they might be.

Mom said to keep running for as long as I can run, and I don't know where I'll end up, but I'm not slowing yet.

I keep going. For hours, I run, and I don't even know what direction I'm headed or how many other packs' territories I've crossed through. I know that if I'm caught by a patrol, I'll be in big trouble for trespassing. I can only hope that if I'm caught, it will be by an Alpha that is merciful and can understand the situation I'm fleeing.

Part of me feels like a coward, that I should've stayed and fought. But my mother has lost so much in her life…. When she was younger, her family was slaughtered in their beds while they slept. My mom was the only one that lived, and that was because she was spending the night at a friend's house. Now, here we are in a similar situation where her family is being attacked again.

How could I possibly argue with her logic?

I couldn't.

And that's why I'm running.

The sun is beginning to come up in front of me. It will be easier for other wolves to see me in the daytime. I have been running for three or four hours and have probably covered at least a hundred miles. Over rough terrain, jumping over bushes and fences, that's pretty good time.

But I can go further, and my mother's words echo in my mind, so I keep going.

I stop for nothing, not even a drink of water or to find fresh game to eat. I keep running until I literally cannot run anymore. By then… it's dark at night, and I am exhausted.

I need to find a shelter, someplace to hide for the night.

In the distance, I can see electric lights and realize I'm close to a village. I know I shouldn't go any closer. I can smell that it's a shifter village. I don't know whose territory I'm in, but I hope whoever it is will be merciful if I'm found.

We are near the mountains, so I hope that perhaps I can find a shelter. Sniffing around, I try to pick up on the scent of minerals or dripping water.

I find a large cropping of boulders and check there until I see an opening big enough for my wolf to climb into.

A cave....

This will work. I'm so tired, and my muscles are aching. Tomorrow, I will have to find water and food. But for now... I will sleep.

As I collapse on the bottom of the cave, my mind goes back to what I've witnessed. People and wolves running, shouts and howls filling the air, the scent of smoke from the houses already lit on fire.

"Run, Tucker, run!" My mother's voice compels me to take off....

I fall asleep reliving the nightmare of the last twenty-four hours over and over again.

CHAPTER 2: BERRIES AND ROGUES

Charlotte

Autumn is always beautiful around where we live. The primary village of Midnight Moon is located just south of a beautiful mountain range that rolls down into the forests that surround our town.

While I would say every season is gorgeous, there's just something about the leaves changing color in the fall that makes the entire place look like something out of a dream.

It's also a great time to go out into the woods to collect wild berries. My friends and I have been doing it every year since we were first old enough to go into the woods alone at twelve, so this time around will be our seventh adventure, and I am looking forward to it more than most.

"Charlotte," my friend Beth says as we head off into the woods carrying our baskets and our backpacks with water bottles and snacks, "how can you be so chipper first thing in the morning?"

I shrug. "I'm always excited to come out into the woods with you and Misty and Hannah," I tell her. The four of us have been best friends since kindergarten, maybe before, and we go practically everywhere together.

"She must've had more coffee than us," Misty jokes. She's trailing behind the others, and I know she's tired because she had a date last night. Most of my friends date, but I've decided not to. I don't see the point. I'm waiting for my fated mate. While they're out having fun with random guys, I'm waiting for the Moon Goddess to deliver the perfect guy to me.

"How was your date with Ryan last night, anyway?" Beth asks her in a sing-song voice.

"Did the two of you make out?" She makes kissing noises until Misty catches up to smack her arm.

"No, stop it! We didn't make out!" We all laugh as we wind our way down the path that leads to our favorite berry patch.

"Did he at least kiss you goodnight?" Hannah wants to know. "Surely, he at least did that much."

I turn to look at Misty who isn't answering and see that her face is turning as red as a strawberry. We all giggle because her non-answer is a definite answer.

"He's so dreamy," Beth says.

"Yeah, but not as dreamy as Charlotte's brother," Hannah chimes in, and the others pretend to swoon.

All but me. "Gross," I say, but I'm not surprised to hear it. All of my friends are always fawning all over my older brother, Eli. To me, he's just a pest. Besides, they don't have to smell his dirty socks after he gets back from training.

"Do you think he'll be Beta someday?" Misty asks me.

"Eli? No. Why would he be? Beta Richard has a daughter." I stare at her like she's crazy.

"I know, but he's Alpha Micah's best friend, right?" she says. "So... maybe he'll just make your brother Beta."

I shake my head. "No, he can't do that. Besides, Zariah will be a perfectly fine Beta." Beta Richard's daughter is a couple of years older than me, so I don't know her that well, but she seems pretty nice to me.

"Well, Eli would make a great Beta, too," Misty concludes. "And a nice mate."

That gets everyone giggling again.

I try not to roll my eyes.

We continue walking through the woods until we get to the place where we usually find the most berries. Sadly, it looks like a lot of them are already gone. "That's too bad," I say, wondering who made it to our spot ahead of us. No one back at the village has said anything about coming out here, that I know of, and as far as I know, no one else ever does.

"We can get what's left and then look for more," Beth suggests.

Agreeing with her, we set out to pick what's there and enjoy the beauty of the forest. The autumn wind has a nip to it, but it doesn't bother us. Wolf shifters rarely have a problem with cold weather.

Once we've picked all of the berries from these bushes, we fan out, looking for more.

I wander around, looking in-between the trees and around bushes, following an old deer path. It leads toward a hill with a large cropping of rocks, one where I'm pretty sure there won't be any berries.

But... I hear something strange. It sounds like something large is walking around up by the old caves. I stop to sniff the air, expecting to catch the scent of a mountain goat or possibly a deer.

What I smell has me stopping in my tracks.

It smells like a wolf... a male... one not from our pack.

I pause just before one of the large boulders, realizing the scent is getting closer.

What if this is a rogue, and he attacks me?

Slowly, I begin to backtrack. I really don't want to have to shift and ruin my favorite jeans, but I also don't want to get eaten alive.

I am about ten feet away from the largest rock when I see something pop up behind it, and my blood runs cold.

A pair of emerald green eyes, glowing at me.

My only thought is, "Run!"

CHAPTER 3: BEGGING AND PLEADING

Tucker

I am staring at a beautiful set of light blue eyes, and when I realize the face of the girl who is staring right back at me is the most gorgeous I've ever seen, I feel panic well up inside of me.

Who is she, and why is she here?

Will she go tell her Alpha about me?

As she begins to back away, I realize I have to say something, and the mind-link won't work because she's obviously not in my pack. I've run too far for that to be the case. That... and there might not even be any survivors.

Quickly, I shift and stand behind a big boulder so she can't see my naked body. She's almost too far away from me by then to hear me, but I have to try. "Wait!" I tell her. "Please!"

She stops in her tracks and slowly turns around, her eyes still wide and her mouth agape.

"Please, hold on a sec. Let me put on some pants so I can talk to you," I tell her.

"Talk to me about what?" she asks, her voice high-pitched and quick, showing me she's at the least uncomfortable but potentially also scared of me.

"Please, just wait?" I beg her. "Please?"

After another long pause, she says, "Fine," and sighs loudly.

I rush off to get my pants from the cave, hoping she's not lying to me. Visions of an entire pack of large warrior wolves coming after me fill my mind, and I can't help but think I might have to leave my new home soon after arrival. I don't want to be chased away again, so maybe I can keep her from saying anything.

With my jeans on and my T-shirt in my hands, I run back out to see her still standing where I'd left her. She looks a little nervous, but not terrified. I decide to keep my distance, so I stop about ten feet from her.

"Thank you," I tell her, noticing the basket with a few berries in it slung across her arm for the first time. "I'm Tucker."

She stares at me, not wanting to tell me her name.

I guess I can't blame her. I swallow hard, trying not to notice how the sunlight catches the golden threads in her hair.

How can someone who's just lost their entire family and their pack be thinking about how gorgeous a girl is?

"I, uh, had to leave my home a few days ago, and I've been staying in this cave, but I don't mean anyone any trouble. I promise, I won't hurt anyone or anything."

"You're living in a cave?" she asks for clarification. "Why? Why don't you come into the village? We have people who will help you."

I quickly shake my head. "No, no thank you. That could be dangerous. I may have been followed, and I don't want to put anyone else at risk." That is part of it, but also, I don't trust anyone in her pack either. Why should I? I couldn't even trust my own packmates sometimes.

I'm fairly certain the reason we were infiltrated is because of a spy, but I have no proof.

"We have a strong army," she contends. "You don't need to worry about that."

I continue to shake my head. "No, thank you. But if you could please not tell anyone I'm out here, I would appreciate it. I won't stay for long, but I need to figure out what I'm doing."

In the distance, I hear another girl's voice shout, "Charlotte? Where are you?"

She looks over her shoulder. I want to run back behind the rocks so her friends don't see me. The more people who know I'm here, the more trouble I'm in.

"Please?" I ask her again.

She grumbles. "Fine!" she says. "But if I hear about anything fishy going on, I'm telling my Alpha. There'd better not be any dead bodies showing up or spies in our village!"

"No, of course not," I tell her. "I'm just one lone wolf, and my home pack is hundreds of miles from here. I wouldn't hurt anyone."

She narrows her eyes. "You ate all of our berries, didn't you?"

I glance down at her basket and recognize that she's picking the same kind of berries I found a few days ago. "I'm sorry," I tell her. It was easier to pick them than to keep killing small game, though I'd done that, too.

She lets out a deep breath as her friends yell her name again.

Charlotte. What a beautiful name.

"I've got to go," she tells me. "You'd better not be lying to me. My big brother is massive, and he could rip your head off." I see her checking out my chest. I'm not massive, but I'm not a weakling. She swallows hard and raises her eyes to my face again. "Just... be careful!"

"I will be, thank you," I tell her.

"You should probably move along before someone who's not so understanding finds you."

I nod. She's right.

But if I leave... I'll never see her again.

She turns around to go but pauses to look back over her shoulder. I can't help but give her a small, grateful smile.

She doesn't return it. She just... leaves. I watch her walk away and breathe a sigh of relief.

But then it occurs to me that even if I stay, I may never see her again.

And I don't like that idea.

I want to see her again.

CHAPTER 4: THINKING AND PLANNING

Charlotte

"Is everything okay, Charlotte?" Beth asks as I catch back up to my friends.

I know that I'm acting strange. I can't help it. The encounter that I just had with the young man—the lone wolf—was unsettling in a way. But maybe that was because I found his story intriguing. Or maybe I just found him to be intriguing....

"Everything is fine," I tell my friends. "I'm just tired. I didn't see any more berries, either."

"You're tired?" Misty asks. "You were so excited to come out here."

"I know." I sigh and try to keep my mind focused so they don't go back over there where I was to see what's really wrong. "But that was before the berries were all gone."

My friends seemed to buy my excuse. "I'm tired, too," Hannah agreed. "Let's head back home."

"Okay," Beth says as we all start walking over to the path that brought us there. "But maybe we can all go to Charlotte's house for a while."

I raise my eyebrows. "Come to my house for what?" I ask her.

"You know," she says, elbowing me. "So we can see if your brother's home."

"Maybe he's mowing the lawn with no shirt on," Hannah adds.

I taste bile in the back of my throat. "Don't make me gag." They all laugh, but my mind goes back to the guy I've just met, Tucker, and I can't help but think about how unbelievably hot he was.

He wasn't wearing a shirt, and his muscles were all so well defined. He wasn't as big as my stupid brother, but he had broad shoulders and a narrow waist. For a moment, I imagine myself pressing my hands against his chest.

I shake my head to clear it. I can't allow myself to become attracted to a rogue. He shouldn't even be here. With any luck, he'll be able to go home soon. I think about his family and the rest of his pack and hope that everything is okay.

The girls come over to my house for a bit, but then they leave, probably because Eli's not home, and now I'm lost in my thoughts.

By the time I go down to dinner, my mind is completely consumed by him. Not because he's so attractive but because I want to help.

He's got to be hungry if all he's eating is what he can catch and the berries he can find.

Also, who wants to sleep in a cave?

But he's told me not to tell anyone, and I don't want to betray that trust.

"Is everything okay?" my mom asks me. "You seem to have a lot on your mind, dear."

"I'm fine," I tell her with a smile, but she just arches an eyebrow at me.

"Did you go out into the woods today?" my dad asks. "To pick berries?"

"We did," I tell him. "But there wasn't a lot left."

"That's weird," Eli notes between shoveling large bites of pork chop into his mouth. "Wonder why not."

I think I know, but I won't say.

"The patrols have been seeing some strange activity out there by Demon's Den," my dad, Martin, says. "Be careful if you go out again."

Demon's Den. That's exactly where Tucker had been when I ran into him. "We're always careful," I assure him, but now I'm nervous. Do the patrols know that Tucker is out there?

"What kind of activity?" Eli asks.

"Just a lot of strange footprints and some carcasses. Looks like there might be a rogue or lone wolf hanging around up there. Until we can find out what's going on, be careful."

"All right," I say, hoping we can change the subject. My mom, Brenda, moves on to another topic and starts talking about something that happened at the hairdresser that day.

Soon enough, my mind wanders back to Tucker. What will the Omega warriors do if they catch him?

I'm not sure. But I don't want to find out. I need to warn him.... The sooner I can get out there to see him again, the better.

I'll just have to make sure that no one sees me. If my parents or anyone else from the pack knows that I'm sneaking out into the woods going to the place where the rogue was spotted, they might follow me, and if they do, he'll be in danger because of me. That's the last thing that I want.

We finish our dinner, and I go upstairs to get ready for the next day. I have training and then work. I am training for battle in case it's in our future, but I'm not a warrior. I have a regular job like a Gamma, even though technically my parents are Deltas—we're a little more important to the pack than some of the other families, essentially, but not Betas or related to the Alpha. I work at the coffeehouse at the moment, but I'd like to work at the bank or possibly become an accountant. Unlike humans, a lot of us don't go to college because our society is so dependent upon one another—we live a simple life and learn our jobs from one another, for the most part, while we are working,

In my room, I think about Tucker and what he's doing. I hope he's comfortable, though I doubt that is possible.

I decide to come up with a plan to make sure he has everything he needs until he can go home or move on.

Even though I've only spent a few minutes in his presence, already the idea of him moving on makes my heart feel heavy in a way I've never experienced before.

CHAPTER 5: SLEEP AND FOOD

Tucker

I spend that entire night sitting in the opening of the cave, waiting, listening. Wondering how long it will take for someone from the village to show up and run me off.

It's been a long few days. I'm exhausted and homesick, and all I want is for this nightmare to end. Part of me is tempted to take that girl–Charlotte's–advice and go into the village and ask for help.

But I'm too afraid. I'm scared that the Alpha isn't as loving and understanding as Charlotte thinks he is, and he might lock me up or return me to the situation I just ran from.

I do want to go back there someday and find out what happened to my parents and my pack, but I can't go back yet. I need to make sure that the situation is safe for me to return. I might be the only hope of my pack. If I have to seek revenge for my loved ones, I need to make sure I'm in the right frame of mind.

I sit there, watching the inky black sky lighten, and I can't help but think of her.

Charlotte.

Such a beautiful name.

Such a beautiful girl.

Her strawberry blonde hair was pulled up in a ponytail, with loose whisps framing her lovely face. Her eyelashes were long and accented her light eyes beautifully. Her complexion was like silk....

I am stupid for even letting my mind wander to her because there's no way she'll want to have anything to do with me.

I am a rogue wolf, and she is clearly an important member of her pack. I think she must be a Delta or something. She didn't seem like a Gamma or an Omega.

By the time the sky turns light blue, with shades of pink and yellow rising over the trees, I am nodding off, wondering how it is that no one has come searching for me.

Even though I'm starving and need to hunt, I can't move. I'm just too tired. I decide to go back to the farthest part of the cave and get a bit of sleep before I go try and find a rabbit or something.

My wolf form is better suited to sleeping on the ground, so I strip and shift, curling up on my clothes and bag, and soon, I am fast asleep.

When I wake up, several hours have passed. I can tell by the way the light is filtering in through the cave opening and the crick in my neck.

Something smells really good....

Puzzled, I get dressed and slowly make my way back to the opening of the cave, alarmed that someone might be out there, trying to use the scent of what I think is fried chicken, to lure me out.

I see a container sitting just inside of the opening. It appears to have a note on top of it. I'm still cautious, but I'm also curious. I don't smell any other wolves or humans, so I come over to it and pick up the note.

"Tucker, I thought you might be hungry. Also, be careful with your carcasses and footprints. Charlotte."

That's all it says.

I look around outside of the cave, but I don't see her. The faint scent of her perfume lingers in the air, so I think it hasn't been too long since she left, but I have no way of knowing for sure.

I open the plastic container to find eight pieces of fried chicken, a roll, and some mac and cheese.

This woman is amazing! She even left me a fork and some clean water in a container.

I have tears in my eyes as I sit back against the cave wall and devour every bite. When I'm done, I quietly take the chicken bones out and use them to set some traps in the woods nearby in hopes that I can catch some small animals to eat later if I need to, like maybe a fox. It's easier to hunt in my wolf form, but it's also dangerous. Other wolves might smell me easier when I've shifted into my other form. I'll heed her words if I catch anything.

I may just decide to stay here a while.... If that's the case, I need a more comfortable cave floor. I find some trees with large leaves that I can weave together to make a mat, and for the rest of the day, I work on that. Later that night, I see I have a badger in my trap!

I've never eaten badger before, but I'm hungry again since it's been a while since I've eaten, so I shift into my wolf and have some dinner.

The only thing that would've made this day better is if I'd seen Charlotte. Not that I'd rather be here than back at home in my house with my family, but at least my stomach is full, and I'm not being hunted—at the moment.

I can fall asleep tonight and dream about happier times—and maybe about a beautiful, kindhearted girl....

CHAPTER 6: QUESTIONS AND DECISIONS

Charlotte

He wasn't there when I went out to bring him something to eat.

I was disappointed. I was really hoping to see him again, even though I had no idea why.

It's not as if that guy is going to end up being my fated mate or anything. He isn't even from around here, and usually, the Moon Goddess has enough foresight to make sure your fated mate is nearby so you can find them.

Still... his story intrigues me, and I want to get to know him better. All of that despite the fact that I know he's going to be leaving soon. He'll likely have to. Our patrols might find him, and if they do, he could end up in trouble for being on our lands without permission.

I don't think that Alpha Micah would do anything to him, though. Our new Alpha is young and understands what it's like to be a kid. The fact that Tucker has been on the run might make Alpha Micah ask a lot of questions, but I don't think it will make him lock him up or anything.

Helping my mom load the dishwasher after dinner, I wonder if Tucker will stay out there all night and sleep on that cold, hard cave floor. I wish there was something I could do to help him.

"Are you all right, sweetie?" Mom asks me. "You seem like you've got a lot on your mind today."

It takes me a moment to snap out of my own thoughts in order to answer her. "Oh, uh, I'm fine. Just thinking about... stuff."

"What kind of stuff?" She hands me a plate to put into the dishwasher, so I do while I think.

"Oh, just what I wanna do with my life. I mean, I know I want to be an accountant, but other than that," I tell her. It's not a lie. Do I want to go out into the woods and look for that rogue who is living in the cave? Do I want to get to know him better? Do I want to move into the cave with him and live with him in the forest? Do I want to run away with him when he goes? I don't think I want to do most of those things, but the fantasy of leaving my life behind for a chance at love is intriguing.

My mom studies my face for a moment as she rinses the silverware. "I think there might be more to it than that, but that's not a bad thing to have on your mind. What brought that on?"

I shrug. "I don't know. I've just been thinking about it."

"Well, take your time and make a good decision. And remember, when you find your fated mate, everything might change." She smiles at me and hands me the last dish to put into the dishwasher.

Once it's in there, I close the door and turn the dishwasher on. She's told me before about how she met Dad at a Moon Goddess Ball when they were both twenty-two. But I haven't ever really paid attention to the story because I didn't care that much.

Until now. "How did you and Dad decide where you were going to live? Since you were from a different pack?"

Mom wipes her hands on a dishtowel as I rinse mine off, and then she hands it to me. "We had to talk about it," she explains.

"I wanted to stay with my family, and he wanted to stay with his, but since my family were Gammas, and he was a Delta, we decided it would be better for me to move here. It would be better for our children."

I understand what she's saying but think it would still be a hard decision to make, especially if one pack was quite far from the other. But then... my understanding is that the Moon Goddess usually tries to make it so that fated mates are close to one another, geographically speaking. Otherwise, it would be really hard for them to ever find one another to begin with.

Obviously, that means that Tucker's not my mate. Not that I ever thought he might be or wished he could be....

"Why do you ask?" Mom wants to know.

I look at her for a second and then move to the refrigerator to get a drink, trying to remember what started this discussion in the first place so I can make something up.

"Oh, uh, I was just thinking... whatever I decide to do, it might have some influence on where I end up living, depending upon whether or not my fated mate is from this pack or another one." I smile at her, and she nods, seeming to have bought my reason.

"Well, hopefully, your fated mate will be someone from our pack," she says. "That will make it a lot easier."

I nod as she lovingly pats me on the shoulder. "Hopefully," I say, taking a drink of my soda. But I don't really mean that.

When I think of all of the guys in Midnight Moon pack, not a single one of them stands out to me as someone I'd like to have as my mate. I mean, sure, there are some hot guys, like Alpha Micah and my brother's friend Alex.... But it's not realistic to think that I would marry the Alpha, and Alex is a little too old for me.

No, I really can't think of a single guy I'd like to marry from Midnight Moon....

But that doesn't mean I can't think of a single guy who intrigues me enough that if I found out he was my mate, I wouldn't be happy....

CHAPTER 7: THANKS AND GOODBYE

Tucker

For the next several days, food shows up at the entrance of my cave, usually while I'm away hunting or when I'm asleep. I hate that I never get to see Charlotte when she drops it off. I really want to see her again, to thank her for her kindness.

And also... just to see her.

She's so beautiful. I've never really seen anyone quite like her before.

Today, I have enough food saved up that I don't need to hunt, and I have plenty of water in a container she left for me to keep—with a note that said so. She's also brought me a couple of blankets and a pillow. If she keeps being so nice, I'm going to practically have a house out here in this cave before too long.

So... I decide to sit and wait for her to come, assuming she will do so.

I don't want her to see me at first, though, because I'm afraid it might scare her away. So rather than hanging out at the entrance of the cave, I take up a position in the woods where I will be able to see her approach the cave entrance, but she shouldn't be able to see me. Hopefully, my scent is masked enough by the various methods I have been using to hide my smell from everyone else that she won't smell me either.

Having a skunky smell around your home isn't great, but it masks just about everything... and he didn't taste that bad either.

I have to sit and wait for a few hours, but eventually, she shows up. I stay quiet, trying not to give myself away. She's so beautiful, though, with the sunlight gleaming off of her strawberry blonde curls, I want to gasp in adoration of such a fine specimen.

Instead, I keep my mouth shut and wait until she's put the food down and is turning around to slowly come out.

"Hi," I say as I break through the trees.

She jumps, lurching backward and into a defensive position, like she's ready to fight.

I hold my hands up. "Sorry!" I say. "Just me."

She looks at me suspiciously, like she might not trust me even though she realizes who I am, but she resumes her normal stance, her eyes regarding me with caution. "Hi."

"Hi," I say again. "Sorry to have frightened you."

"You didn't," she says, even though that's obviously a lie.

"Good." I pretend to believe her. "I just wanted to thank you for everything you've brought. It's really nice of you to do that."

She shrugs. "You're welcome." Looking around, she adds, "Maybe I should bring some skunk repellent."

Snickering, I say, "That's on purpose. I figure it'll keep the other people from your village away."

"Right," she says with an understanding nod. "Clever." She gives me a half-smile, and both of us stand there, uncomfortable. I want to say more, but I'm not sure what to say. I don't want her to leave.

But it seems pretty clear that she's going to. "I should get back home," she says.

"Already?" I ask. It sounds desperate, but I can't help myself.

She shrugs. "Well, yeah. I mean... unless...." She looks around and then refocuses on me. "Why would I stay?"

"I don't know," I admit. "I just thought maybe... we could talk for a bit?"

"Talk?" she repeats, and I nod. "About what?"

"About... life. How's your pack? What do you do there? Where are your friends? How's your family?"

"Okay...." She holds up her hands for me to stop. "Someone is lonely."

"Yeah, I guess so." How could I not be? I'm used to spending the day with my friends and family, and I haven't seen another person or wolf for... days.

"Well," she says, "my friends are at work. My pack is fine. I work at a coffee shop right now. My family is fine." Then, she shrugs again, like that's all she has to say.

I am not satisfied. "What's it like working at a coffee shop?" I ask her.

She sighs. "Boring," she admits. "I want to be an accountant, but I'm not ready for that yet. So I'm trying to get some work experience before I try to get a job at the bank."

"And... what do your friends do?"

"Uh... they work at various shops in the village," she says.

"Like what?"

She seems leery of telling me, but she manages to get out a few sentences about the other girls that were out here the other day, I presume, and I listen and nod, even though I really don't care.

"What does your dad do?" I ask her.

"He's a Delta," she says. "He helps with defense, mostly."

"And... your mom?"

"She stayed at home with my brother and me when we were growing up, so now she mostly hangs out with her friends and does charity work. She spends a lot of time at the daycare center."

"That's cool," I tell her. "She sounds a lot like my mom."

"What did your mom do?" she asks, and then she corrects herself. "Or does she do, I guess."

I can't help the wave of sadness that washes over me. I don't know if my mom is alive or not. "She... uh... did a lot of charity work, too. She... was the Luna."

Charlotte's eyes focus on me for a moment, and I wonder if maybe I shouldn't have told her that. "The Luna?" she repeats.

I nod.

"So... your father was the Alpha?"

I nod again.

"Which means that you're...."

"Screwed," I say and then I laugh a little, even though it's true.

She says, "Tucker, my family can help you. If we can find out what happened with your parents' pack–"

"No," I tell her. "My mom told me not to come back."

"But–"

"Thank you, Charlotte, but I have to trust that she knows–knew–what was best. For now."

She lets out a deep breath. "Okay. But if you change your mind... let me know."

"Thanks," I tell her.

"Well, I should get back home," she says. "I have to go to work soon."

I don't want to see her go, but I don't blame her. Standing around talking to me sounds super boring. "Thanks again for everything, Charlotte."

She gives me a small smile and lifts her hand before she turns to go.

I watch her leave, wishing there was something I could say to make her stay.

Maybe in another life, I would have actually gotten to become Alpha of my pack. Maybe she could've been my fated mate and become my Luna.

But now... none of that will ever happen. I'm not an Alpha's son anymore.

I'm just a rogue, a wolf without a home.

CHAPTER 8: WANT TO DANCE?

Charlotte

I spoke to Tucker!

The smile on my face for the rest of the day is apparent. All I want to do is run back to the cave and see him again.

It's silly. I know that. He doesn't belong to our pack, and I'm really not even sure why he is here. I don't know how long he'll stay. But I do know that when I talk to him, I feel a rush to my heart.

What that means exactly, I am not sure.

I just know that I want to see him again.

For the next few days, I go out to see him as often as I can. Rather than just dropping off food or something else like that, I wait and look around each time. He is always nearby. We sit and talk to one another, sometimes for hours.

I know I have to be careful because if anyone finds out that he's out there, he could get in trouble. I think Alpha Micah will be kind if he finds out what the situation is, but I don't know for sure.

Days turn to weeks, weeks turn to months... I go and see Tucker as frequently as I can.

Both of us change. He grows stronger, more rugged from living outside for so long. I get my banking job and am busier at work. Still, I make time for him. No one seems to be suspicious at all that I am going out into the woods on a regular basis. They think I'm just going for a run, though I always take a backpack with me. It carries the food and other items I hand off to Tucker on a regular basis.

From time to time, I try to talk him into going into the village with me. I tell him that everything will be fine, that he will become an accepted member of our pack in no time, but he still dreams of the day when he will go home, back to his own family, his own pack.

He doesn't know how he will decide it is time, but he will go—one day.

When he leaves, he will take my heart with him. I don't know that he is my fated mate. That can only be determined at a Moon Goddess Ball, but I do know that I love him, and that's just as powerful.

He doesn't know it, though. I haven't told him. Sometimes, I think that he might have feelings for me beyond friendship, too. A time or two, he has brushed a loose strand of hair behind my ear, and his fingertips have grazed my cheek. But that has been the extent of our touching.

I want more, but I don't want to lose his friendship, so I keep my mouth closed and dream of being in his arms.

One day, almost two years after his arrival, the two of us are sitting in the cave, looking at the cryptic markings he found on the cave wall long ago. We stare at them from time to time, trying to figure out what they mean. It is his only form of entertainment.

"We are having a Moon Goddess Ball Saturday night," I say, keeping my tone light.

Tucker's eyes widen. "That sounds fun," he says, nonchalantly.

"Yeah," I agree with a nod of my head. "Have you ever been to one before?"

He shakes his head, wrapping his arms around his legs. "No, I've never been. I wasn't quite old enough when I... when I left."

It's still hard for him to talk about his pack. I don't blame him. "I haven't either," I tell him.

"We haven't had one in a while."

"Why is that?" he asks.

"I'm not sure," I admit. "I think because there weren't a lot of funds. We've had these issues with a neighboring pack for a long time, too. I think the leaders didn't want a ball when we might be going to war at any minute. But that's still the case now, and we still have that threat."

"Well... I'm sure you'll have a great time," Tucker says, dropping his head and biting his bottom lip.

My eyebrows arch. Why is he acting that way? Does he not really want me to go?

"You know..." I begin, "if you wanted to go–"

"No, thank you," he says quickly.

"But there will be people there from other packs," I assure him. "No one will know who you are or where you came from. I can get you a suit."

He shakes his head, his lips drawn into a tight smile. "No, I wouldn't be comfortable."

I take a deep breath and nod.

My dreams of Tucker going to the ball, of the two of us locking eyes across the dance floor and realizing what I think I've known in my heart all along, that he is my fated mate, and we will run to one another and wrap our arms around each other, spending the night dancing, kissing, and whispering that we love one another... all of that slips away.

"Well, if you change your mind," I tell him.

He doesn't look at me, only returns his attention to the drawing on the side of the cave. A man with a shovel, an explosion of purple light from the ground, others standing back in wonder in both human and wolf form. I have no idea what it means, but it's interesting. I can't even tell how old it is. It doesn't look ancient. We have decided it is just some sort of a story someone drew here, possibly to entertain their kids.

An uncomfortable silence settles over us. It's clear that the mention of the ball was a bad idea. After another few minutes, I finally say, "Well, I should probably go," and get to my feet, wiping the dirt from the cave off of my bottom and my legs.

Tucker stands, too. He has to lean over a bit because he's so tall, and the ceiling is low here. As I walk out, he follows me. "Charlotte, you know, it's not that I don't want to go with you, right?"

Outside of the cave, I turn to look at him, my eyes wide. Do I?

"Right," I say, but I have my doubts. Maybe if another girl asked him, someone he was attracted to, he'd say yes. Maybe I've been imagining things all along, and he really doesn't like me like that at all.

"I just... don't want to take any chances, that's all."

I know he means about being discovered out here. "Right," I say again. "See you later, Tucker." I lift my hand to wave at him and then turn to head back to the village.

Maybe I won't be in such a rush to come back next time. My heart is heavy with sadness as I enter the village....

Maybe I won't go to the ball either. If Tucker isn't my mate, maybe I don't want to know who is.

Chapter 9: The Scent of Love

Charlotte

The night of the Moon Goddess Ball, I don't want to go. But my friends are persuasive. We are all over at Autumn's house, getting ready, and even as I watch them fix their makeup and take turns working on one another's hair, I am lagging behind.

I am slowly going about doing the same things. My hair is halfway done, and I am finishing putting eyeshadow on my left eyelid, my right already brown, but as I look at myself in the mirror, all I can think about is how badly I wish Tucker was going with me.

"What is your deal, Char?" Misty asks me. "You look like someone just ran over your dog or something."

"I'm sorry," I tell her, trying to force a smile that looks more like a grimace. "I'm just... thinking about work."

"Well, stop thinking about it!" Hannah insists. "This is the biggest night of our lives. We're going to find our fated mates—finally!"

I smile at her, but if this is the biggest night of my life, then I don't even want to go to the ball. I don't want to meet some guy and find out I'm bound to him. I don't want to discover that some dorky guy I've known since kindergarten is destined to be my husband. Once the bond is recognized, it's nearly impossible to ignore. While rejection is a possibility, speaking those words will curse the entire pack. So no matter who it is I find myself attached to, I'll be attached to them forever.

And I don't want to be bound to a single soul that will be present at this ball.

I finish getting ready and stand to look at myself in the floor-length mirror in Autumn's bedroom. I picked out this gown before I brought up the ball to Tucker. At the time, I was hoping he would agree to go. I'd even rented a suit I thought would fit him, just in case, under the guise that one of my cousins from Bright Beam pack might be coming. But I had to cancel the rental earlier in the day because Tucker had declined my invitation.

He'd declined me.

"You look so beautiful," Autumn says, wrapping her arm around my shoulders.

"Thank you," I say. "So do you." Her gown is black, and she looks elegant. Mine is bright blue, and it brings out my eyes.

I do feel beautiful, but I'm still not happy.

I am dreading this.

The four of us decide it's time to go. The others are laughing as we head downstairs and pose for pictures. "I'll send these to your mothers!" Autumn's mom promises.

My mom will love that. She wishes I was getting ready at home, but Autumn's room is a bit bigger than mine.

Besides, I didn't want them around Eli. They all act too goofy when my brother is nearby. I know that at least one of my friends is hoping that they'll find themselves mated to him.

As we walk over to the event center where the ball is being held, Hannah says, "So... how will we know, exactly?"

"Simple," Misty tells her. "Whenever you lay eyes on them, you'll smell all of your favorite scents. You'll be compelled to go to them, and you'll know as soon as you see their face that they're feeling the same about you. It's like magic."

"Well, I hope my magic is strong," Autumn says. "I don't want to be confused."

We walk in and take a look around. The decorations are lovely. Lots of silver and stars with moons highlighted everywhere to honor the Moon Goddess. There are plenty of snacks and drinks, and everyone is dancing to loud music coming from the corner of the room where a band is set up.

I look around and see some other friends. Lifting my hand in a wave, I smile. But I'm still not happy. My friends drag me out onto the dance floor so that we can all dance to a fast song together. I try to break out of my funk and have some fun.

As the night wears on, my friends break off. Sometimes to dance with cute boys who ask them that are not their mates, and eventually, pulled by their favorite scents, they head across the dance floor, drawn to a particular boy.

I don't wait around to see who is paired off with who, though I do see my brother dancing a lot with a girl I didn't think he liked much—Alice, Beta-to-be Zariah's best friend. My friends will fill me in later.

I feel drawn to no one, and in a way, I am thankful. Not everyone who is here tonight will find their mate.

I am beginning to realize I am one of those who will not.

The later it gets, the more tired of all of this I become. I decide perhaps it is time for me to leave. I don't even see anyone worth telling that I'm slipping away as all three of the friends I've come with are locked in the arms of different men.

Deciding to slip out the door, I step out into the night near the forest, using a side door.

Immediately, my lungs are hit with the scent of strawberries, my favorite. It's faint, but I smell it.

Closing my eyes, I take a deep breath and try to figure out where it is coming from. Could someone be baking a pie?

No, it's definitely not an actual fragrance in the air—it's in my head.

It's coming from my mate.

Sighing, I prepare to go back inside, to find him, but then I realize, it isn't coming from inside where the ball is being held.

It's coming from behind me... from the forest.

Quickly, I turn around and start walking through the woods, stopping a few feet in to take my shoes off. My feet are tough, and my high heels are sinking into the damp forest floor.

Carrying my silver heels, I walk carefully through the woods, following my nose. The scent is getting stronger the further in I walk.

When I see the caves in the distance, my heart lights up and tears begin to glisten in my eyes.

Could it be...?

It has to be!

I don't know how it's possible, he's come from so far away, but it has to be!

I walk up to the area around the caves and see Tucker standing in the open, his face illuminated by a silvery moonbeam. He's never looked more handsome than he does right now.

With his nose raised to the air, he asks me, "Do you smell... cinnamon?"

All I can do is smile and laugh. "No. I smell strawberries," I tell him.

His forehead wrinkles as he drops his eyes to me. "But why are we smelling—" He stops talking, and I only have a one-word answer for him.

"Mate."

CHAPTER 10: MATES

Charlotte

The word hangs between us as Tucker stares at me, intently. "Mate?" he asks.

I nod. "You smell it, too, because we are mates, Tucker. You and I are fated to be together."

"But... how can that be?" he asks me as moonlight illuminates his hair, shining off his rippling muscles.

"I don't know," I admit. "But it's true. Can't you feel it?"

Silently, he nods at me, and I continue to slowly walk closer to him until I am standing in front of him, waiting to see what he will do.

Tucker slips a finger beneath my chin to lift my face toward his. In the nearly two years that we've known one another, we've barely ever touched. But now, I can hardly keep my hands off of him. I want to feel his muscles beneath my palms; I want to drag my fingernails down his back and dig into his flesh, holding him tightly against me while my tongue dances with his.

He says nothing else, only lowers his warm lips to encapsulate mine. I rise up slightly on my tiptoes to meet him, and when his tongue darts out to probe between my lips, I welcome him in, lifting a hand to the back of his head. My fingers splay, and I grab onto his hair as his tongue reaches further and further into my mouth. I want to taste him from the inside out.

Tucker lifts me off of the ground and I wrap my legs around his waist. No words are needed as he carries me into the solace of the cave, his home, and takes me to the back where his makeshift bed lies on the ground.

With him on top of me, I can feel just how badly he wants me. His erection is rock hard and presses against my inner thigh. I begin to rub against him, no longer in control of my body, and he finds the zipper in the back of my gown, yanking it down.

We don't rush, though. This is my first time, and he knows it. I have no idea whether it's his first time or not, and I don't ask. I just want to savor every moment. I'm not in heat, so there's no reason for us to worry about protection. I want to feel every inch of him inside of me, flesh to flesh.

He kisses my neck, and I lift my head, wondering if he will mark me now or wait. Since a mark is an obvious sign that two mates have made love, I hope that he'll wait. But then... I also want to know I'll be his forever.

Tucker slides my bra straps aside and finds my breast with his mouth. I lift my pelvis and press down on his head with my hand, not able to get enough of him. When he lifts off of me, I feel cold and alone, but he is only removing his pants. He strips naked in front of me, and I get a chance to see what's been driving me crazy all this time–I want him inside of me

Before he lays back down, he yanks my panties off, and I unhook my bra. We are naked together now, only the two of us, this place illuminated slightly from the faint moonlight at the cave opening, but it seems like the rest of the world is entirely gone, and it's just him and me.

With his tongue pressed against mine, I spread my legs for him, and he pushes inside, twisting his hips slightly to get past the barrier. Pain radiates up through my core as he stretches me to my limits, but as he slowly begins to move his hips back and forth, and I start to find his rhythm, the pain subsides, and all I feel is pleasure.

His palms caress my skin, his lips taste every bit of me he can reach, and he works in and out of me, grinding as he goes, hitting me in all of the right places. I can't help the ethereal moans that leave my lips like a siren's song on the wind. He feels so good, and I want more and more of him.

My mind grows dizzy, and I feel my muscles tightening around him and going into spasm. Tucker keeps me there, lost in a fog of ecstasy, for what seems like an eternity before he begins to grunt and then I feel his warm essence fill me.

Finally, I open my eyes and look into his. The way he is gazing down at me lets me know that the love I feel in my heart is returned. We are one now, fated mates, soul mates. Lovers.

Tucker lies down next to me and pulls my body against his. I want to tell him how much I love him, how he makes me feel like eternity is ours to explore together, that no one will ever take us away from one another. But all I can do is rest my head on his chest and listen to his heart beat.

Exhaustion washes over me, and I feel myself fade away. Just before I lose consciousness, I hear his voice say, "I love you, Charlotte. I love you so much."

I want to reply that I love him, too, but my lips will not move.

I know it isn't necessary, though. He already knows.

Chapter 11: Sneaking In

Charlotte

The sun isn't as bright as usual when I awake and strain to look around my room to see why my alarm hasn't gone off.

It only takes a second for me to realize what the problem is.

I'm in the cave—with Tucker!

"Oh, shit!" I mutter sitting up and looking around for my clothes. Out in the front part of the cave, I can hear the sound of my phone alarm going off as I must've dropped my dress a ways back and my phone was in a secret pocket.

"Are you all right, Charlotte?" Tucker, my mate, asks me as he groggily wipes sleep from his eyes.

Holding one of the blankets I have given him over the last couple of years against my body, I scramble to my feet.

"Yes, fine," I tell him. "I just... don't know what time it is." Judging by the anger in my alarm and the sun streaming in, it's way past the time I'm usually up. I don't have to work today because of the Moon Goddess Ball being held last night, but my mother—is going to kill me!

Hurriedly, I get dressed, trying to ignore the weight of Tucker's eyes on my body.

"I'm sorry, babe," he says, getting up and sliding his jeans on. I find myself slowing as I catch a look at his naked backside.

Shaking my head, I continue to get dressed.

"It's not your fault. It's just... no one knows where I am." At least, I hope no one knows.

Once I'm dressed I come back to him and kiss him quickly. "See you later?" he asks me.

I nod. I'm not sure how I'll make that work, but I will.

I rush out, grabbing my shoes and hurrying back home.

As I run, I turn off my alarm and note that it's only 6:42. There's a chance my mom is still asleep, especially if she was up most of the night wondering where I was.

Goddess, I hope that's not the case.

Most of the town is sleeping in today because of last night's festivities. I hope to find my house the same way.

When I reach the back door, I pull it open carefully, knowing it will creak as it always does, but it's not too loud. I have my shoes in my hand, so I tiptoe into the kitchen, headed for the stairs.

I am just about to go up them when I hear a loud voice booming from the living room.

"Where the hell have you been?"

I jump and nearly drop my shoes. Turning around, I see my brother standing there, his hands in the pockets of his wrinkled suit pants, his tie undone, his jacket off, and the top three buttons of his shirt unfastened.

"Goddess, Eli!" I say, whisper-shouting. "You scared the shit out of me!"

"Do you think we haven't been scared all night?" he counters. "Hell, Mom was ready to send the patrol out for you. I finally got her to calm down by lying to her and telling her that you spent the night at Autumn's house. But none of your friends know where the hell you've been. I tried following your scent into the woods and ended up with a nose full of skunk. Now, let's try this again. Where the hell have you been?"

It is obvious he is angry, and I really can't blame him. I am glad he covered for me, though. "With... my mate," I tell him, knowing lying will make it worse.

His eyes widen. "And who is that?"

"You don't know him," I say. "He's from another pack."

"And you went out into the woods with him last night to do I-don't-even-want-to-imagine-what?"

I narrow my eyes at him. "Yeah, like you're a virgin."

"We're not talking about me, Charlotte. You're my little sister. Whose head do I need to pound for taking advantage of you on the night you met?"

"We didn't just meet!" I insist. "I've known him for two years!"

He is giving me a skeptical look, and I can't blame him. That doesn't seem likely.

I'm going to have to tell him everything or else he's going to insist on telling Mom and Dad and probably his best friend, who just happens to be the Alpha.

Reluctantly, I walk into the living room and sit down on the couch, hating that I know my brother can smell Tucker all over me. I can also smell Alice, his new mate, apparently, all over him. But he doesn't smell like sex.

I do know that he's not a fan of Alice's, so that's rather funny.

I don't laugh, though.

"What's going on?" Eli demands as he sits across from me in my mom's favorite chair.

I tell him the truth, starting with when I first met Tucker two years ago and ending with last night–though only that I went out to see him and realized he was my mate, not the details. When I am finished, I beg him not to tell the Alpha.

"If he ran all of this way from a pack in the northeast, but he's the son of an Alpha, why hasn't he ever bothered to find out what happened to his people?" Eli asks, his tone conveying he doesn't believe me.

"Because he's afraid to," I tell him. "And he doesn't know what to do. It's just him. Not an army of warriors."

He shakes his head. "I'm going to have to look into this."

"Fine. But please... don't tell Micah. Not yet anyway?" I am begging him.

He glares at me. "You are walking on thin ice."

"I know. Please?"

"For now, I will keep it to myself, but if I find out this guy is lying to you, I will pound him right through the ground, and he can go find another pack in China or whatever the hell is on the other side of the planet from us."

"Thank you," is all I can say, even though I want to tell him to stop being a jerk. He shakes his head at me in disapproval. So I ask, "So... about Alice," and smirk at him.

"Son of a bitch," Eli says and gets up. "I'm going to bed. Goodnight."

I can't help but giggle as he walks out of the room. I knew he didn't like her. Now he's stuck with her–forever.

I bet she will grow on him, though. I decide to go take a shower and go to bed. I will have a lot of explaining to do when my parents are up. I hope they will at least give me a couple of hours, though.

I need time to think.

And time to figure out what to do about Tucker.

CHAPTER 12: MEETING THE BROTHER

Tucker

I didn't see Charlotte for a couple of days, which was disconcerting. I thought I would see her again later that day, after she left in a hurry that morning, but she didn't come back.

Perhaps she wanted to see if I would come into the village to find her. Maybe I should have.

But I didn't. I was too afraid to.

I had no idea how the people of her village would react to me.

The longer I sat out in the woods in the cave by myself, the more I realized it was time to get my life together.

I need to find out what happened to my family and my pack.

Whenever Charlotte does come back, and I have to hope that she will because we are mates, I want to tell her that I'm ready to go home.

And I want her to come with me.

It's evening, the second day after we discovered we are mates, and I am sitting in the opening of the cave, looking up at the sky as the dusk falls and turns the woods shades of orange like a campfire is burning in the distance, lighting the sky on fire.

My heart is heavy. I miss her and hope that I didn't do something wrong.

When I smell her scent growing near, I hop up and rush over to the place where she usually appears. I'm so caught up in the fact that she's approaching that I fail to notice that other scents accompany hers until it's too late.

"Charlotte!" I exclaim as soon as I see her. "I missed you so much!"

I rush over to hug her, but she is not smiling, and as soon as the two men behind her come around the corner, I realize why.

"Don't be mad, Tucker," she says to me, stopping in front of me, but she doesn't reach for me, and I drop my arms before I embrace her.

One of them looks friendly enough, but the other, the one who has facial features similar to Charlotte's, looks like he wants to drive me right into the ground.

"What's going on?" I ask.

"This is my Alpha, Micah," she says, gesturing to the friendlier of the two. "And this is... my brother. Eli."

Over the years, Charlotte has talked about her brother many times, and usually not in a good way. They don't seem to get along very well. I've always wanted to meet him to tell him to be nicer to his sister, but now that he's standing there, glaring at me, I'm thinking now is not the best time.

"Hi," Alpha Micha says, lifting his hand and then offering it to me. "It's nice to meet you, Tucker."

I hesitate but end up shaking his hand. He seems nice enough. And not very old to be an Alpha. Maybe only a couple of years older than me.

"Eli!" Charlotte barks.

"Hi," her brother begrudgingly says, but he doesn't offer me his hand.

"Hello," I say to both of them.

Charlotte begins to answer my initial question. "Eli caught me coming back home the other morning, and I had to tell him the truth. He told Micah—and some of his other friends."

I feel sick to my stomach. After all of this time, they finally know about me.

"We want to help," Micah says. "We've looked into it, and your pack was taken over by a neighbor a couple of years ago, we assume at the time that you left. You're from Lost Sun pack, right?"

I nod. He's right.

"And the other pack was Cosmic Chaos pack?"

I shrug. "I have never known for sure. But probably." Cosmic Chaos pack had been formed out of another pack's lands when a group of rogues grew very powerful.

Alpha Micah nods. "The good news is, from what we can tell, most of your pack members are still alive. They've just been submitting to the Alpha from Cosmic Chaos for the past few years. The bad news is that Cosmic Chaos has a strong Alpha, Randall, who isn't just going to roll over and die."

"And the other bad thing is we don't have jack shit to help you with," Eli says, still glaring at me.

Alpha Micah looks at him a moment, sighs, and says, "While that's partially true, if you want to go back, I'm prepared to send a small detail with you, especially if Charlotte goes with you. But you will need to rely on your pack members and your allies in the area to overthrow Randall and defeat him once and for all. I've been in contact with the Alphas from Wind Walker pack and Sunbeam pack, and they're willing to help you, but they want to speak to you."

My eyebrows arch. "You've already spoken to them?"

Alpha Micah nods. "That's right."

"Wow... thank you." I wonder if my father is still alive. If so, he would be the rightful Alpha. What about my mother....

Charlotte must be reading my mind. "We couldn't get any information from inside of the pack, so we don't know if your parents are still alive or not. I'm sorry."

All I can do is nod. If I try to speak, I might start crying, and I don't think that Eli would appreciate a man who cries.

"We'll leave you two to talk it over, but don't feel like you have to keep living in the woods, Tucker," Alpha Micah tells me. "You're welcome to come into the village and stay for as long as you like. We have cabins."

"Thank you," I tell him. He extends his hand again, and I shake it. Eli reluctantly sticks his out, too, and I shake it before the two of them turn and leave Charlotte and I alone.

"Are you mad?" she asks, and I can tell by her expression that she's afraid I'm angry at her.

"No, baby. Of course not," I tell her, finally getting the chance to take her into my arms.

"It's not your fault if your brother caught you coming in."

She wraps her arms around me, and I kiss her, deeply.

When we finally come up for air, I have to ask her, "Would you really consider coming with me?"

"Of course, I will," she says as if it is a silly question. "I love you, Tucker. I want to be with you, no matter where you are, and you belong back at your pack, as a leader. As the Alpha."

I can't help but smile at her, even though I'm nervous to find out what's gone on back there. But now, with Charlotte by my side, I feel like I can do anything.

CHAPTER 13: RECLAIMING THE ALPHADOM

Tucker

Going home is nerve-wracking in a way I can't describe, but I'm glad it's finally happening. I'm ready to see what the situation is.

I'm ready to find out whether or not my parents are still alive and to throw off Alpha Randall. With Alpha Micah's help, I feel confident I can finally make this happen.

Charlotte is alongside me, and I feel stronger and more confident than I ever have before, even if her brother continues to glare at me like he wants to rip my head off every time I look in his direction.

Alpha Micah was kind enough to spare a few of his best warriors and a vehicle. Driving is a lot faster than running had been when I'd left his home years ago.

When we arrive on the outskirts of my territory, forces from Wind Walker and Sunbeam pack will be waiting to join us. I should be able to use the mind-link to get information from inside of my pack to find out where Alpha Randall and the other warriors are. The sun is beginning to set, and as soon as it is dark, we will shift and take the Alpha by storm.

The driver of the vehicle pulls to a stop, and I feel my breath catch in my throat. I get out and take a few steps away to be alone. This is it. The moment I've been waiting for for over two years.

"Mom? Dad?" I call, using the mind-link.

It is quiet for a moment, and I fear the worst—that they are both dead.

Then, I hear a high-pitched voice saying my name. "Tucker?" I can tell my mom is on the verge of tears. "Is that really you? Are you nearby?"

"I'm here," I say. "On the outskirts of our pack lands, near Wind Walker pack. Where's Dad?"

Again, it takes a moment for her to respond. "He passed away, son," she tells me, and I feel a heaviness in my heart. I thought that might've been the case, though I couldn't say how I knew. "Where are you, Mom?"

"I'm in the Alpha's home, our old home, though it's been rebuilt after the fire. I'm a maid here now, honey. What are you planning to do?"

The idea of my mom scrubbing toilets in our old house makes anger boil up inside of me. "I'm going to kill Alpha Randall!" I tell her.

"You can't do that, dear. He's too powerful. He has hundreds of warriors guarding our pack lands."

"I have hundreds with me, too, Mom. Wind Walker and Sunbeam are helping me. And I have some warriors from Midnight Moon pack."

"Midnight Moon pack?" she repeats. "I don't even know where that is, honey."

"It's where I've been these last two years. And it's where I met my mate, Charlotte."

"You met your mate?" I can hear the love gushing in my mother's voice. "Be careful, dear. Alpha Randall was a rogue. He will fight dirty."

"I know, Mom. I love you, and I'll see you soon."

I go back to report what I've discovered to Eli. He's already working with warriors from Sunbeam and Wind Walker to coordinate our attack. I will leave it to Charlotte's brother to lead the attack while my main objective is finding and killing Alpha Randall.

Charlotte wants to fight, too, but I already told her I'd be too worried if she was out there, so she's agreed to stay back until the battle is over. Some of the women from Sunbeam are here to stay with her.

Before I shift, I hug her and kiss her deeply, ignoring the grunt from her brother. "I love you so much," I tell her.

"I love you, too. Be careful."

I nod at her, and as she walks away, I feel like my heart is leaving my body.

But then... the battle is on.

I strip and shift along with the others, and we set out to go reclaim my homeland.

The battle starts when forces from the two surrounding packs and Midnight Moon storm into the village unexpectedly. We have completely taken Alpha Randall's men by surprise. Many of them haven't even shifted when we attack. I watch as wolves pummel human men to the ground, ripping their throats out. Sunbeam and Wind Walker warriors know the distinct scent of my pack mates and won't harm them, but the Midnight Moon warriors are more cautious, being sure not to hurt anyone who belongs with me.

My mom has already spread the word to our people that it's me attacking, and as they are freed, my people join in with us, shifting and attacking.

By then, Randall's men realize what is happening, and a wave of warriors in wolf form come out to meet us.

I can't speak to Eli directly in our wolf forms because Charlotte and I haven't marked one another. We are not yet joined as one pack. Still, I can tell by his expression he wants me to go find the Alpha.

So I do. I run between the attacking warriors, none of which are fast enough to slow me down, and I head for my own home, seeing most of it has been rebuilt since the fire.

I burst through a window that has strategically been left open, obviously by my mom, and take a look around.

I can smell Alpha Randall and know exactly where he is, hiding beneath the stairs.

As I approach, I shift so I can open the door with my hand. It's locked, but I manage to rip it right open anyway. Then I shift back into my wolf and find him cowering in the corner, his knees drawn up to his neck.

"Now, listen, Tucker," he begins, "I can explain everything."

I don't want to hear his excuses. I lunge at him, grabbing hold of his leg and chomping down, but he shifts, and now he's also a wolf, stronger and able to fight back against me. There's hardly room for the two of us in this crawl space beneath the stairs, so I keep my teeth in his leg and pull him out with me.

His teeth sink into my shoulder, and I flip him over, pulling away from him. My shoulder muscle rips, but I don't care.

I need to get my teeth into his throat.

The battle wages on between us, and though I have the upper hand, he is strong. We tussle around the living room, breaking vases and picture frames.

I manage to get on top of him again, and try to sink my teeth into him once more, but he's kicking me off of him with his back legs.

Out of nowhere, a tuft of white fur emerges on my left, and with the two of us fighting him, Alpha Randall has no chance. The female wolf sinks her teeth into his neck and rips. Alpha Randall stills beneath me.

"Mom?" I say, using the mind-link. It's been so long since I've seen her, I've almost forgotten what her wolf looks like.

"Welcome home, son," she says. She rests her head on my uninjured shoulder, and we stand like that for a few minutes until I run out to check on the battle.

It's nearly over. With the help of my neighbors and Midnight Moon, Randall's warriors are all either destroyed or surrendered, bloodied and battered.

In the distance, I see a light blonde wolf with strawberry streaks and know that Charlotte is coming to find me.

I run to her, and the two of us fall to the ground, our front legs around one another.

We've taken back my pack, avenged my father's death, and now... we can be together forever.

I wish I could tell her how much I love her, but for now, all I can do is look at her with adoration in my eyes.

Epilogue

Tucker

"By the power of the Moon Goddess, I pronounce you man and wife!"

My entire pack claps as Charlotte and I kiss. Not only are her parents here, but so are some delegates from her pack, including the Alpha and his wife.

We've had to wait a bit to get married because of issues back at Midnight Moon, but now that Charlotte and I are married, I never want to let her go.

I kiss her even more passionately, and everyone continues to cheer.

"Now, we start our lives together, officially," Charlotte says, and I lift her hand into the air to celebrate.

In the months since I've been back home, there's been a lot of work done to restore our pack to what we formerly were. We've also built a high wall around our village so the likes of Randall can never get in again.

Charlotte and I head to our new home, my new Alpha house, which has been built near my old home, where my mother will stay. I can't wait to mark Charlotte and make her mine forever.

The public ceremony is over, but the private one will begin soon enough.

As we walk, I look at the faces of all of my people and smile. I've been so glad to get to know them again. I know they will be partying without Charlotte and me. She stops to say goodbye to her pack members, and I wait patiently, saying thank you to some of my own pack members. We have decided not to attend the reception because I am impatient to get her home and mark her.

I love her so much, I can hardly stand to wait the few minutes it takes for her to hug her parents and tell her brother goodbye.

I thank her Alpha and his wife, and then we head on.

In our own home, in our own bedroom, in our own bed, I look down into her eyes. They are wide with pleasure as I continue to make love to my beautiful wife. "I love you, Charlotte," I tell her, our rhythm beginning to pick up speed.

"I love you, too, Tucker," she says, her fair skin glistening with a sheen of perspiration.

I drop my head and bite the soft flesh of her neck as her teeth sink into my shoulder. There's a sharp pain, but then it dissipates, and I know, Charlotte and I will be together forever.

She falls over the edge, moaning and panting, and I join her shortly, spilling my seed, hoping we will have an heir to the Alphadom soon.

Then, I collapse next to her and pull her to my chest. "Thank you for believing in me, Charlotte," I tell her.

She kisses the mark on my shoulder near my neck and says, "Tucker, you will always be my rogue–and my mate. And now, you're my Alpha."

I kiss the crown of my Luna's head and close my eyes.

While being a rogue was hard, being her Alpha makes it all worth it. I can't wait to see what this life brings us next. As long as Charlotte is by my side, I can handle anything.

The End.

ABOUT THE AUTHOR

ID Johnson creates characters you'll want to have as your best friends with antagonists you'll love to hate. Her love for all things princess-y compelled her to write her first medieval romance at fifteen, and she hasn't stopped writing since. Now, her plots are a little more complex, her topics a little more mature, and her romances often more intense, but she's never lost the love she felt the first moment she breathed life into a character over twenty years ago. If you love feisty paranormal heroines, damsels who cause distress, or historical ladies who know how to light up a room, then pull up a seat, get out your eReader, and meet ID Johnson's friends. Soon enough, they'll be your friends, too.

For the most up-to-date information, subscribe to Johnson's newsletter http://eepurl.com/ci-iSX

Twitter

Facebook

Email ID Johnson at authoridjohnson@gmail.com

Also By ID Johnson

Steamy

She's My Beta and My Mate

WebNovel

Dreame

The Clandestine Saga

Titanic

http://eepurl.com/ci-iSX

DEVIL'S MAGIC

TIA DIDMON

Blurb

A Proposal. A Portal. A Prophecy.

Serena is Dying. When her chance for one last adventure turns out to be a deal with the devil, she learns that losing her soul isn't the worst part.

She agrees to retrieve an artifact from another realm, with the help of a sexy werewolf, hellbent on seducing her. But they learn the true power of the relic Lucifer covets.

Will she complete her deal with the devil and ensure humanity's destruction, or will she forsake her world and risk eternal damnation?

Chapter 1

We regret to inform you.

Serena's tears dripped onto the paper, causing the ink to bleed. The words swirled together in a black river, rolling down the page. Her doctor had given her the prognosis in person, but it wasn't real until she read the words.

The artfully crafted medical advice on what to expect over the next few months and the various pain management methods did nothing to change the truth. She would die.

Serena scrunched the letter in her hand before throwing it on the ground. She grabbed her tie-dye purse and slipped it over her suede jacket. The fringe strips hanging from her sleeves were a current fashion statement, now whispered of death. She stood from the bus stop bench and headed down the street.

A couple holding hands while roller skating on the street laughed as they whizzed by. The California sun basked them in fortune and beauty. A future Serena would be denied.

She wiped her tears with the back of her hand and ducked into a black door lining the street. The sign 'Rejected Dreams' caught her attention. While she'd never noticed the shop before, the scent of cinnamon and sage offered a respite from the darkness consuming her.

The door chimed as she entered, but no one met her at the entrance. The dark interior was lined with tables full of grimy lawn tools, electrical devices, and used clothing. Multiple glass display cases were lit with various gold and silver jewelry as Billy Idol's new song played in the background. She surveyed the discarded items of people's lives. She was the last of her family. Who would she pass her mother's jewelry to? Grief swamped her. No one would miss her when she was gone. She covered her face with her hands as silent sobs racked her body.

"Now, now, child. Whatever it is, there's always a solution." His thick Haitian accent drowned out the background music.

She sniffed. "There's no cure for cancer."

His eyebrows arched, making his skin appear more youthful. "You gonna sit there and complain, or you gonna make the best of the time you have left."

Serena clutched her bag, allowing the anger to dissipate. She wasn't sure if it was the sweet-smelling herbs, or the painful truth of his words. She couldn't change her fate, but she could go out on her terms. "What do you suggest?"

He beckoned her to a covered table at the back. "What if I could offer you one last adventure?"

The shadows in the room swallowed her, masking the rest of the shop. She could see the various items, but it was like looking through a cloud. "What is this?"

"This is an opportunity." He pulled off a black satin cover, revealing a small table with strange symbols carved along the top. "I can't tell you what your adventure will be, but I guarantee it will last longer than the few months you currently have."

She sucked in a breath. "How did you know that?"

"Death hovers beside you like a dark hummingbird. It sucks the nectar of your life force as we speak. You won't see the next full moon."

Serena sat, running her fingers over the hand-carved symbols. The characters were scary and comforting. "What does the symbol mean?"

He glanced at the wolf. "That is the prisoner."

She touched one that looked like a goddess praying to heaven. "And this one?"

He tapped the symbol with his finger. "That's you. This is your adventure should you choose to accept it."

"There are pictures of monsters, volcanoes, and objects I don't recognize. How can this be my adventure? Is it some sort of fantasy resort?"

He smiled, but there was no warmth in his eyes. "Many refer to it as the garden. It may look like a resort, but it is where your adventure begins."

Her hand fell to her lap. "I have no money. My mom was diagnosed two years ago. Our savings went to her medical bills. I don't even have the money to pay for my treatment."

He crouched beside her. "If I asked for something other than money. What would you offer?"

Serena swallowed her fear. Her pain. What would she trade for a few weeks of happiness? "Anything."

He stood. "Your payment is acceptable."

Serena squinted. "I can give you anything."

He backed away as the dark mist swirled around her. "When you meet the caretaker, tell him I have fulfilled our agreement."

Serena opened her mouth, but no sound escaped as her world shattered around her like a broken mirror.

CHAPTER 2

The wind tugged at Serena's hair, causing her to roll over on the soft mattress. She pulled up the thick cotton comforter before the powerful smell of salt water, fresh fruit, and spices permeated the air. Her eyes snapped open as the memories from the store resurfaced.

She sat up, threw the covers to the side, then stood on the bamboo floor. The sheer curtains billowed in the briny breeze as she stepped onto the veranda.

Was she dreaming? The bedroom looked like a five-star tropical retreat with hand-carved furniture and unique artwork.

Sandy beaches, swaying palm trees, and lush undergrowth accented the crystal blue water in the distance. The tropical paradise spanned the ocean side, but no other buildings were in view. If it was a resort, it was a private one.

The room had a single closet full of clothes. She grabbed a simple cotton blouse and blue capris, slipping them over her bra and panties. Her clothes were missing, but she intended to find out who took them.

She ducked into the bathroom, washed her face, and tied up her long black hair into a messy bun before opening the bedroom door.

The hallway was empty with decor similar to the bedroom, and potted plants were placed at intervals along the corridor leading to the stairs.

Her hand slid along the decorative wrought-iron railings as she descended the steps.

The entrance was large, with floral couches and brown wicker coffee tables. She made her way to the connecting dining hall, finding large tables and handmade chairs but no people.

Her heart fluttered as she ran through the massive entryway doors. A large lizard sunned himself on the beach as she turned, taking in the majestic hotel.

"Welcome to the garden, Serena."

She spun, losing her footing on the soft, white sand, and fell. She looked up at the tall, dark-haired man in a white suit. He was good-looking, but his eyes were unnerving. The gold hue swirled with amber flakes like glitter on autumn leaves. "Where am I?"

He held out his hand. "Some call this a gateway, others call it limbo. I see it as a garden with infinite possibilities."

Serena allowed him to help her up, then dusted the sand from her knees. "How did I get here?"

He smiled, but it didn't reach his eyes. "You told the Bokor you wished to have one last adventure. That wish was granted, but like every service, it comes at a price."

Her hands clutched the thin cotton of her pants. While the sun warmed her skin, ice traveled through her blood. "Who are you?"

"I have many names, but you may call me the caretaker."

"The caretaker of what?"

He spread his hands' palms up as if worshiping the sun. "Of Lucifer's Garden."

Serena's heart skipped. "Lucifer, as in the devil. Are you saying that I'm dead? That I'm in hell?"

"No, Serena. This is a gateway, an oasis that connects the realms. A rest stop for the trajectory of your life. Only you can determine your next destination."

She rubbed her forehead. "As in heaven or hell?"

He huffed. "If it were only that simple. The question you should ask is which heaven or hell."

She nibbled her lip. "I don't understand."

He glanced down at the beach. "You will."

"What do you want from me?" she asked.

His eyes flickered with white flames within the gold. "There is another resident on the island. I need you to assist him."

"How?"

"I need an object retrieved. You will help him."

Serena couldn't decide if her medication pushed her into some form of medical-induced psychosis, if she was dreaming, or if she had died. Her paradise was turning to hell.

The caretaker walked toward the hotel. "Come along, Serena. You have little time."

The pain in her chest felt as real on the beach as it had at the bus-stop bench. She trudged along behind the caretaker, shocked when they entered the hotel.

It was no longer furnished with floral coaches and bamboo coffee tables. The stone floor was littered with seaweed and wet sand. She glanced back. But the backdrop was no longer a blue ocean and white beach. Jagged rock surrounded her, making her jump when water trickled over her bare feet. "Jesus Christ."

The caretaker whirled. "I recommend you refrain from praying or cursing. Neither will do you any good."

She followed him through the dark, dank cavern until it opened into a small room. Low growls echoed against the stone.

The caretaker pointed at the beast chained to the wall. "This is Merek. You will assist him."

Serena backed away until her back hit the course rock wall. "Is that a werewolf?" she stuttered.

The caretaker nodded. "They are unruly and ungrateful creatures, but they possess certain abilities. One in which I need."

Serena shook her head, pursing her lips.

The caretaker walked over to a wooden table with leather whips, chains, and other implements Serena didn't recognize. He picked up a large whip with serrated barbs of steel attached to the end. "Then he dies."

She ran in front of the chained beast, putting her hands up. "Why would you beat him? What did he do to you?"

The caretaker shrugged. "Nothing. He won't cooperate. He made a deal, and if you renege on a deal here, you die, and Lucifer gets your soul."

Serena had assumed dying was the worst thing to happen to a young woman. She was wrong. "I'll help him. Don't hurt him."

The caretaker nodded. "Of course, you will, Serena. That's why I chose you." The chains fell from the wall, releasing the beast.

His yellow eyes bored into Serena as he resumed his human shape.

He looked like a Greek God with sun-kissed skin and long dark hair that tumbled to his shoulders. His vibrant yellow eyes receded to a brilliant green as his muscled arms pulled her against him. His fingers wrapped around her neck.

"What have you done?" Merek hissed.

CHAPTER 3

Merek felt Serena's pulse quicken under his fingers. Her neck was slender with satiny smooth skin. Her pupils dilated when his hands circled her throat. She had no idea he couldn't hurt her, that her scent drove every sane thought from his head, or that his wolf was pushing for things he had long forgotten. "Why are you here, Serena?"

She swallowed hard. "I'm dying. I thought I was opting for one last adventure. Like a safari or an exotic cruise."

Merek gazed into her steel-blue eyes. They were rimmed with silver and were as unique as she was. He could sense lies, and she told him the truth. "You didn't sign a contract with Lucifer?" He let his fingers fall from her throat as the room wavered. The stone walls with metal shackles dematerialized into a lush jungle, with birds screeching, insects buzzing, and a roar of a wild animal.

Serena looked around. "Where's the caretaker? How did you do that?"

Merek waved his hand in a circular motion. "This place isn't real. It is a portal. A gateway that intersects the realms. You are from the last human world. The only fertile realm left in existence. Lucifer will protect it, at all costs."

Serena frowned. "Why would the devil protect us? Doesn't he want to destroy everything?"

Merek arched an eyebrow. "And then what? When every realm is gone, how will Lucifer enslave new souls?"

She shook her head. "I assumed that's what he wanted."

"It may have been his goal at one time, but even Lucifer learns and matures. World after world perished or became infertile and infested with the creatures of his creation. He discovered his immortals couldn't produce children."

Serena's eyes narrowed. "Why are you here, Merek?"

"I made a deal with the devil. My world was on the brink of destruction. While we are immortal, we are infertile. We were starving and killing each other. I made a deal to restore order in our realm. I am banished from my world, but I have restored balance."

Her forehead creased. "That's an awful price to pay."

He shrugged. "I was dead either way. At least my family has a life."

"There has to be some way for you to return to your world."

He shook his head. "There's no reneging on a deal with the devil."

She sighed. "I don't have a lot of time, Merek. I have less than three months, so I suggest we use that time wisely."

Merek inhaled her fresh spring scent. "Time is stagnant in Lucifer's Garden. No time passes here. Do you feel sick?"

She frowned. "No."

"You will remain as you are until you return to your world."

She huffed. "If I stay, I'm the devil's puppet, and if I return, I'm dead. Those aren't stellar options."

Merek touched her cheek with his finger. "You do not understand, Serena. Lucifer will never let you return. He brought you here. He wants you here. There is something special about you."

Serena swallowed dry air. "What?"

"I don't know, but I feel it."

Serena nibbled her bottom lip. She didn't know how sexy the innocent action was, especially for a wolf who hadn't had contact with a woman in a long time. "The caretaker said you were to retrieve an artifact. Is that correct?"

"Yes."

Her eyes narrowed. "Did he specify what you had to do with it?"

"No."

She smirked. "Then let's get it and re-hide it. That should fulfill your deal and mine."

Merek's lips twitched. "I like you, human."

Her eyes roamed over his body. His muscles tightened as his body responded to her inspection. He stepped closer to her as she spoke. "Where is the artifact?"

Merek looked down at her perfect features. Her long black hair fluttered in the subtle wind. "It's here, in Lucifer's Garden. That's why I am here."

She swallowed hard, meeting his intense gaze. "But you refused to retrieve it."

"Yes."

"Why?"

"I don't know what the artifact does. And if Lucifer wants it, then it isn't good."

"Where can we put it, so Lucifer or the caretaker won't have access to it?"

He searched her face. "There is only one place the caretaker can't access."

"Where?"

"A fallen realm."

CHAPTER 4

Serena swallowed dry air. They had been walking for hours on the narrow trail. "Are you sure it's here?" The lush green canopy blotted out the sky with only snatches of bright sun peeking through. Ropy vines snaked down the trees, curling around the trunks in suffocating loops. The dense undergrowth sprouted across the bed of rich soil and rotting vegetation, creating a soft, green carpet beneath her feet.

Merek stopped on the trail that never seemed to end. "It is irrelevant which direction we walk. The garden can alter its appearance at the caretaker's whim."

Serena touched his muscular arm. "If he can change the trail, our surroundings, how do we know we're going the right direction?"

Merek's eyes flashed with amber. "Do you think Lucifer chose me for my good looks? I have a gift. While all weres are excellent trackers, if I'm shown an item, I can find it in any realm."

Serena sucked in a stuttered breath. "This isn't the first object he's asked you to retrieve, is it?"

Merek shook his head. "I have traveled to many worlds, but my ability to traverse the realms is ending. I have refused to retrieve this artifact. The next trip into a realm will be my last."

"Why?"

"The travel between realms is toxic. A few trips and you will feel sick but will recover. The more foreign a realm from your own, the worse the effects when you return."

Serena snapped a bamboo leaf from a nearby plant. She waved the leaf in front of him. "Why do this? I mean, is this even real?"

Merek stepped closer to her. "My usefulness has ended. I cannot return to my home, and I cannot exist in another realm. I ask for your help to get this artifact and hide it from Lucifer and the caretaker. My future is an eternity as the caretaker's plaything. Yours is death. We can do this one thing to ensure my family goes on and that your world remains out of Lucifer's grasp."

Serena swallowed hard. "So, we die either way, but we can make a difference to our world's safety."

"I know it isn't much. But it is all I can offer you."

Serena shrugged. "I asked for one last adventure. Playing hide and seek in another realm certainly qualifies."

Merek pointed down the trail. "The entrance is just up there."

She followed him as he walked. "I'll take your word for it."

They heard the snarling before the creature stepped from the foliage onto the trail in front of them. It pointed a gnarled grey finger with black curved claws. "Return to your realm. Only death awaits you here."

Merek took off his shirt. "You have guarded the artifact for centuries, Solass. I must retrieve it and hide it in another realm. It is time for you to take your eternal rest."

There was a flicker in the old were's eyes. Relief. Excitement. Anger. "If you best me in combat, the artifact is yours. Be warned. I am a mephitic."

Serena peeked around Merek's back. "What does that mean?"

Merek's body balked out. "His claws are venomous, but so are mine."

Serena grabbed Merek by the arm. "You guys killing each other won't help me."

Merek winked. "Trust me."

He removed his pants before shifting into his were form—the large muscled grey wolf with black curved claws.

Solass nodded a salute before he attacked.

Merek jumped the moment Solass moved. They met in the air that vibrated with ferocious growls. Both went for their opponent's neck. Blood stained both wolves' fur when they returned to the forest floor.

The wolves backed away, waiting for something.

Serena crouched down beside Merek. "What's going on?"

Neither wolf moved—the smell of rotting vegetation mixed with the acrid odor of iron. When Serena thought they would resume the attack, Solass shifted to his human form.

He sat on the ground. His smile sad as he gazed at Merek. "It's been a long time. I have missed my mate. I waited for this opportunity, but to join her, another of my kind had to fulfill my agreement with Lucifer. Only another mephitic were, with stronger venom, could replace me. Thank you for ending my enslavement." He motioned to Serena. "Do you know who she is?"

Serena approached the dying werewolf kneeling before him. "You know who I am?"

Solass nodded. "Not who, what."

Serena swallowed hard. "What am I?"

"The mother of the future," he whispered.

She shook her head. "I don't know what that means."

Solass raised his hand to her cheek, touching her softly. "I am sorry. I must spare him the pain of what's coming." His claws sprang from his fingers before he slashed her throat.

CHAPTER 5

Merek attacked Solass. His claws ripped open the ancient were's chest, spraying blood across the vegetation. He knelt beside Serena, cradling her head in his lap before ripping open her shirt to inspect her injuries. He clamped his hand over the pumping wound, attempting to stem the river of blood. There was one outcome for such an injury. Death.

She shivered against him. "I'm sorry. I was destined to die."

He whispered in her ear. "Don't leave me. You're the first person to give me hope. A reason to live, even if it's only for a day. I want our first kiss. Don't deny me."

Her hand snaked up around his neck, attempting to pull his face toward hers as her strength waned. Moments from death, she would give him what he asked for. How did a monster deserve a miracle like Serena? "Don't leave me. I just found you."

The sky thundered as dark clouds rolled over the crystal blue, turning the perfect paradise into a smoky cauldron of danger and despair. The caretaker emerged from the foliage. His eyes blazed with golden fire. "This cannot be. She must survive. Save her."

Merek looked up at the handsome creature who oversaw the garden. "Why did you bring her here? Was it to punish me?"

The caretaker knelt. "You must save her."

"I'm forbidden to turn a human. Lucifer would annihilate my entire realm for such an infraction. I will join her in death, but I will not ensure my realm's destruction."

The caretaker's eyes turned red. "You will save her, Merek. Then you will complete our deal."

Merek squinted. "Lucifer?"

Lucifer's anger was a living force, destroying the natural beauty surrounding them. "Serena doesn't have much time. That has been the downfall of her entire existence. She was destined to return to the garden. Give her your blood. You and your bloodline are exempt from my rules."

Merek paused as his canines sprang from his gums. "You understand the consequences of me turning her."

Lucifer's eyes flared. "I do. Both you and her will have eternal safe-haven in the garden should you complete your mission."

Merek's heart fluttered. It was a gift of possibility he'd never considered. "I want a day with Serena without your interference."

Lucifer rolled his eyes. "I have better things to do than interfere with your sex life. Retrieve the artifact, and you will have eight hours off my radar."

Merek bit into his wrist. Blood welled up, dripping to the ground as he placed it over her mouth. "The venom from Solass' claws is already in her system. If she is powerful enough, her turn will be pure."

Lucifer stood. "That has never been a guarantee. She will live, but her species is undetermined."

Merek hissed. "You would have me turn her, knowing she could turn into a mindless creature. One of your failed experiments." While his words whipped with his anger, he prayed she would not only survive but become his mate.

Lucifer shrugged. "Creation is a learning process. There will be failures and successes. We will find out which of these applies to Serena."

The caretaker's eyes returned to golden fires. "Is there anything else you require?"

Merek shook his head as Serena moaned. "Why do you serve him? Do you have an actual name?"

The caretaker glanced around at the lush foliage. "I made a deal with Lucifer and am bound by the terms of our agreement. My birth name is irrelevant since my species no longer exists. There's no realm for me to enter. Not even in death."

Merek held Serena closer to his body when she convulsed. While it had been centuries since one of his brethren had transformed, the fear of an impure turn wrapped around his soul like a vice. "How is that possible?"

The caretaker walked away, entering the foliage. His voice echoed before he disappeared. "You know far less than you think you do."

Serena sucked in a stunted breath. "What's going on? My body feels like it's on fire. Everything hurts. I thought death was peaceful."

Merek grabbed his discarded shirt, tucking it under her body as a barrier to the damp earth. "You're not dying, Serena. I gave you my blood. If your turn is pure, you will be a were creature."

She struggled to swallow. "I will be a werewolf?"

He wanted to reassure her. To tell her they'd have a life together, run in the forests of Lucifer's Eden, but he wouldn't lie to her. "I can't guarantee what you will turn into."

"I may not be a wolf? What do you mean by my turning being pure?"

He kissed her forehead. "Majority of the immortals turn into creatures that have no consciousness. They're starving versions of the were or vampire society. The creatures feed but are never sated. They destroy their realm."

"I don't want that."

Merek scrunched his eyes closed. "I won't let that happen."

"How will you stop it?"

His eyes blazed amber as he met her pained gaze. This was the one truth he could promise her. "If your turn is not pure. I will kill you."

Chapter 6

Serena panted through the pain. Fire burned through every internal organ, reshaping and reforming into something else. "How long will the conversion take?"

Merek caressed her hair. "The conversion will take several days in your current state. I could speed the process by biting you, injecting you with more venom. The pain will pass soon, but you won't be fully were for twenty-four hours."

She swallowed hard. "Can I turn here; in the garden, I mean."

Merek shook his head. "I don't know. Turning no longer exists in my realm. All humans converted centuries ago."

She scrunched her eyes shut. "Do it."

His teeth bit into her shoulder as pain radiated through her neck and chest. She took ragged breaths until it receded. Tissue melded together, reverting her skin to its perfect condition. Her eyes snapped open as the wounds closed. "That was quick."

Merek stared at the smooth skin. "It was too quick. It should have taken longer for the venom to saturate your body. Are you still in pain?"

She sat up, wrapping her arms around her knees. "I feel warm inside. I have stomach cramps, but my internal organs don't feel like there being seared from the inside out."

Merek stood before holding his hand out to her. "Let's head into the cave. It can provide shelter until we decide our next move."

His hand slid around her waist, holding her to him as they entered the cave. It wasn't like the one that had caged Merek. This one had smooth walls, with Egyptian hieroglyphs painted on the walls. "I've seen nothing like this."

She pointed to a black figure on the wall. "These are Egyptian gods. This isn't my forte, but I think that is Anubis."

"Then the artifact originated from your world. That's why no were could retrieve it."

She shook her head. "No, the caretaker said you needed to retrieve it, and I needed to help you."

Merek rubbed his chin. "That makes no sense. Solass would have retrieved the artifact himself if he could have. He guarded it because that option was not open to him." He pointed to a set of glyphs. "Do you know what this means?"

She ran her finger along the smooth stone. "My mom was an archaeologist, but I never had time to pursue that career. I recognize some symbols." She pointed to three glyphs grouped together. "This is a warning. Only a summoner can retrieve the artifact."

"What is a summoner?"

She pursed her lips. "Someone who possesses magic."

Merek clenched his fist. "No witches or warlocks in my realm turned pure. It forced us to hunt them down and kill them."

Serena sucked in a breath. "Witches turn into one of those starving zombies."

Merek frowned. "They aren't zombies, but yes, magic has an adverse effect during conversion."

Serena stared at the glyphs. "There's a ward around the artifact. I need a root in order to make a potion to counteract the effect."

His eyebrow arched. "You know how to make potions?"

She met his gaze. "My mother was a practicing Wiccan."

"She taught you her recipes?"

Serena smiled. "We made lotions, soaps, and potions. It was the reason she liked to travel. To find rare ingredients. She died of cancer a year ago. They diagnosed me two days after she died."

Merek hugged her. "I'm sorry, Serena. That is a tough break."

She pushed out of his embrace. "If we can collect the ingredients, we'll need a fire to let the mixture simmer for a few hours."

"The caretaker wants us to retrieve this artifact. Everything we need will be available to us. In fact, I think it already is."

"Why do you say that?"

Merek took her hand and led her to an adjacent cavern. The middle of the room had a fire pit with smooth stones. There was a shelf full of jars and dried leaves. "I'm guessing what you need is already here."

She frowned. "How did you know this was here?"

He pointed to another cave. "I am a tracker. I can sense what I'm looking for. The artifact is in that cave."

Serena huffed. "How convenient."

Merek touched her cheek. "We stick to the plan. Lucifer wants the artifact retrieved. He will help us attain it, but he will expect us to give it to him. We hide it in another realm."

Serena nodded. "You start the fire. I'll combine the ingredients."

There was a calm in the familiarity of putting ingredients together. Reminding her of when she was young, she and her mother would make herbal soaps or ointments. She got the adventure she wanted, and this way, her death would mean something.

Merek laid blankets beside the fire. He stoked the amber flames before sitting down.

She brought the pot to the fire, placing it on the smooth stone in the middle. "This will simmer for a few hours, then we can retrieve the artifact."

Merek patted the spot next to him. "We should get a few hours of rest. Once we open a portal, Lucifer will be after us."

Serena sat beside him, snuggling into his shoulder when he wrapped his arm around her. "I thought I would be sad when this day came. I'm glad I met you and learned about the other realms. There's more to life than I thought."

He touched her cheek. "I feel fortunate to have met you as well."

Serena gazed at the flames that engulfed the iron pot. "I wish I could have run as a wolf. That would've been cool." She stared up at him. "What's it like?"

Merrick smiled. "It's been a long time since I ran as a natural wolf. Since arriving in the garden, I have been in our warrior form, but running as a wolf is one of the most freeing and beautiful experiences. It was the only reprieve I had from an eternity of loneliness."

Serena frowned. "Why were you lonely? Did you not have family in your old home?"

"I have family, but no mate."

"You would've found someone had you stayed in your realm."

Merek shook his head. "I met every unmated female. None of them were my mate. I believed I was cursed until you walked into the cave."

Her heart skipped. "What are you saying?"

He took her hand, kissing her fingers. "You're my mate, Serena. I have waited centuries for you, and all I can offer you is one night."

She took his face in her hands. "I'll take it. Some people can live a lifetime in a few moments. We will have the next few hours.

Thunder rolled, and lightning cracked in the background when his lips touched hers. The light pressure ignited a fire in her blood she had never experienced. A pulsing raw power surged through her body, making every nerve ending ultra sensitive. She moaned into his mouth as his tongue swept between her lips.

Merek wasn't kissing her. He was devouring her. He traced her lips, moving to her neck, circling her collarbone with featherlight flicks of his tongue as he removed her clothes.

She could only cling to him as her bra fell to the ground.

His hands explored her body, inflaming her skin with each masterful caress. Merek's need and his arousal seemed to fuel the storm outside. His hunger more powerful than anything nature could conceive. "I gave up believing there was an end to the nightmare of my life. If tonight is all we have, then I thank you for this gift. This miracle."

His voice was raw with hunger, passion, and conviction that matched her own. He was wild, untamed, and sexy, but he was hers for the time they had left. She clung to him. This moment of happiness, this adventure, had her thanking the heavens.

He lay her down on the blanket. She had never felt so wanton as she lay naked before him. Her eyes glued to his body as he removed his clothes.

Merek was chiseled muscle in tanned, perfect skin. A Greek God unlike any other. Her breath hitched as he knelt between her legs before kissing her stomach, working his way to her breasts.

Her body arched as he sucked a nipple into his mouth, growling his approval at the rush of liquid between her legs.

She wished she could stay in that cave forever with her sensual lover. Floating on the sea of sensation and erotic ecstasy.

She tensed when his thick cock nudged her entrance.

He stilled, tipping her chin to meet his amber gaze. "Serena, are you okay?"

Her body hummed like a live wire. She had never wanted anything more. Still, the fear of the unknown was a palpable opponent. "I've never..."

He kissed her so long she forgot what she would have said. Her body was a flame of fire and lust. She couldn't think straight, her mind and body all centered on the Adonis that held her. She would've done anything for him to sate the savage passion raging through her body.

He nudged her entrance, causing a sting of pain before it subsided. "Serena, I want you to know, if I had time, I would have mated you. That the centuries I waited, bound to the garden, were worth this one night with you."

He surged forward, breaking through the thin barrier of her innocence. She gasped into his mouth before the storm intensified. Lightning licked through her blood, sending jolts of electricity over her skin. She gasped at the unexpected pleasure racking her body.

His arms, like steel, wrapped around her in an unbreakable vice, yet his lips continued to worship her mouth. His slow, thick strokes intensified as his body tightened like a spring.

He pumped into her, taking her higher and higher. Two souls locked in the clouds, soaring for eternity. She teetered on the apex, begging for release when the tsunami reached its peak.

Pleasure ripped across her body, causing her to cry out. She clamped down on him as she came, taking him with her. They spiraled in never-ending ecstasy as beads of sweat coated their bodies in glistening beauty.

Serena was on the verge of falling asleep when Merek sat up. His eyes flashed with anger. "This can't be it. I've waited too long for you. I can't accept your death."

She reached out, pulling him back down beside her. "I need to rest. The potion needs to simmer for another hour. Lay with me."

Merek settled beside her. She lay her head on his shoulder, waiting until his breathing was slow and even.

She dressed quietly before grabbing the potion. A tear ran down her face as she slipped away.

The adjacent cave containing the artifact was small. Light and smoke drifted from the hollowed-out altar in the middle, flicking shadows along the wall. They reached with showy fingers, grasping the night.

She poured the potion into the hole, waiting for the smoke to dissipate. She pulled back her sleeve, holding her arm above the stone crevice.

"Don't do it, Serena." Merek snapped.

She paused, staring at the man she loved. "I can't let you throw your life away. Mine was already over." Her hand lowered into the darkness.

Power surged through her body as her heart stopped.

CHAPTER 7

Power surged within her, breaking the spell surrounding the artifact. Serena blinked as powerful arms encircled her waist. The growl in her ear caused her to focus on the steel object in her hand.

She withdrew the dagger from the magical well that had been its home for centuries. The metal warmed against her skin, but the blade was dull. "What is so special about this? It looks like a child made this weapon."

Merek touched her arm, forcing her to lower the strange blade. "This dagger was Lucifer's first creation. He imbued it with the power of purity. His father blessed it prior to his fall from heaven. It is his only holy creation."

Serena flipped the dagger in her hand. Unlike other weapons, someone forged together the hilt and blade. Foreign markings adorned the handhold. "What does it do?"

Merrick sighed. "The dagger can cleanse a fallen realm."

Serena shook her head. "I don't know what that means."

"The fallen realms started with a single infection. This dagger can destroy the source."

She ran her fingers over the blade. The thin cut stung, forcing her to snap her hand away. "Shit! It didn't look that sharp."

Merek grabbed her free hand, pulling it up to his face. It healed, leaving a gray scar. "That's a silver burn. You are a were. But you possess magic, don't you, Serena?"

Serena closed her scarred fingers. "I was never like my mom. I could do little things. Call an object to me or settle an angry animal. This time my power was like a force attempting to break free."

Merek rubbed his forehead. "I had hoped that if I saved you, you'd be able to return to my realm, but beings of magic turn into starving mindless creatures. You cannot go there."

She grabbed Merek's arm. "If I'm not dying, I can return to my realm. You could come with me."

He shook his head. "Serena, you carry the were virus. If you return home, you risk infecting your realm. It's not a blessing to be immortal. The women in my realm cannot have children. The virus makes them sterile within a year."

She nodded. "Let's worry about where to go after deciding what to do with the artifact. I wonder why Lucifer wants it?"

Merek glanced at the blade. "He wants to resurrect the fallen worlds."

She slipped the blade into her belt. "Why? Isn't Lucifer all about death and destruction?"

Merek frowned. "Every realm has a different version of Lucifer and his story. Some are accurate, some are not, but none know what he's capable of or what he will do to accomplish his goal."

She swallowed hard. "What does he want?"

"Only Lucifer has the answer to that. Let's hope we never find out."

Serena looked around the cave. "Where to next?"

Merek walked to the cave entrance, then drew a symbol on the wall. A doorway formed in the rock. "We go to the dispensary."

Serena joined him in front of the strange door. "What's the dispensary?"

Merek held up his hands, forming a circle. "Think of the garden as a nucleus. All the other realms move around us but are only accessible at certain times. We will choose a realm with an auto-return, one that permanently tethers to the garden."

Serena blinked. "How many realms are there?"

"Thousands, but many are barren and no longer accessible."

Serena frowned. "Wouldn't a barren world be the perfect place to hide the dagger?"

Merek shook his head. "Life creates the tethers. Once a realm is barren, it's lost to the garden forever."

"That sounds bad. How do we tell if a realm is tethered to the garden?"

He took her hand and led her into the dispensary.

Doors of various shapes and sizes cluttered the room. Many had markings, while others were bare. Several doors had one or two countdown timers.

She turned around as doors appeared, then disappeared. "How do we choose?"

Merrick pointed at a black door with a single timer. "The doors with a single timer will return us in the time allotted. This one is eight hours."

Serena pointed at a door with two timers. "What does that mean?"

Merrick glanced at the gray door. "That realm is tethered to the garden. You must find the exit before the time expires, or you're trapped in the realm forever."

Serena pursed her lips. "Yeah, I'm not down for the magical door scavenger hunt. How do we choose between the doors, preferably one with a timer?"

Merek shrugged. "Only Lucifer knows what's behind each door. Pick one and hope for the best."

Serena looked up at him. "You want me to choose. Why?"

His eyes were sad as he looked down at her. "You are a were with magic. If you open a door from Lucifer's Garden and place the artifact in another realm, then only another were with magic can retrieve it."

"What are the consequences for relocating the dagger?"

Merek's eyes flickered with amber. "The penalty for unsanctioned travel between realms... is death."

CHAPTER 8

Serena fell forward, clutching her stomach as the contents relieved themselves on the dusty ground before her. "I feel like a human salt and pepper shaker."

Merek knelt beside her, rubbing her back as she vomited. "That is an accurate description of inter-realm travel."

She sat back on her heels, taking deep breaths before noticing Merek's beard. "Is facial hair another side effect?"

Merek rubbed his face. "I have not grown a beard since I transformed."

She cleared her throat. "What does that mean?"

Merek surveyed the dusty landscape. Partial structures and abandoned vehicles dotted the sand and rock. The wind whipped against them, causing tornadoes of sand to swirl around them. The brown fog made their whereabouts impossible to discern. "Judging by my beard, there is a two-month time discrepancy. Time shifts are common between realms, but if I'm growing a beard, then I am aging. We are not immortal in this realm."

Serena stood up, dusting the sand from her knees. "We are only here for eight hours. I don't think it matters."

Merek grabbed her hand. "Provided we don't get hurt. We will not heal here."

Serena nodded. "Be careful. Got it. Now, where do we hide the dagger?"

The low growl echoed through the mist. They knelt, looking for the source of the sound.

Merek pointed at a cement structure that looked like an old chimney. "Over there. We are wide open here. We need some cover." He grabbed her hand, pulling her behind him.

Serena touched the weathered stone of the chimney. The colored mortar and intricate design denoted pride of ownership. "What happened to this place?"

Merek surveyed the fog. "Lucifer happened."

There was no warning. It was as if the creature appeared from nowhere. She would've been dead if Merek hadn't stepped in front of her, taking the brunt of the attack.

She assumed the thing was once a man, but his humanity was barely recognizable. His skin hung in gray folds over his skeleton frame. The long, hooked fangs snapped together as it snarled and drooled, attempting to bite Merek's neck.

"Run!" Merek shouted.

She heard the growls in the fog as more creatures approached. She spotted a cross in the distance. It appeared to hover in midair as brown mist swirled around it. She bolted toward the church, praying it offered safety.

Serena sprinted through the brown mist encrusted with sand and dirt. The boarded-up church had no visible entrance. She bounded up the broken steps, banging on the plywood that covered the window. "Is anybody in there?" She shouted. When she received no response, she proceeded to the rear of the building.

She found a contraption mounted on the back panel. "Is that a dumbwaiter?" She tugged the rope that moved the cart from the ground to the roof.

She was about to climb in when something yanked her backward. The fetid breath and angry growls had her grabbing for the dagger before she turned.

Her arm whirled, connecting with the creature's chest as his fangs grazed over her neck.

The shriek made her cover her ears and crouch down as the vampire fell to his back, clutching the dagger in his heart.

She expected him to explode in flames or die quickly. He cried and shouted, with each syllable becoming more and more human. His skin returned to a human hue. Dark smoke lifted from his body like ash from a fire. Instinct had her yanking the dagger from his chest, waiting for blood to erupt and end his suffering.

She watched in horror as the wound closed. The smell of burning flesh assaulted her nose, causing her to gag.

His eyes turned from red to blue. "You're the one."

She touched his chest. The dagger-shaped scar looked like a tattoo. "I don't know what happened?"

The man sat up. "That is the purity dagger."

She held up the dagger as the blood burned away. "How do you know about this weapon?"

The man pointed at the church. "I was pastor here when the infection hit. There are scrolls in our archives that mention that dagger. I thought it was a myth."

Serena glanced at the church. "How do we get into the church?"

He nodded, allowing her to help him to his feet. "Follow me."

She followed him to the side of the building, where he removed a panel and activated the retinal scanner. He put his face to the camera before a steel door opened. He entered the church.

She stepped inside. The door slammed shut, startling her. "That was more high-tech than I was expecting."

The pastor smiled sadly. "The energy core for the defense system could power a small city. It wasn't designed to guard a church, but this was the last haven. When my flock abandoned the church, I programmed security to allow a human retina to open the door. I never expected it to be me."

Serena glanced around the interior of the church. Benches, candles, and a wooden altar reminded her of home. "I'm not alone. I have to find Merek and bring him back here."

The pastor nodded. "Your friend won't last ten minutes out there. I suggest you hurry."

CHAPTER 9

The security door closed with a hiss when she exited the sanctuary. She raced toward the area she had last seen Merek. Angry growls echoed around her as the fog swallowed the outline of the church.

She pulled the dagger, holding it like a talisman when the first creature attacked. This time she held onto the weapon after stabbing her assailant.

The first vampire fell to the ground, clutching his chest, but three more surrounded her. She gripped the dagger like a talisman when the next creature attacked her. She plunged the blade into his heart before the vampire fell to his death. Another one bit her arm, forcing her to drop the blade as another creature ravaged her shoulder.

Serena knew Marek instantly, even in were form. A sense of safety washed over her as she locked eyes with his beast.

The wolf ripped the head from the vampire at her shoulder, giving Serena the chance to kick the one attached to her arm. She scrambled for the dagger, then stabbed the surviving vampire.

She knelt beside the growling wolf. "We need to get to the church. The dagger reverts them to their human form. I saved the pastor; he has a safe place."

Merek shifted to his human form. While naked and bleeding from multiple lacerations, he was magnificent and sexy as hell. "We won't last eight minutes here, let alone eight hours, if we don't go there now."

Serena led Merek back to the church. She opened the side panel and placed her eye in front of the retina scanner, causing the door to open. They entered the church, turning as two vampires followed before the door shut.

The pastor stood in front of a basin, filling it with water. He motioned to Serena. "Put the dagger in the water."

She grabbed the dagger, doing as a pastor instructed. When her hand touched the water, power flooded her body—the empty silver goblets beside the basin filled with water as her wounds healed.

The pastor stepped back. "You are more than just a messenger. You are the mother."

Serena didn't have time for his cryptic message. Merek was fighting both vampires. One bit his shoulder, forcing him to shift to his were form.

She grabbed a cup of water, and threw it at the vampire. She expected him to revert to his human form, but he exploded in fire and ash. "What just happened?"

The pastor pointed at the vampire fighting Merek. "Some are beyond the point of saving. The power of purity can bring forth life or destroy it."

She grabbed another cup, tossing it at the fighting men. The vampire screamed when the water touched his skin. He collapsed to the floor as ash and smoke lifted from his body.

Merek shifted to human form as the pastor and Serena joined him. They watched in fascination as the vampire reverted to human. He held up a hand. "Thank you." Then slumped into unconsciousness.

The pastor knelt beside him. "Help me get him into the other room. There are beds set up."

Merek and the pastor took the man as Serena flexed her hands. She felt different, more powerful than before. The hair on the back of her neck bristled, warning her of the danger.

She swung around as the diseased wolf emerged from its hiding place. They hadn't noticed him sneak in with the vampires. This one was more cunning. He had waited for an opportunity to get her alone. His eyes flared red as saliva dripped from his canines. The creature was beyond saving.

The goblets were merely inches away but seemed like miles as the wolf sprang. Her fingers grappled for the metal cup as the creature propelled her backward with its attack.

The power inside her rose, blasting the creature away as she shifted.

Her wolf was white with gray tips on its fur. Her eyes blazed with amber fire as she circled her prey. They growled at one another before a third wolf joined.

Merek returned to the congregation room and rushed to her side. His teeth flashed as fur rose on his back. He stood beside his mate, facing down the creature ravished by disease and fate. The two wolves attacked in unison, ripping the throat of the aggressor. He was dead before his body hit the floor.

Merrick shifted first, kneeling beside Serena. "Honey, I need you to shift. It's not safe for you to stay in this form. Your magic encases you like a shroud. If we stay here, you will turn into the creature we just killed."

Serena shifted into his arms, tucking her arms over her breasts when she realized her clothes didn't survive her transition.

The pastor handed Merek two robes while keeping his eyes averted. "Put these on. Fill the cups with water and add a few drops of blood to each one. We will put them outside. The starving creatures will drink. We will save those that can be redeemed. The fallen will die."

They slipped on the robes before Merek went to the basin. His fingers caressed the water before turning to Serena. "This happened in my realm. We didn't know what purified the water. One day we were starving, going mad, and the next, we were turning human. That was centuries ago."

The pastor nodded. "Only a traveler can traverse the realms with a blessed object."

Serena joined Merek at the basin. "I'm a traveler?"

The pastor looked her over. "Did you bring the dagger from your world to this one?"

Serena shook her head. "We took the dagger from Lucifer's Garden."

"I suspected you were the mother," the pastor said. "We have a prophet, but I didn't believe it until today."

Serena shook her head. "I don't have any children. I was dying of cancer until becoming a were."

The pastor grabbed an old book from the shelf. "The prophecy says the mother will come from another world, then enter the garden. There she meets her mate, and they conceive a child. They travel to a fallen realm, but restoring it causes her unborn child to be untethered. The one true traveler."

Serena touched her stomach. "What does untethered mean?"

Merek rubbed his forehead. "We're tethered to the realm in which we were born." He glanced at the pastor. "Serena couldn't get pregnant in the garden. Time is stagnant there."

"A pregnancy can't progress in the garden," the pastor interjected. "You need an active realm for your child to grow. I recommend you stay here until your daughter is born."

Merek caught Serena's arm when she swayed. "This can't be happening. I'm supposed to die, not have a child or..." She plopped onto the bench.

Merek sat beside her, taking her face in his hands. "Look into my eyes, connect with my wolf. I need to know if what he says is true."

Serena's wolf rose to meet the gaze of her mate. Her vision blurred before clearing. She met his fiery amber eyes. "Well?"

Merek pulled her against his body. "I can't confirm it's a girl, but you are with child. The pregnancy is new, maybe eight weeks along."

Serena pulled back. "What are we going to do? We will return to the dispensary. Do we pick another door or ..."

Merek kissed her cheek. "I have one card left to play. Trust me." He took her hand, turning to the pastor. "Protect that dagger with your life."

"Serena had a pure soul before entering the Lucifer's Garden. Lucifer attempted to use her to acquire the dagger, but he can no longer touch her. A blessed artifact can only travel between realms with a pure soul. Your child will possess unimaginable power. You must protect her from Lucifer at all costs."

Serena huffed. "I guess you don't play Russian roulette with mother nature."

The pastor frowned. "I do not know what Russian roulette is, but Lucifer believed he could circumvent the rules of the realms. His actions ensured your creation. His attempt to use you guaranteed your daughter's."

Serena swallowed hard. "Does the prophecy mention my daughter?"

"Your daughter is Lucifer's creation," the pastor added. "The rules of the realms do not bind her. Neither good nor evil, but not tethered to any world. She will be a liberator or a destroyer of the realms. While her birth is preordained, her story is yet to be written."

Merek tipped her chin up to meet his gaze. "You are a miracle. Our child is a miracle. Trust me to keep you safe."

She kissed him. "I do trust you. What do we do now?"

Merek drew a symbol in the air. It lit on fire as he glanced at the pastor. "Good luck."

Serena raised her hand to wave at the holy man, but darkness engulfed her.

CHAPTER 10

Serena grabbed her stomach as she fell to the ground inside the dispensary. Merek helped her to her feet before she glanced up at the timer above the door. "It's dark. How do we know what happens to them?"

"You don't," the caretaker said, causing them to turn around. His golden eyes roamed over Serena's body. "You resurrected a lost realm. I didn't believe it was possible."

"What now?" Serena glanced at Merek, then at the caretaker.

The caretaker shrugged. "You've fulfilled your debt and are free to return to your own world."

Merek stepped forward. "She can't. Serena is were and my mate. She could infect her realm with the were virus."

The caretaker looked at Serena. "Yours is the last fertile realm. Lucifer owns Merek. He is tied to the garden, but you have a choice. You may choose to stay here with him, but if you do so, you'll be bound to the terms and conditions of the garden—forever."

She placed her hand on Merek's. "I can't let what happened in that broken world happen to my home. I go where my mate does."

Merek's eyes narrowed on the caretaker. "You didn't need me for the artifact. You wanted me to turn her. Why?"

"I needed her to live." The caretaker's eyes flared.

Serena glanced between the angry men. "Why me?"

The caretaker's eyes softened when he looked at her. "You're special. I wanted you to have a life."

"Was my pregnancy part of the plan?"

The caretaker sucked in a breath. "That's not possible. The child's conception would've happened in the garden and..."

"I'm pregnant," Serena said.

"You are the mother." The caretaker's eyes flared with golden flecks. "I wanted the prophecy to be true, but the chances of those elements coming together at the perfect time were impossible."

Serena smoothed the robe she wore. "The pastor said my child cannot grow in Lucifer's Garden. What are the consequences of me staying here?"

The caretaker rubbed his chin. "You must return to your world long enough for your child to be born. Once she's born, you must continue to travel."

Serena frowned. "How do we travel if we aren't returning to the garden? Merek says that excessive travel makes you sick."

The caretaker pulled an amulet from beneath his dark suit. "This is my personal amulet. It is the last of its kind. Unlike the dispensary, it will choose the next realm randomly. It will protect you from the effects of realm travel. Hold Merek's hand before you activate it." He held it out to Serena.

She took the amber stone that looked like a cross between Topaz and Opal. "It's beautiful. Why is it the last of its kind?"

The caretaker's eyes flickered with gold. "The amulet only works if its owner is alive. My species has passed. When your child is born, the amulet will form a small crystal. Gift it to your daughter. Make sure she never takes it off. It will shroud her from Lucifer."

Serena's heart stuttered. "You think Lucifer will hurt her?"

The caretaker took Serena's hand. "I can stall Lucifer for a couple of human years, but once he's aware of her existence, he won't stop hunting her."

The caretaker released her hand and walked to an octagon with two timers. He tapped the door, causing it to open. "Go, save your daughter."

Merek took her hand as he stood in front of the portal. "Are you ready?"

She squeezed his hand. "I never imagined a life, let alone one filled with love, excitement, and family."

Merek's eyes flickered. "I love you, Serena. Are you ready for our next adventure?"

The End.

About the Author

Tia Didmon is a USA Today bestselling author of provocative paranormal romance. When Tia isn't busy writing about sexy shifters
and dreamy demons, she spends her time binging The Order and reruns of The Vampire Diaries, cooking with her daughter, and serving her cat. Her love of writing stems from a self-diagnosed book addiction.
Subscribe to Tia's newsletter

For a free book and to start your journey through Tia's supernatural world today go to www.TiaDidmon.com

ALSO BY TIA DIDMON

www.TiaDidmon.com

Shadow Shifter Series

Mortal Curse -

Mortal Mate-

Mortal Reaper-

Mortal Queen-

Mortal Magic-

Mortal Guardian (WIP)

Mortal Demon (WIP)

Mortal Princess (WIP)

Dragon Rules Series

Dragon Rules-

Legion-

Bram-

Conner-

Thorn-

Draco -

New Immortals Series

Valentino's Kiss-

Dante's Desire-

Jordane's Hunger-

Tovan's Temptation-

Immortal Christmas-

New Immortals Box Set-

Jenner's Justice-

Cascade Cougars Series

Virgin Mate-

Enter The Lair-

Hunter's Passion-

Shifter's Eden-

Cougars Christmas-

Wild Seduction-

Feral Attraction-

Shifters Storm -

Supernatural Midlife Mystique Series

The Prime of my Magical Life

All Good Magic Comes to an End

Sweet Magical Destruction

KILLIAN'S QUEST

MAGGIE ADAMS

Blurb

Diana Zamaroni's community is different than most. Paranormal of all kinds and humans cohabitate amicably in her small village. Peace rules their slice of the world. At least until one cold winter night ...

Killian Arroyas is one of the infamous vampire twins born to the leader of the US contingent of Paranormal beings. His twin, Royas, has killed their parents and sent Killian on a quest to find his mate before Royas can kill him too. Fortunately, he knows exactly where she is ...

But can Killian convince Diana that they are meant to be together before his evil twin descends on the town and destroys their peaceful existence?

CHAPTER 1

Grafton, Illinois; a haven for the paranormal

Diana Zamaroni glided across the worn floors of her general store, Ned's Shed and Sausage Shoppe. Her long legs and ample hips sashayed to the beat of the music blaring from her old stereo. The lime green microfiber dusting shoes she sported on her feet had her twisting and turning around the tables to Frankie Valley and The Four Seasons.

She belted the lyrics to "Oh What A Night" as her gray-haired cat, Birdie, watched from his spot near the cash register. She turned to make a final sweep when a fierce howling rent the air.

Birdie jumped, hissed, and raced into the kitchen.

Diana shook her head, making her long, dark ponytail whip back and forth. "It's just the wind," she shouted. "Get over it."

A crash of glass in the kitchen had her scurrying around the counter, mumbling curse words at her skittish cat. "I swear if you've broken...."

She came to a standstill as someone crashed through the window, sending shards of glass twinkling across the floor. He landed against the stainless-steel island.

"What the..." she whispered and darted over to the person who lay unconscious. She knelt to check for vital signs and found none. She put a trembling hand to her mouth and realized the stranger was dead. She reached for the phone in her pocket.

A pale hand gripped her ankle. She screamed, falling back onto her butt.

"No," he whispered with a ragged breath. "You run."

She stared with mounting horror as realization pounded her brain. *Not human, a vampire.*

"Run, please," he croaked.

She crawled across the kitchen floor and reached in the back of a cabinet for her grandmother's silver teapot in case of more intruders.

The vampire tried to sit up.

"You stay away!" she shouted and ran toward the delivery door.

Uncanny howls rent the air. Claws scratched against her screened-in porch at the back of the building.

"Run," the vampire whispered again.

It was too late. A werewolf ripped the door off its hinges. His eyes darted about the room and landed on the vamp.

Her pulse raced. Her throat constricted with fear. She didn't think she could be more terrified—no escape, the werewolf blocked the exit. She doubted she'd make it to the front.

She screamed when he lunged at her, scratching her arm. She grabbed a cast iron skillet from the stove and swatted it.

The beast barely flinched and clutched for her again.

She dashed around the countertop and spied the candle lighter she used to light the pilot light of her ancient gas stove. She seized it as the werewolf yanked her ponytail, pulling her to him.

Flicking off the safety, she lit the flame and ignited the fur on his face.

The wolf shrieked and let her go.

She snatched the bacon grease can atop the stove shelf and threw it as he advanced. She jabbed him with the lighter flame again and again.

He caught her wrist, twisted, and squeezed until she dropped the lighter, but the flames already licked across his fur. He yelped in pain and retreated out the broken door, batting the fire on his body.

She sighed in relief and tripped over the vampire crawling toward her. His fangs elongated, then he passed out.

Diana scooted around him. She needed help and tried to locate her phone and found it in scattered pieces on the floor. "Well, hell," she mumbled.

She glanced at the vampire.

He'd tried to warn her. He told her to run, so maybe she'd give him the benefit of the doubt until he came to.

Still, the vamp had a lot of explaining to do.

Chapter 2

"What did you do?" She looked at his injuries as she dipped the washcloth into a water bowl and gently dabbed the large hole in his side. It didn't look good.

His eyes fluttered, then he murmured, "Silver kills."

She glanced at the silver teapot on the floor.

"No, side," he said.

She gently grazed the spot. "Oh, is it a bullet?"

He nodded. "You need to go. He'll be back."

"Well, I can't just leave you in the store like this to die," she said gruffly. "Sorry. I didn't mean to sound mean."

"Need blood," he muttered.

"Will deer or pig blood do?" Living in a paranormal community like Grafton, she had all sorts of supernatural happenings that a mortal general store didn't have.

"No. Human." His voice faded fast.

The stranger had tried to warn her, even save her. She dashed over to the teapot and grabbed it. "You may take my blood, but once you're sated, you better let go, or I'll shove this teapot in that hole without hesitation. Do you understand?"

He didn't respond.

She shoved her wrist to his mouth. "Do it." She turned her head away and squeezed her eyes shut, holding tightly to the teapot, waiting for the pain, but nothing happened.

Opening her eyes, she noticed he was unconscious again. *He must be too weak.*

She reached for the paring knife near the cutting boards.

You can do this, Diana. She let out a whimper and made an incision on her wrist with the knife. Blood spurted. "Oh God, I'm gonna die." She raised her wrist once more to his lips.

Within seconds, his eyes popped open, and he greedily sucked the warm blood from her veins. Funny, it didn't hurt. She thought it would, but it was more like a gentle suckle.

An unexpected sensation coursed through her veins. Tender desire pooled between her thighs at the apex of her womanhood.

After a few more seconds, she tried to pull away, knowing full well if she didn't, she'd succumb to the passion and give not only her blood to this mysterious stranger. This was why so many fell victim to vampires—the great need.

He held onto her wrist with a firm grip.

She yelped, then whacked him across the face with the teapot.

He withdrew his fangs.

She tried to stand up, but she was woozy and managed to make it only to her knees.

He tugged her arm, and she wanted to wallop him again, but she dropped the kettle. Her energy zapped.

"May I?"

"Why not?"

He lifted her wrist, licked it, and sealed the wound.

"Thanks for not killing me," she whispered, leaning against him, slightly embarrassed that she had shrieked in the first place.

"I would never kill my heroine. Thank you for saving me." He closed his eyes. "Give me a minute."

Diana noted his voice seemed stronger.

Before he drank blood, he couldn't even pierce her wrist.

She rubbed her wrist absently as she studied him. Chiseled features, dark black hair with a hint of gray at his temples. His body, or what she could see through his shredded shirt, rippling with muscle.

He shivered.

"Are you cold?" She wondered aloud.

He was a vampire and assumed they always stayed that way. He ticked up one side of his mouth in a semblance of a grin. "No, are you?"

"You shivered. And yes, I'm freezing." She glanced at the thermostat, which read seventy-two. The wintry December wind blew through the shattered window.

"I'm healing," he explained. "Humans usually don't like vampires, yet you helped me anyway."

"Don't be ridiculous. We aren't like that here. This is a small paranormal community, and we take care of each other. Oh, I'm Diana, by the way—Diana Zamaroni."

"I know. I'm Killian Arroyo."

"You're one of the twins." Her grandfather loved telling the story about the birth of identical twin vamps born within minutes of each other to the former leader of the paranormal council of the Midwest several hundred years ago.

"How do you know me?" She clutched the teapot to her chest. "Why are you here?"

He raked his fingers through his silky black hair. Then the silver bullet popped out from the injury and rolled toward her. She watched the hole heal completely.

She picked up the bullet and offered it to him, then realized her mistake – silver.

"Keep it. I don't want it." He grimaced. "As to why I'm here, that's a bit complicated, but I came to save you."

"Me? Why do I need saving?" Diana stood and poured the bowlful of bloody water into the sink.

He sidestepped the question as he came to his feet. "Although we were twins, my elder brother became leader when my parents were killed. He has always been wary of me. He covets my power."

"Power?" Her head tilted to the side.

"I'm a day walker."

Vampires that could walk in the daylight were rare. "Your parents were killed?"

"Yes." He stepped toward her.

She felt the familiar pang of desire again. *Weird.* Was he using glamour on her?

"My mother was human and easy to kill. My father, well, that took some cunning."

"What happened?" Diana suddenly became afraid.

"My brother killed my parents to rule as the leader of our region."

"And now he's after you," she added.

"I'm the only one able to challenge him. Therefore, I'm a threat. When I claim my mate, I will become a leader. My power will outrank his, and Royas will go mad with mate lust."

"What's that?"

"It's when a vampire cannot find his mate, or his mate may have died. It's not simply a 'want' to mate for us; it's a 'need.' We go insane, dangerous, and measures must be taken to subdue us."

"And what does this have to do with me?" she asked but already knew the answer. Diana tried to absorb everything. Her eyes wandered into the store. It seemed ages ago she'd been dancing and carefree, content with her life.

"Royas knows I will confront him to save my mate, to save you."

CHAPTER 3

Diana stared at Killian's face in fascinated horror. She brushed an errant bit of hair from her face. They sat side by side with their backs against the counter, only inches apart.

His mate? Shaking her head, she tried to clear her mind. She backed away from him.

"Please, don't," he commanded.

"I need space." *Mated to a dark-haired, day walking, silver-eyed vampire?* The thought terrified her. "I don't understand. I'm nobody," her voice cracked. Hell, she was on the verge of a full-blown panic attack. *Tonight was too much—werewolves, dying intruders, and now her mate was a vampire leader?*

Strong arms closed around her. She struggled against his chest— no match for him, but she continued to fight. She felt his erection stir. "Oh my God, you're hard!"

"Stop. You're going to injure yourself," he said. "And I can't help it. I'm not going to do anything about it. I would never hurt you."

"Because I'm your mate?"

"Yes."

She stopped pushing, and his arms relaxed. Sure, he was sexy as hell, even in tattered clothes. Her body responded to the potent chemistry he exuded. Sensual thoughts ran through her head—fantasies of Killian taking her on the floor of her kitchen. Her nipples tightened painfully, a reaction that had nothing to do with the wind whipping through her cold kitchen and everything to do with the man holding her.

Killian noticed as well. "You are experiencing the sexual pull from finding your mate. It will pass."

That comment snapped her back to attention, and she twisted out of his arms and stood. Hands on her hips, she was no longer aroused but angry. "Are you telling me you did this to me? How did you even find me? Why am I your mate?"

"I've had you on my radar since you were born." He came to his feet. "As to why, well, you just are. Your body, your soul, your mind knows it's true. We're drawn to each other." His arms reached up to gently massage her shoulders. "I feel it, too."

Diana put some distance between them.

"In normal circumstances, I would court you," he said, his voice low, seductive. "I would gently bring you to my bed. You would know the sensual touch of the man who will love you, take care of you, and keep you safe forever. Unfortunately, there's no time. You need to believe me, now." He closed the space between them, then cupped her cheek with one of his enormous hands. His intensity willed her to recognize the truth.

Diana shivered with need as his hand ran down her neck. She should move away, but the feel of his cool hand caressing her collarbone as he ran his right index finger over and around to the special spot right between her throat was intoxicating.

"Ah, Diana, how I would love to continue, but now is not the time." He kissed her softly on her forehead and stepped back.

The spell broke.

She stumbled against the kitchen counter, her face an expression of astonishment and embarrassment. She believed him. No one had ever made her feel so wanton with a simple touch. Whatever the reason, she was his mate.

"Careful, my love." Looking down at her footwear, he grimaced. "What in the hell are those?"

Oh God, she'd completely forgotten she was wearing dusting shoes! Leaning down, she stripped them off quickly and threw them towards the sink. "It doesn't matter."

He caught one, examining it closely. "Ingenious!" He bashfully admitted, "I'm a bit of an inventor. Until my brother decided to assassinate me, I led a rather quiet life."

Diana rubbed her forehead in consternation. "You talk like his betrayal doesn't bother you."

"Long story for another day. I know you're confused. This is a lot to take in, but you must know," he said, brushing his lips against her temple, "that you are mine, and I protect what is mine."

She felt a soft flutter against her bare feet and marched across the room to grab her cat, forgetting about the shards of glass.

"Ow!" she cried, hopping on the other foot only to injure that as well. Birdie dashed back into the store.

In a flash, Killian was at her side, pulling the glass out and licking the blood from her toes. Satisfied that she was healed, he placed her on top of the counter, swept up the glass, and disposed of it in the large trash receptacle.

With a slight smile, he said, "I need to rest. I should be fully recovered in a few hours. You must stay here by my side." A statement, not a request. "Where do you sleep?"

Diana bristled. "Don't tell me what to do. Even if you think I am your mate, I am my own person." At his pointed look, she acquiesced, almost as if she needed to please him. "My apartment is up the back stairs."

"I apologize for my bluntness," he said humbly but with a twinkle in his eye. "I want you badly. Your scent, your blood, makes me..."

Diana blushed but changed the subject. "Where's Birdie?" She looked around. The cat had wandered back into the general store. She found her sitting at her favorite place near the cash register. Satisfied her cat was safe, she reached for the light switch on the wall behind her and turned off the lights.

Killian lifted her in his arms.

"What are you doing?"

"I'll carry you. No sense in you injuring yourself again. There could be stray glass." He started up the stairs.

She wrapped her arms around his neck and tucked her head under his chin. He had powerful arms, and her weight didn't appear to strain him at all. She reveled in the blossoming closeness with him.

"What are we going to do about Royas?"

"I like it when you say 'we.' There's no sense worrying. It's dawn, and he will soon sleep, and so will his werewolf, his scout. Normally, I would simply confront him. Kill him and his minions. But I have you, and he knows it, so we run after a few hours of rest. Contact who you must and get the people you love out of harm's way. I'll figure things from there, understand?" His look brooked no dissent.

She nodded complacently as they entered her room. He placed her on the edge of the bed. "I mean it, Diana," he commanded and walked into the bathroom. "Stay here. Don't make me chase you down. There's no time."

"Are you sure about that?" she asked. "Running doesn't seem like the answer."

"We don't have a choice. I don't know who is with me and who's against me. I don't know how many he will bring. It's best to retreat until I have the upper hand."

"Oh, alright," she said with an eye roll.

He left the door slightly ajar.

She heard the shower running, so she grabbed her slippers and raced down the stairs. Technically, she disobeyed. But she had to warn the community. She jogged to the middle of the town, went into the bell tower, and climbed the stairs as fast as possible. She grabbed the bell rope and tugged with all her might.

An unfamiliar clang rang loud and clear through the night, then she exited the building. Vamps, witches, shifters, and humans surrounded her in a flash.

"Trouble?" inquired Carlton Spark, the local hardware store owner.

She quickly relayed the evening's events. "Killian Arroyos came into my store, injured—a werewolf hunted him. I managed to get rid of the wolf, but he will be back, and with him, Killian's twin, Royas."

"Why are they here?" Sarah McVie glanced at the rest of her gathered coven.

"It's complicated...." Diana started.

"You're his mate," Leonard Cavanaugh, the town council leader, declared. "I became aware of this information when Killian's parents were killed. Killian knew Royas would come for you, so he's come for you himself."

Diana glanced briefly to the ground. "Yes, and he's dragged this town into it. He's sure we need to retreat, or Royas will kill anyone in his path until he finds me."

"Nope." Leonard smiled. "We fight. You're one of us, girl. We fight for our family."

Her eyes grew misty. "I don't know how many he will bring."

"Then we best get prepared." Sarah hugged her and led her coven away.

Diana turned and looked at her second-floor apartment. Killian stood in the window with his arms across his massive chest. She connected with his feelings. He was ready to pounce, but he needn't bother. He didn't know who his friends were, but she did, and they looked at him too.

CHAPTER 4

Minutes later, Diana walked into her bedroom.

"I told you to stay put," Killian growled.

"I won't stay put because you command me. Besides, I had to alert everyone." Diana tried not to notice just how sexy he looked, lying there on her bed, fresh, clean, smelling of man, and she noted he was also naked and hard as a rock.

Before she embarrassed herself by jumping him, she turned away and began rifling through her dresser. She grabbed her flannel pajamas and warm wooly socks. She headed into the bathroom. "You better get used to me telling you no," she remarked. "I'm pretty independent."

With that, Diana slammed the door and locked it. She rested against the back of the door for a moment. The sight of him in such a state nearly took her breath away. It had been a long time since she'd seen a man in such good form. Although she tried her best to be nonchalant, her heart was beating a mile a minute, and she hoped he couldn't tell. Turning on the shower, she then divested herself of clothes.

She shrieked when a cool hand slid down her back. "What the hell?"

Killian silenced her with a scorching kiss. In a flash, he lifted into the shower. Warm water caressed her skin... *or was that Killian?*

"We may not have much time, but I can give you this." He kissed her neck as water cascaded over her hair and slushed around her shoulders. His fingers threaded through her long strands, and she sighed with pleasure.

"Hand me the shampoo," he whispered.

She did as he asked, feeling his fingers gently rub her scalp. Bubbles flowed down her body, and the comforting scent of lavender vanilla soon filled her shower.

"Rinse," he said, turning her around and fitting her to him as he leaned her head back, cradling it in his large palm.

She closed her eyes and gave in to the sensual indulgence.

His soapy hands warmed her breasts, and her breath hitched. He molded them to his hands and slid ever so gently across her body, down between her breasts, lingering along her stomach. She arched, wanting his touch on her most private parts.

He chuckled. "Not yet, sweet," he murmured in her ear. "Soon."

She shivered as he lathered her legs and toes, then returned to caress her bottom, kneading it so close to where she wanted his touch, and then she shifted around and kissed him feverishly.

Diana could feel his erection against her. She wiggled, standing on tiptoe, trying to entice him.

He smacked her bottom to still her movements, and she gasped. "Let me love you," he whispered as he crouched down. "Let me show you how beautiful you are to me." He moved his lips lower, and she practically fainted from the pure pleasure of his devilish tongue.

"I'm sorry I could not court you the way you deserve." He licked at her sensitive nub. "But you are mine, and I will do everything to keep you safe." He stood, once again taking her mouth.

She held onto him with fierce abandon and sighed when he finally released her go. "I know you only want to run because you found me," she told him as he dried her with soft towels and took extra time applying little nips and kisses of pleasure. "But we can trust this community. I've known them all my life."

"We would be putting our lives and theirs on the line." He picked her up and cradled her against his chest. "But that is for the evening to decide, and now is our time." He carried her to the bed, gently sat down, and crawled beside her.

Diana watched as Killian's eyes roamed her body, claiming her with his possessive stare. When his gaze landed between her thighs, she spread her legs and savored her arousal to his visual caress. If she had any doubt, it fled at that moment. Watching Killian's face turn from cool beauty to passionate lover was immensely arousing.

Killian grasped her arms and clasped both hands above her head. "Do not move them," he commanded. Her body suffused in erotic heat as his fingers glided between her breasts, down her stomach, and her saturated folds.

She moved her hips, needing more. "Please, Killian." She reached for him, but he reclaimed her hands and tortured her with pleasure.

She quieted, eager for his next sensual torment.

"You are mine," he uttered as he came on top of her.

His kiss was warm, yet his skin was cool to the touch. The sensations caused by fire and ice were more than she could handle. Her body tightened, ready to orgasm. He brought her back from the edge by twisting his fingers in her hair and tugging. She writhed with pleasurable pain.

"You will do as I say, come when I say," he demanded, looking deeply into her eyes.

When she nodded, he threaded his hands through her hair to bring her mouth to his once more. His cock probed, and she opened her legs wider, ready to receive him. "My mate, Diana. Tell me you believe."

"Yes, I believe. Please."

He shifted, every muscle in his body rippling with pent-up need. "You will never be free of me, Diana. You will always be mine."

Killian buried himself within her with one powerful thrust. The heat inside her body caught fire and triggered her release. She flexed her hips against his groin with a primal scream, grinding wildly against his rock-hard cock. Diana gasped as the ecstasy of her orgasm began building even higher. She urged him on, digging her heels into his ass and ignoring the bit of pain his faster movements caused.

Her tight channel closed around him as he lifted her hips to embed himself even deeper within her. Her back arched as a thousand jolts of electricity battered her body, centered on her core. Killian pumped faster, and Diana turned her head, baring the vulnerable curve of her neck. His fangs sunk into her flesh with an erotic pain that sent her over the edge once again.

She grasped his shoulders, and her nails bit into his flesh. The marks on his shoulder beckoned her, and she found herself with the overwhelming urge to taste him as he tasted her. She licked at his wounds, finding him sweet and intoxicating. She pulled away slowly, feeling his warm release flooding her womb as his blood ran down her throat.

They fell onto the pillows with a deep sigh of satisfaction.

Killian rolled, keeping his cock deep within her as she floated down from heaven. He held her lovingly, possessively, his hands comforting her as her breathing returned to normal. Still trembling in the aftermath of the most extraordinary experience of our life, she wished she could find the words to express her thoughts. He was her lover, her mate.

So much had happened in the past twenty-four hours, but one question remained. Diana hated to ask, to break up their sensual moment, but time was of the essence. "Do we fight or run, Killian?"

"If we run, we continue to run. If we fight, we may die." Killian kissed her head and pulled the covers up around her. "The thought of you in peril, Diana...." His voice choked with emotion.

"I know, love. This is new for me as well. But I've always been a fighter. And we are better, stronger, together, aren't we?"

He touched her cheek lovingly. "You are sure about your people? This is what they want as well?"

"Yes, love." She kissed his hand. "The danger is here. There's no way Royas will let them go unscathed. They didn't turn you over to him immediately. They know they have no recourse."

"Then we fight." Killian moved her to his side, tucking her within his embrace. "Sleep. It will be all right. I'll see to it."

As Diana drifted off, she realized he would do everything to keep her and those she cared about safe, even at the risk of dying himself. But what he failed to understand was that she would do the same.

CHAPTER 5

Diana came awake slowly with a gentle kiss from Killian on her brow.

"It's time, love," he whispered in her ear.

She stretched, feeling more energized, even stronger. She was truly blessed if this was what Killian's love did for her. She sat up, flinging off the covers. *But a bit of luck wouldn't hurt.* She darted into the bathroom to fish the silver bullet that came out of Killian from her pants pocket.

He quirked an arrogant eyebrow from the doorway.

"It's my lucky charm." She smiled as she stood in front of him. "It brought me my love, my mate."

Shaking his head, he kissed her hungrily. "You no longer doubt me. That's good. My blood is powerful and will help you if you are in danger." With that, he lifted his wrist, piercing his skin. The blood began to flow, and he held it up to Diana. "Drink."

She shook her head in the negative. *Drinking blood? Nope. Not ready for that.*

"Either drink, or I'll bind you to the damn bed," he said. "I'll not have you facing Royas without being fully armored. Now drink!"

Diana frowned but grabbed his wrist and licked the blood. It was warm. Odd, he was cool to touch, but his blood was warm. She licked again. It didn't have that metallic taste like hers, but rather like mulled wine. She suckled his wrist, the need for more overtaking her. She heard Killian groan in passion. Surprised, she released his arm and looked at him. He was fully aroused.

"Get dressed," he panted, pulling away to put some space between them. "I want you badly, but now is not the time. The others are gathering near the bell already."

She obediently donned her clothes and braided her hair with shaky hands. She was still aroused. Unfortunately, Killian was right. Now was not the time.

Gone was her passionate lover of this morning; Killian was all business now. She bounded down the stairs to the street and greeted the townspeople, who were armed with what they could find as the sun was beginning to set.

Killian addressed the crowd. "We know Royas will be here soon. He will bring an entire contingency with him. Leave now if you wish to avoid the confrontation."

An old crone approached the group. "My coven and I have set a hex for protection around the town's perimeter. It is as powerful as we could make it, so only the strongest and most determined should be able to breach the walls. This is our home, and we will not be defeated!"

Diana could feel the apprehension in Killian. "Thank you for standing here with us. I respect your right to defend your homes and families, but if I say retreat, you run. Find your safe spots as Leonard has designated. He knows what to do. Royas will not go down lightly."

"No, brother, I will not." A gravelly voice boomed across the town square. Before the assemblage could disburse, the skies filled with winged creatures, their battle cries mixing with the shrieks of surprise and pain as the rogue vampires and werewolves set upon the townspeople.

"Retreat!" Killian shouted. His large body seemed to grow before their eyes as he pushed Diana behind him. "Show yourself, coward!"

Diana covered her ears as the fearful noise of battle rang out. She wanted desperately to close her eyes but could not look away as her friends and neighbors faced the onslaught of evil or headed into the trees.

Killian nodded to her to follow the retreat as several vampires advanced on him. "Go!"

She ran through the streets toward the forest, only turning back once when Killian's war cry rent the air. Her beloved threw himself into the fray as if he alone could save them all. Her feet hit the pavement at a fast clip. Many of the townspeople were ahead of her.

Abruptly, she was seized from behind, but it was Killian. He grabbed her arm, pulling her along as they ran toward the meadow at the edge of town, away from the trees' safety.

"Stop! Where are we going?" Diana pulled away, digging in her heels.

He turned, and she cringed in horror. It wasn't her beloved Killian. No shock of gray at his temples. It was his brother, Royas. He increased his grip until Diana feared her arm would snap.

"Let me go, please," she whimpered.

Royas laughed. "Pathetic. He has a whiney human as his mate. That's why I will continue to be a leader. A new world order is due, and I will see it done."

"No, you will die on this day, brother." Killian stepped from a side street.

Royas pulled Diana against him. "Watch her die and know there's nothing you can do."

Diana shared one last look with Killian. She wanted to hear his vow of love, but he said, "I will always remember how we met, my fiery Diana."

Memories of their encounter flashed through her mind. The window, the fire, the taking of her blood, the silver bullet... She reached in her pocket as Royas' hot breath descended upon her neck. With lightning speed, she shoved her arm up, tossing the silver bullet into the vampire's open mouth.

Royas stumbled, releasing Diana to clutch his throat. "What have you done?" He croaked out as he fell to his knees.

Killian pulled Diana to his side. "My mate, a mere human, has killed you, brother. Your faction has been defeated. You should have spent more time on strategy than on strength. We didn't retreat; we simply surrounded you. In your haste to get to Diana, you allowed my people to regroup and defeat yours."

Royas clawed at his throat. Blood poured from the slashes he made. He screamed in agony, then fell silent. His body collapsed onto the cold earth and turned quickly to ash. The cold winter wind scattered his remains until nothing was left.

Killian lifted Diana to his chest for what seemed an eternity. When they finally separated, they headed back toward town hand in hand. "How did you know I was in trouble?" Diana asked.

"I sensed your fear, love. Our union heightens my senses," he murmured. "Yours will as well, given time."

The town square came into view, where folks tended the injured. "I wish that I hadn't brought the fight to your town. Perhaps one day, they will forgive me."

The cheers erupted as soon as they were spotted. The shifters, vampires, witches, and humans crowded around them, slapping Killian on the back, demanding to know how Royas was defeated. Diana took it all in stride, but Killian seemed somewhat embarrassed at the attention.

"You'll get used to it," she remarked as the folks began to disperse finally.

"To what?" Killian glanced at her as he healed an owl shifter's arm with a bit of his blood.

"Friends," she said.

Killian looked around at the remarkable people in this small community. "Yes, but only with you by my side."

Diana kissed his cheek. "I wouldn't have it any other way."

The End.

ABOUT THE AUTHOR

International bestselling author **Maggie Adams** lives in St. Louis, Missouri, with her husband, four kids, and four of the sweetest, smartest, and most talented grandchildren ever to grace God's green earth. She began writing at a young age, concentrating on creative writing of poetry, short stories, and comics. It wasn't until she read her first historical romance novel at the age of fourteen that she found the romance genre gave wings to her writing soul. She finds humor in everyday life, as her books often reflect, and believes in happy ever afters, no matter what the circumstances.

Her first novel, Whistlin' Dixie, debuted in the top 100 of several book lists and made the tiny town of Grafton, Illinois, a reader's romantic escape. There are five more books available in the series: Leather and Lace, Something's Gotta Give, Love, Marriage & Mayhem, Forged in Fire, and Cold as Ice. She also released a companion cookbook featuring the recipes from the series as well as tried and true comfort food from generations past entitled, The Coalson Cookbook of Memories.

In addition to the Tempered Steel series, she is the author of the spinoff paranormal romance series, Legends. The first novel, Legends: Catori, garnered her recognition in the USA Today's Happily Ever After section of Lifestyles. Legends: Kermode, followed in 2019 and Legends: Piasa is coming in 2021 along with the final book, Legends: Amarok, is coming 2022.

In 2019, Maggie also began releasing her over-forty series, Hell on Heels. The first two books in the series, Minx and Jinxed are widely available. Look for Sphynx, the next book in the series, to be released in the fall of 2022.

She has collaborated on several charitable anthologies and has enriched older stories into stand-alone novels, including her women's erotica bundle, Lustful Legacy.

You can sign up for her FREE newsletter to keep in touch, find events and signings for the year and get exclusive sneak peeks into works in progress!

She's also been known to gift books randomly. Website Go to www.MaggieAdamsBooks.com

ALSO BY MAGGIE ADAMS

www.MaggieAdamsBooks.com

Lustful Legacy -

Hell on Heels - Jinxed

Legends Series - Catori

Piasa -

Getting Lucky

Whistlin' Dixie -

Leather and Lace -

Something's Gotta Give -

Love, Marriage & Mayhem -

Forged in Fire -

Cold as Ice -

A TWIST OF MAGICAL FATE

USA TODAY BESTSELLING AUTHOR

BRENDA TRIM

BLURB

Evil witches, murder plots, and sexy shifters. Just another day in my life.

I wasn't meant to be part of the magical world. I was born a mundie and stolen from my parents by an evil witch. They say the first three years of your life establish the pathways in your brain. I wonder what mine looks like having endured countless painful experiments that finally turned me into a dragon shifter.

Layla saved me from becoming a homicidal maniac, much to Myrna's dismay. I'm tired of being this evil witch's pawn, and when she plots to maime one of the nicest women I know and kill everyone in her support system, I have to do something.

Risking life and limb, I get a warning to Hattie, but will it be too late to keep Myrna from ruining Hattie's life, leaving her barren and childless?

Chapter 1

"What the hell went wrong this time? I followed everything down to the letter. I'm close to figuring this out. I know it. Get me another witch for my table, now, Tsekani!" Spittle flew from Myrna's mouth, making my gut clench along with my fists.

Anger washed over me, followed quickly by hatred and shame. I was twice Myrna's size and shifted into the biggest dragon you'd ever seen. You'd think a strong guy like me would be able to tell this small woman no and walk away. My vision turned red when I couldn't stop my head from dipping in acknowledgment.

This vile witch's lab was all I'd ever known. I have no idea if she gave birth to me. I looked nothing like her. My skin was olive toned whereas hers was pale as cream. My hair was black as night, and she had hair the color of wheat. The biggest difference between us was our eyes. Mine was dark brown and slanted, while hers were blue and round.

My sister Layla grabbed my hand. We'd grown up within this macabre place, and neither of us could stand it. Looking at Layla, I reconsidered the doubts that had been plaguing me about my parentage.

Perhaps Myrna had given birth to us both. Layla shared my black hair. She also had brown eyes, although hers were a lighter shade than mine. Layla's facial features resembled Myrna's more than mine. Maybe we had different fathers. Mine had to be Asian like me.

I had always dreamed that I was someone else's child. No way could I be the product of a tyrant like Myrna. She used to keep Layla and me locked inside our rooms in the basement. We spent most of our time talking to each other through the space at the bottom of the panel.

We got to see each other when Myrna took us out so she could inflict some treatment or another on us. I craved contact and love and eventually managed to pick the lock on my door and Layla's with a talon when I partially shifted. Layla gave me the contact I needed along with my name, and I did the same for her.

Life really became hellish when Myrna started forcing Layla and me to gather subjects for her to torture. Until that point, all of Myrna's twisted thrills were taken out on us. It was a relief not to watch my sister endure some horrendous procedure. I wished we could go back to being Myrna's focus. It was much harder being the one to bring an innocent into this nightmare.

My anger burned like lava through my veins when I thought about my childhood and what Myrna had done to us. Our rage was pointless because Myrna used her magic to ensure Layla and I did what she asked.

Refocusing on the matter at hand, I couldn't help my hesitation to jump and do Myrna's bidding. She was asking us to get her another victim. "Please don't ask us to do this again."

Myrna got in my face and grabbed my chin, her fingernails digging into my skin. It was her not so subtle reminder that she could make me obey her. "Do I need to remind you who has the power here? I made you what you are, and I will destroy you if you question me again."

Layla held up her hands. "He understands, don't you, Tseki? We're going now."

Myrna pushed my head, then let go of me. "Remember, she has to be in her child-bearing years. The last one was too close to menopause to be of any use." The awful witch grabbed a potion and shoved it in my hand.

Bile in my throat, I held myself rigid as I turned and stalked out of the lab. Myrna kept her work space hidden in the basement. The space was dark and smelled of chemicals mixed with too many herbs. There was also an electric energy hovering in the air that felt like needles stabbing me all over. The feel of that had changed over the years becoming sharper by the day.

I stopped in my bedroom and grabbed my jacket before joining Layla in the hall. Her room was across from mine. Myrna had the space beneath her home divided into three sections. Our rooms took up less than a quarter and were separated from her house of horrors by thin walls. I think she purposefully made sure we could hear the cries of the babies and screams of the others. It was one of her favorite methods of reminding us she could do the same to us if the urge struck her.

"I don't think I can do this again," Layla whispered as we moved from the basement's cement floor to the wood of the steps.

"I'll do it. You can go get dinner." I would do anything to save Layla more trauma.

My hands shook as I hurried across the kitchen tile and out the back door. We weren't allowed into the main part of Myrna's home. I'd made the mistake of exploring the kitchen when I was little. I lifted my hand, my heart racing at the sight of the scars on my palm.

Layla grabbed my hand, twining her fingers with mine. "I'm not letting you do this alone. We stick together, remember."

I smiled as we walked down the quiet street and headed downtown. "What do you think she's doing this time?"

Layla tugged her hand out of mine to wrap her arms around her torso. "At least it's not a kid this time."

I shuddered, recalling the one-time Myrna had forced us to find a child for her. Layla and I refused to kidnap the little girl, which made Myrna go into a blind rage. The beating was so bad I was convinced that we wouldn't live through it. It was our shifter sides that saved us then. By that point, our animals were fully integrated with our bodies, so we didn't have scars.

"One day, we will be free of her," I promised Layla.

Layla scoffed. "She will never let us go." Layla was right. Myrna made us what we were, which is why she was able to control us. "And even if we do find a way to escape, we won't be able to hurt her."

"Mark my words. Myrna will get what's coming to her one day," I promised.

Layla shrugged one shoulder. "I hope you're right. I'd settle for finding out who she took us from. Don't you ever wonder whether our moms miss us?"

My head jerked in Layla's direction. "What do you mean? I've always thought she was our mom. In fact, I was thinking about that before we left."

Layla shivered as she moved closer to me. "I used to think so, too, but I found her looking through a notebook in the lab a few months ago, and I read a passage over her shoulder. I'm happy to report she is not biologically related to us. She took us for one of her sick experiments."

Despite the awful scenario we were facing, a smile spread across my face. "That's the best news I've ever heard. And it makes sense why she called us by numbers until we named each other. You lifted a weight from my shoulders."

I stopped and pulled her into a hug. "So, you want to get a coffee?" I'd offer her dinner, but we had very little money. I hadn't been able to sneak away and earn any in a while, so I was running low.

Typically, on cases like this we would stall as long as we could. Of course, in the end, we would have to head to the witch headquarters, where we would find Myrna's next victim. How that group of witches didn't see Myrna for who she really was baffled me. She was a member of the coven where several people had gone missing, yet they didn't suspect a thing. That bitch had them all fooled.

Layla shook her head. "I'd rather get this over with. My stomach isn't up for diner coffee right now."

Bright lights blinded us as a car pulled over to the side of the street. My heart stopped when the driver leaned over and rolled down the passenger window. "Change of plans. Get in."

Layla and I shared a look before we got in the back. Trying to gauge Myrna's mood, I leaned forward. "Are we skipping the procurement?"

Myrna narrowed her eyes. "No, you idiot. I can't perfect my potion without someone to test it on. There's no need for you to sneak around outside headquarters. Catherine told me Margo has a few friends coming in from the west coast. Taking one of them won't raise as much suspicion."

I wanted to scream at Myrna's callousness. Warning Margo and her friends would be a more fruitful option, but I couldn't talk about what Myrna had done to anyone. I'd tried more times than I could count. Every time Hattie, the coven's High Priestess, came to visit, I tried to tell her everything to no avail.

Layla smoothed the A-Line skirt she was wearing as Myrna told us that she would enthrall the victim and send her out of the soda fountain downtown, where the witches were celebrating their reunion. Little did they know how this little gathering would end. My fists clenched as I fought the desire to punch Myrna.

Pain blasted through my head as my anger took over. Nausea quickly followed while I stopped imagining my dragon biting Myrna's head off. Her magic was strong and so deeply ingrained in me that I couldn't see a way out no matter what I had promised Layla.

"Did you hear me?"

I shook my head, preparing to have Myrna lash out at me. Layla pushed my shoulder. "Of course, Tsekani heard you tell him to drive her home and return for you. He's a lot of things but deaf isn't one of them."

Myrna lifted her chin, narrowing her eyes. "I'll have her subdued, so she won't put up a fight. Keep her in the lab until we return, Layla."

Before either of us could respond, Myrna was out of the car. I grabbed Layla's hand before she got out of the vehicle. "Thank you for saving me just now."

"We stick together. Besides, I could guess that you were picturing some truly inventive torture for she, who we cannot name. No one deserves to be punished for hating on her," Layla replied, then hopped out of the vehicle.

"I wish I could say it was creative. My dragon wants to bite her head off." I was so connected to that side of me that I found it difficult to believe I wasn't born with him. Myrna had magically fused us together just like she had done with Layla and her wolf.

Layle shrugged one shoulder. "There's something to be said for simplicity."

My chuckle died on my lips when a short brunet woman wearing a white top tucked into her brown plaid A-Line skirt walked around the corner of the building. Her grey eyes were glazed, and her movements were jerky.

I choked on the bile that burned the back of my throat and fought my helplessness. My dragon roared in my head while I clenched my fists. Layla had hunched over next to me and was fighting just as hard.

By the time the victim was at the car, I'd given up trying to overcome Myrna's directive and opened the back door, gently nudging her into the seat. Layla slid in next to her while I got behind the wheel and peeled out of the parking lot.

Myrna might get pissed that I caused a ruckus, but I was too pissed at the moment to care. I hated myself for doing this to an innocent woman. I had no ability to disobey Myrna, and there was no way out of the situation, either. I'd tried running away, committing suicide and asking Hattie for help.

It didn't take long before I turned into the driveway and parked. Layla and I lead the young woman through the back door. After ensuring Layla and the witch reached the lab safely, I returned to the soda fountain.

My blood chilled when I noticed the mundane police cars parked in front of the establishment. Pulling over, I got out and approached the scene. Part of my mind wondered if I could talk to a mundie about our situation. The warning pulse of pain, told me not to bother.

Myrna was hugging Margo when I reached them. "I can't believe she would just run off like that. I only met her for a brief minute, but she seemed like a good girl. Let me know if I can help in any way."

Margo sniffed and rubbed her eyes. She was beside herself, as were three other girls standing behind her. "Thank you. I'm going to ask the coven to scry for Sarah's location as soon as the police are done."

You would never know Myrna was upset by that idea. She smiled sadly and nodded at Margo. "I'll be there to help."

Margo wiped her cheeks with her hands. "Be ready later tonight. I don't want to wait."

Myrna promised she would be there before she turned and walked past me without a word. I was tempted not to catch up. She hadn't ordered me to, so I could stay there. I didn't move for several seconds. Layla's trembling figure got me running to catch up. I was barely in the backseat before Myrna pulled away from the curb.

"She's perfect. At the perfect age and easily controlled," Myrna told me as if I cared. I tuned her out and laid my head back against the seat.

Myrna jumped out of the vehicle with a spring in her step. I, on the other hand, drug my feet. By the time I reached the basement, Myrna had Sarah on the table without her skirt on and was poised above her with a knife. "It's time to see what that potion did to your eggs."

I crossed to Layla who was scowling at Myrna. Given the lines around Layla's mouth and eyes, she was the one thinking up creative torments. My shoulder nudged hers. I forgot what I was going to say to Layla when Sarah groaned.

Myrna sliced into her abdomen and used magic to open the wound. Using a pair of long tweezers, she poked and prodded Sarah's organs. The woman cried out as her head started thrashing from side to side.

Myrna walked to the potion she'd created earlier. "Drinking didn't do the trick. Let's try pouring it directly on the ovaries. One way or another I will find a way to magically render Hattie sterile, then I can convince her to make me the heir to her Pleiades magic."

Sarah's cries increased as Myrna poured the liquid into her abdomen. Myrna watched for several seconds then grabbed individual herbs and tossed them inside Sarah's open abdomen. I couldn't stand what she was doing to Sarah but refused to think too much about it for fear of being debilitated by pain. I needed to keep my wits about me when Myrna got like this.

Sarah passed out as Myrna continued poking and prodding. An hour later, Myrna finally stopped. She must not have liked what she'd seen because she lifted the instrument in her hand and threw it across the room. "What do I have to do to create a potion that will render someone barren? It shouldn't be this hard!"

Myrna took off her gloves then turned to face us. "Get rid of her. She's of no use to me anymore."

Layla was trembling as Myrna stalked out of the room. I crossed to the table, praying Sarah was still alive. "She's alive. We need to get Sarah to the hospital. She's going to live. C'mon."

Layla shot into gear, grabbing the gauze and pressing it over the open wound. Together we wrapped Sarah's stomach wound then I picked her up. Layla grabbed Sarah's skirt and the car keys as I headed up the stairs.

I laid Sarah across the backseat then got behind the wheel. Layla put the woman's head in her lap as I took off. The hospital was across town. Thankfully traffic was light, and we made it in record time.

Layla pointed to a darkened side of the hospital parking lot. "Park there. We will be less likely to be seen. It's also close enough that we can leave her right outside the door."

I shoved my emotions deeper and climbed out. Layla was already outside holding Sarah. We snuck along the hospital side, pausing when we reached the corner. I poked my head around and held up my hand as a couple left the emergency department. I waved her forward when the coast was clear.

We hurried over, and Layla carefully laid Sarah right in front of the doors, making them automatically open. I had to pick Layla up and carry her away when she didn't make a move to leave.

I didn't stop until I had her in the car. Needing to see if Sarah had been found, I started the car and slowly drove around the building so we could see the front. The breath I had been holding whooshed out.

"They have her. They'll save her," I said.

Layla sat in the passenger seat sobbing. "She's a fucking monster. I want to go to Hattie and warn her. We can't let Myrna take this from her."

I threw up my hands. "How do we do that? We can't say one bad word about Myrna. It's not even a matter of living through the pain to get it out. She has spelled us, so we can't even speak a word."

Layla sobbed as I pulled out of the parking lot and headed home. "We have to at least try. She kills a piece of me every time she makes us do this shit. I can't take it."

I rubbed the ache in my chest. I knew what she meant. "We will do whatever it takes to try and tell her."

I knew what Layla meant when she said it was killing pieces of her. Somehow the two of us had maintained a semblance of empathy in everything we had endured, and I'd be damned if I allowed this bitch to take one more thing from me.

CHAPTER 2

My fists were clenched at my side as we walked up the stairs leading to Nimaha, Hattie's house. Layla and I returned home last night to find Myrna in the middle of one of her episodes.

Myrna was always crazy, but there were times that she didn't sleep for days on end while she concocted some experiment or another. Typically, it would lead up to her hunting for the right victim and ending like it had with Sarah. This time it worked in reverse.

After having us dispose of Sarah, she returned to the basement and resumed working on the potions to make Hattie sterile. Layla and I watched helplessly as Myrna made one mixture after another before proclaiming she'd gotten it right. Her assertions when she was in this state were her most dangerous.

I'd watched people die at her hands every time she came up with a plan, potion, or tonic during her episodes. Thankfully, these only happened a few times a year. Or conversely, unfortunately; they happened a handful of times each year.

My stomach was in knots as we waited for Hattie to let us into her house. The Pleiades witch was one of the nicest women I'd ever met and didn't deserve what Myrna was going to do to her. Chances were, the potion in Myrna's purse would kill Hattie rather than render her unable to have children.

I didn't know much about the nature of Hattie's magic, but I knew enough to know shit would get much worse if she died. The young woman opened the door with a smile. "Myrna, so good to see you. I'm glad you called. Your idea about doing something for that poor friend of Margo's is brilliant."

Myrna embraced Hattie, then passed her and entered the house. "It's such a tragedy. We need to find out who is preying on witches in Camden."

I choked on my saliva as my desire to wrap my hands around Myrna's neck took over too quickly for me to banish it. Hattie hurried forward and patted my back. "Are you alright, Tseki?"

Nodding, I allowed her to budge me inside. Once over the threshold, my body relaxed. I always felt at home when we visited Hattie. I wasn't sure if it was the witch herself, her familiar, or the pixies living on her land, and I didn't care.

"I'm alright. Thank you, milady." I bowed to her because to me she was royalty.

Hattie placed a hand on my shoulder, her blonde hair falling over one shoulder as she lowered her head to mine. "I've told you to call me Hattie."

I straightened and cringed when I noticed Myrna's glower. Ignoring her, I smiled at Hattie. "Habits are hard to break."

Hattie chuckled and wound one of her arms through mine. "You've done a great job raising Tseki and Layla when they were orphaned. It's not easy raising shifters when you're not one."

Myrna waved her hand in dismissal. "I admit it hasn't been easy, but Layla and Tsekani are my pride and joy. The two things I have succeeded at and have never been able to reproduce."

Hattie let go of me as her forehead furrowed. "Have you found other abandoned shifters? We will need to get the pack leader involved next time. He was pretty upset when he discovered you'd kept Layla without telling him."

"I was referring to having no children of my own, yet," Myrna replied.

"*You and Hattie both have plenty of time to find a partner and have children. I tell her all the time not to rush these types of things.*" Tarja's voice in my head always startled me when we came over. I'd tried communicating with her several times with the same results, so I'd given up a long time ago.

"I know I have time. I just want to fill these walls," Hattie replied. "The house is too quiet after my parents' deaths."

I wasn't sure what happened to them but I'd wondered if Myrna had been behind that, too. I couldn't say for sure because I was too young, but it seemed like something she would do.

Myrna wrapped an arm around Hattie's shoulders. "I know what you mean. It's why I adopted Layla and Tsekani. And why I come over so often."

"It's nice having the company," Hattie admitted as she waved at Mythia, a pixie that helped her around the house. "Thank you, Thia. I'm famished. Please help yourself, everyone."

My mouth watered as Hattie waved a hand over the food spread across the island in her kitchen. There were skewers of meat, fruit, cheeses, and crackers. Myrna had never cooked a meal for me in my life. There was a point she would give us raw meat. That changed with time; now, she bought us packaged foods more often than not.

Layla and I remained by the archway we'd just walked through. Myrna wouldn't like us eating until Hattie insisted. Myrna filled a plate then set it on the counter. "Would you happen to have any iced tea?" She asked Hattie.

Hattie bounced on her feet. She was older than Myrna, but still a young woman and beautiful inside and out. "Mythia just made some fresh peach tea. It's delicious. You have to try some."

Myrna took the potion out of her purse when Hattie turned her back to get the pitcher out of the fridge. "That sounds delicious. I love ripe peaches in the summer."

Myrna slipped the vial into Layla's hand then glowered at her. Layla inclined her head and closed her fingers around the vial. My heart dropped to my feet. I hadn't been aware she was forcing Layla to add the potion to Hattie's drink.

Now I knew why she had brought us along. Myrna was all about not raising suspicion, which was why she remained at the soda fountain while having us take Sarah to the house.

"Aside from watermelon, peaches are one of my favorites." Hattie set the tea down before getting several glasses out of a cupboard.

Hattie poured two glasses then turned to face us. "Would either of you care for some tea? And, come join us. There is no need for you to remain over there."

"I would love some," Layla said as she joined them.

I walked over, as well, and took a place next to Hattie. "No, thank you."

Hattie handed Myrna a glass then gave one to Layla and took a sip of her own. The second she set the glass down, Myrna pointed to a plant in the backyard asking if it was lavender. Hattie loved her plants and was engaged in the conversation with Myrna over the thing. Layla's hands were shaking as she added the potion to the tea.

I wanted to grab her into a hug and reassure her that she had no choice but couldn't because Hattie was turning back to the island. My mind raced with a way to keep Hattie from taking a drink. Myrna and Hattie discussed how they could help Sarah and find the person behind her abduction and attack while they ate.

I half listened as various options raced through my head. My heart stopped in my chest when Hattie picked up her glass. I acted without thinking and knocked into her arm making her drop her glass. It hit the tiled edge of the island and dropped to the wood floor where it shattered.

I gasped, my hand flying to my mouth. Myrna would make me pay for this one, and I didn't regret taking action. I'd saved Hattie from a horrid fate if she even survived the tonic Myrna had created.

The one thing about Myrna in her manic episodes was she worked in a flurry and never stopped long enough to take notes. During one of those times, she perfected her desire to create a shifter, proving she was more powerful than mother nature. And it was why she hadn't been able to do it again. She couldn't recall exactly what she did.

"I'm so sorry, milady. I should have paid closer attention to how I was moving." I let her see exactly how sorry I was.

The look in Hattie's eyes went beyond grateful and didn't fit the situation. Did she know? I opened my mouth to ask her then groaned when my skull felt like it would split open.

Myrna grabbed my arm. "Are you getting one of your headaches, Tsekani? We'll have to get you home."

Standing upright, I shook my head. "I'll be alright."

Myrna's hand tightened on my bicep. "No, it's best if we get you to bed. Thank you for having us, Hattie. We will talk again soon."

Myrna didn't wait for a reply as she hauled me out of the house with Layla behind her. She practically shoved me in the backseat. She jumped when Hattie put a hand on her arm. "Is everything alright? You don't have to leave. Tseki can lay down upstairs."

Myrna took a deep breath as she closed the car door in my face. "That won't be necessary. His medication is at home." She hugged Hattie, trying to throw off any suspicion. "If he starts throwing up, it gets ugly. Let's talk tomorrow."

Hattie nodded and watched as Myrna and Layla got inside the car. I was surprised when Myrna drove slowly down the driveway. She sped up when she got to the main road.

Her silence meant I was in deep shit. My heart raced and my stomach dropped to my feet. My dragon roared in my head urging me to shift and take off. I'd try when she parked the vehicle. It would be my only chance. If I played my cards right, I could grab Layla and take her with me.

I opened my door the second the vehicle stopped. The shift started to come over me then stopped when Myrna barked an order for me to shut it down. She held a finger in my face. "That just got you a hundred more. Try me again and you won't survive the night."

"No, he won't survive two hundred lashes, Myrna. You don't want to hurt him like that. You need us," Layla said as she tried to reason with the psychopath."

Unable to do anything else, I marched inside the house and went right to her work room. Once there, I took off my top and sat in the chair backward. Looking over my shoulder, I watched as Myrna entered with her leather bullwhip in her hand. "At least now you're making things easier on yourself. You will not interfere with my next attempt on Hattie. Neither of you will."

There was power behind her words that I felt locked something in my mind. I ground my teeth against the order knowing there was nothing I could do now to stop her from acting.

My jaw clenched as she struck my back using a whip. Once she got the rhythm going, the implement would continue until all the lashes were delivered.

Myrna got in my face as I jerked and cried out from the blows. "Two hundred should teach you not to interfere with my plans. Clean this place up when it's done, Layla."

With that, the vile woman left the room. Layla rushed to me and went to her knees. She grabbed my hands as tears flowed down her cheeks. I couldn't respond to her and tell her I'd be alright. Thanks to Myrna, I was part dragon and had a sturdy composition.

Layla's image swam as my vision wavered. All I knew was red hot pain. It seemed to take forever before the whip stopped.

Honestly, I wouldn't have known it was done if Layla hadn't picked me up from the chair and carried me to my bed.

I was thankful that we had stopped Myrna from poisoning Hattie. She couldn't recreate what she'd done, so I called it a win. I knew Myrna would try again and come up with another potion. I'd find a way to stop her that time, too.

Layla chewed on her lower lip while laying me down, then crouched by my bed. "Your back looks like raw hamburger. I'm afraid to touch it and cause you more pain but if I don't clean it'll scar for sure."

"I'll survive you cleaning my back. But scars are sexy, Layla. I'll find Mr. Right someday, and he will love me regardless."

Layla was wrecked as she worked on my back. "We need to get you out to the mountain so you can shift. It'll help you heal faster."

I tried to tell my legs to swing over the side of the bed but they didn't move. The little energy I had left escaped as the adrenalin drained from my system, and my eyes slipped closed. The sting of the cleaner nearly made them fly back open. The trauma of the beating made me pass out as my dragon roared to be let out.

CHAPTER 3

Sweat poured down my back, making the pain worse. Layla had cleaned the flesh then woke me to get me out of the house so I could shift. I tried to tell her no, but I couldn't afford the time it would take me to heal in my human form.

Apparently, Layla had overheard Myrna talking with someone about physically attacking Hattie. It was the only thing that could have gotten me out of that bed so soon after being whipped two hundred times.

"I can shift here," I told Layla as I was forced to pause for the second time in as many minutes.

We weren't nearly far enough into the forest, but it would have to do. It was close to dinner time, and if what Layla had overheard was right, Hattie would be set upon after she finished dinner at a local seafood restaurant.

Layla shook her head as she scanned the area. "I can still see the houses from here. The last thing we need is for a mundie to see a giant green dragon."

"She's right." A deep sultry voice agreed.

The pain was momentarily forgotten as I whipped around to see the sexiest guy alive leaning against a tree trunk a few feet behind us. Layla jumped in front of me with a snarl.

The guy held up his hands. "I mean you no harm, and I'm not trying to encroach on your territory. I'm merely passing through and caught the scent of blood. I'm Murtaugh, by the way."

Layla narrowed her eyes. "Why would you follow blood? Are you a rogue suffering from moon sickness?"

I tried to shove her aside. Something about Murtaugh drew me to him. "I'm Tsekani, and this is Layla."

Layla glared at me. As I was about to tell her he was safe, a hand landed on my shoulder, sending warmth through me that eased some of the pain. "I understand her wariness. I was merely worried a shifter was injured and in danger of being discovered. I don't suffer from moon sickness, and I'm not a rogue. My pack is in North Carolina."

So, he was a wolf shifter like Layla. My nose wasn't working well under my current condition, but I thought I sensed a canine in his scent.

Layla straightened. "Thank you for your concern. We're fine." She made a move to continue, and I grabbed her hand.

"I can't continue, L." I tried to convey my weakness without having to say anything aloud. I didn't want to admit such a thing to this sexy guy. My legs were about to give out.

Murtaugh spread his arms out. "Perhaps I can be of assistance. I'd be happy to carry you. There's a clearing just beyond those trees that should work."

Layla's eyes narrowed even further. "We've got this. I can help him."

Murtaugh chuckled, the sound rumbling through me. "Alright, I admit, my offer is an excuse to carry a good-looking guy and be his hero."

Layla rolled her eyes as a smile spread across her mouth. My mind played out a mini battle for and against having Murtaugh carry me. Before I said anything, Layla extended her hand in my direction. "Tseki deserves a knight on a white horse. Be careful with him and move quickly. We have a mission that requires our attention."

I shivered as Murtaugh pressed his chest to my side and lifted me with one arm under my knees and the other across the lowest part of my back where I was injured the least. "Wrap your arm around my neck. I'd ask what happened to you, but I have a feeling it'd be a long story, and you have a mission to complete."

It felt good to put my arms around his neck. I wanted to tell him what had happened but knew I couldn't. "I paid the price for helping a friend. She's still in trouble which is why I need to shift and heal quickly."

Murtaugh moved swiftly through the trees. "These wounds are hardly going to heal with one shift. You'd need to spend a few hours in your dragon form for them to go away."

I sighed, wishing I was having a different conversation with Mr. Sexy. "I just need to heal enough to stay upright and awake long enough to help my friend."

"She must be some friend to make you go to such lengths for her," Murtaugh replied.

Layla pointed to the ground. "This is good enough. We aren't visible from the street. Thank you for your help."

Murtaugh jolted but recovered quickly, setting me carefully on my feet. "I'll stay close in case you need me again."

"Can you keep an eye out and make sure no one gets close?" I stumbled a few steps away from him not waiting for his response. I needed to shift before I threw up again. I'd already shown him enough weakness. I didn't want to completely turn him off.

I was aware of the eyes on me as I dropped my pants and took off my shoes and socks. I buried my toes in the ground as I called up my dragon. The shift took much longer than normal and hurt like a bitch. Aside from being a nice distraction, Murtaugh's presence made me bite back the scream that wanted out.

I was panting from pain when my dragon finally took over. The urge to curl up in the wild flowers was strong. Hattie could be under attack at that very moment, so I clenched my jaw and forced my body to return to its human state.

Layla rushed to my side with a bottle of water and my shirt. Murtaugh stayed at the periphery of the clearing with his eyes focused on me. I approached him after getting dressed. "Thank you for your help. I'd appreciate your discretion about what you saw."

Murtaugh laid a hand on my shoulder. "I won't tell a soul. I have to say, you looked like you were close to death a second ago. I've never seen a shifter recover from such severe injuries so quickly from one shift. Anyway, I'll leave you two to the task that brought you out tonight."

With that, the sexy shifter loped away. I wanted to go after him. I almost did until Layla placed a hand on my shoulder. "We need to find Hattie."

Shoving Murtaugh to the back of my mind, I followed Layla back through the woods and toward downtown. The walk seemed to take forever and was agonizing. The skin of my back had begun healing but there was so much flesh missing that it was still a raw mess.

My fatigue slowed us, which I would never forget because we'd arrived too late. By the time we reached the restaurant, Hattie's attacker had a knife buried in her abdomen. Layla and I took off running from down the street and were shouting for him to stop.

I couldn't get a clear image of him as he stabbed the knife into her abdomen repeatedly. There had to be a spell at work on Hattie's attacker. As for Hattie, her magic crackled across her hands as she flung spells at the man brutally stabbing her. When she managed to shoot a lightning bolt into her attacker's torso, he yanked the blade free with a shout and took off running.

There was a split second when I caught sight of brown eyes on a pinched face. It was too brief for me to be able to identify who it had been. Layla and I didn't bother following the culprit as we skidded to our knees next to Hattie. Layla pressed a hand over her lower stomach. "Who should we call, Hattie?"

Hattie groaned as her eyes rolled back in her head. I looked at Layla and balled my hands into fists. We should have come straight here. We might have been able to stop this from happening if we'd been here sooner.

"The waitress called for an ambulance," a mundie man said as he rushed out of the restaurant. "Did you see the guy that did this? It was too dark for me to make anything out."

I shook my head as I focused on Hattie. "I couldn't see him, either." My mind raced as I tried to figure out a way to keep her from being taken to the hospital, but I came up empty.

The sound of a siren echoed in the distance, telling me all I could do now was pray they wouldn't be able to detect she was a witch. I picked up her hand and cradled it in mine. We had to find a way to get out from under Myrna's thumb. My soul was crying out in my chest.

"We will make sure you are alright, Hattie. I'm so sorry we failed you." Emotion burned my throat while helplessness made me want to rail at the unfairness of it all.

"*She was ambushed and taken by surprise but she saw you running toward her and knows you tried to help her.*" Tarja had never spoken to me outside of when we visited them at Nimaha.

"*Is she okay to go to the hospital?*" I whispered the words, unsure if the familiar could hear me or not.

"*That's the best place for her to get emergency help. She's been seriously injured and is losing too much blood. I fear what will happen if she isn't treated immediately. Please have Myrna contact Esme to come and see her at the hospital. I cannot contact her unless Hattie is in her presence.*" So, it was my contact with Hattie that allowed her to talk to me.

My stomach lurched at the mention of Myrna. I didn't reply because an ambulance pulled up at that second, and two men rushed to Hattie's side. "We've got her," one of them assured Layla as they began caring for Hattie.

We watched as they put Hattie on a stretcher and loaded her into the back of the ambulance. The guy who had spoken to Layla paused before getting in next to Hattie. "We're taking her to the hospital. You can meet her there. She will likely want to see friendly faces when she wakes up."

I grabbed Layla and started following the ambulance as it pulled away. "We have to make sure Myrna can't hurt her anymore."

Layla lifted a handwritten note. "I wrote this after I heard what Myrna was planning. I blacked out twice, but I managed to jot down the basics."

My eyes widened as I stared at the paper.

Layla had written down *Myrna's attack and stolen families bound help*. It would be enough to inform Hattie about their condition.

"What are you two doing down here?" I practically jumped out of my skin when Myrna barked at us.

Layla snatched the note and stuffed it into her pocket. "Tseki had to shift so he would be of use to you. We were on our way back when we saw a man attack Hattie. We were heading home to tell you."

Myrna narrowed her eyes at us. "The house is in the opposite direction. Get in the car."

I hated that I had no choice but to do as she asked. She was smiling from ear to ear. "Was she seriously injured?" The question should've been in a grim tone, not a gleeful one.

I swallowed bile as my back bitched at me for the pressure of the car seat. "According to Tarja, it was bad."

Myrna's eyes widened as she jerked the wheel over the middle line of the road. "What? She was there?"

Layla narrowed her eyes at me. I shook my head. "No, she wasn't. I have no idea how she managed to tell me she was seriously hurt, but she asked that you have Esme come and heal her."

Myrna scowled. "I'm not calling Esme until I know the spelled athame took her ability to have kids."

I had no words for how awful Myrna was. I didn't want her attention to stray to us more than it already had. Layla had a note for Hattie; if we played our cards right, she could slip it to her soon.

Myrna's smile vanished as we rushed through the doors of the hospital. She was panting when we reached the nurse's station. "My friend was attacked and brought in an ambulance. I need to see her."

The woman at the desk lifted her hands. "You must be Hattie Silva's friends. She is in surgery right now. Have a seat in the waiting room, and I will take you to her room when she is done."

"Thank you so much." Myrna's voice cracked, and she sniffled before heading to the chairs the nurse pointed out.

Myrna paced the waiting room for what seemed like hours. With the mundies milling about the hospital, she couldn't talk freely, which was a blessing. I was certain she would discover Layla's note.

I jumped to my feet when I saw the nurse finally approach us. "She made it through surgery and is in her room. I can take you to her now."

Myrna gasped and threw her hands over her mouth. "Thank goodness. Can you tell me what happened to her?"

The nurse shook her head as we followed behind. "That is confidential information. The doctor will be in to speak with Hattie shortly. Then your friend can tell you what she wants you to hear."

Myrna rushed to Hattie's side the second we entered the room, playing the concerned friend perfectly. There were even tears in her eyes. "Oh, Hattie. I'm here."

Hattie's eyes fluttered open. "Myrna?"

"Yes. I'm here. How are you feeling?"

Hattie's gaze shifted to us. "You came to help. You saved me."

Myrna flashed a scowl in our direction before focusing on Hattie. "Tsekani needed to shift, and they saw you on their way home. They couldn't see who attacked you. Did you get a look at them?"

Hattie shook her head. "He had a spell...hiding his identity." Hattie's face was pale, and her breathing was uneven. It was obvious she was in pain.

A knock at the door made us look back. A tall man wearing a white lab coat walked into the room. "Ms. Silva, I'm Dr. McNabb. I performed your surgery. How are you feeling?"

Hattie grimaced. "Like my insides were carved out with a blunt knife."

Dr. McNabb frowned as he approached the bedside. "That's a fairly accurate description. I'd like a few minutes alone with Ms. Silva, if you three would excuse us."

Myrna squeezed Hattie's hand. "We will be right outside."

Layla and I walked into the hall before Myrna since we were closer to the exit. The closed door was no barrier to shifter hearing, so we heard every word the doctor said as he told Hattie that her uterine artery had been severed among the damage. He'd been forced to remove her uterus and one of her ovaries.

Hatred burned in my throat as I glared at Myrna. She had forced Layla to relay everything said and was practically jumping with joy over the news. It was disgusting. Myrna had her mask of grief back in place when the doctor left a few seconds later.

Myrna stopped short at the sight of the tears in Hattie's eyes. It made me wonder if she regretted her actions. I dismissed the idea when Myrna sat next to her friend and took her hands. "What happened? What's wrong?"

A sob burst from Hattie as she told Myrna what the doctor had said. "What am I going to do, Myrna? I have to have an heir to pass the magic to."

Myrna patted her hand. "You will find someone to gift the magic to when the time comes." The glee underlying Myrna's voice was unmistakable. The vile bitch had gotten what she'd wanted.

"It's not supposed to be this way. I can never have a family." Hattie's heartbreak nearly shattered me. I wanted to hug her close and tell her I would be her family.

"You will always have me and the coven. You aren't alone. Plus, you have the business you just started," Myrna told her in an attempt to placate her.

Layla was pointing at Myrna and shaking her head frantically. Hattie sniffled and her tears stopped as she frowned. "I'm sorry. I'm really tired and need to get some rest."

Myrna nodded and got to her feet. "I'll call Esme to come and see you tomorrow. Call me if you need anything."

Layla rushed to Hattie and hugged her before Myrna could say anything. I caught sight of her slipping her hand beneath Hattie's pillow. I approached the Pleiades and bent to give her a hug, as well.

"Under your pillow," I whispered in her ear as I let her go. "I truly am sorry we didn't reach you sooner, Hattie."

Hattie shook her head from side to side. "You two saved my life. I will never forget that. Thank you."

My heart was pounding in my chest as we left the hospital. All I could think about was the note and how Hattie would respond. Would she understand and find a way to rescue us? For the first time in my life, I thought there might be more than hell in my future.

CHAPTER 4

"Do you think Myrna knows about the note?" Layla brushed the herb debris off the counter into her open palm. "I mean, it's been two weeks, and she never gives us a second alone with Hattie during our daily visits.

"She would have whipped us until we died if she knew. The real question is whether Hattie understood. I mean, it seemed obvious to me but I would have thought she would make a move before now to help us."

I'd given up hope of ever getting free of Myrna's vile clutches. Initially, I thought Hattie was trying to communicate with me. After the third visit, I realized it was wishful thinking. She had Tarja who could tell me anything she wanted us to know. The only thing I could think of was that she either didn't know what Layla meant or she wasn't going to interfere with Myrna's projects.

The one good thing to come from Hattie's horrendous attack was that Myrna had backed off the experiments and hadn't tortured Layla or me for fourteen days. She was so busy baking food to take to Hattie. She was trying to convince Hattie that she cared about her.

The look Hattie had sent me when we took her a casserole at lunch made me wonder. Was she trying to tell me something? It sure seemed like it, and I couldn't stop replaying it through my head. Was she hurting? Did she need our help?

"But she's always trying to get us alone. The only reason she wanted to do that is to tell us the details of her plans." Layla dumped the remnants in the trash can and brushed off her hands.

Was that what she was trying to do? My mind replayed Hattie's request for me to take the casserole to the kitchen that morning. She had told Myrna to wait for her in her office before walking away. Myrna hadn't listened and continued to the kitchen with us. That was when Hattie had thrown me a look I couldn't decipher.

"If that's the case, we should pay her a visit tonight as soon as Myrna goes to sleep. Is there a sleeping potion in here we can add to her wine? That would ensure she doesn't catch us." I moved to the bookcases against the wall and started sifting through the vials on the shelves.

Layla joined me. "That's bri...what was that?"

I was already moving to the door and heading for the stairs. "I have no idea but the screech of tires isn't a good thing."

"Maybe it's the paranormal police," Layla whispered behind me as we walked through the kitchen.

An explosion blew me back into Layla before we reached the living room. Loud voices made me scramble to my feet and rush for the other room. Layla ran into my back when I stopped short at seeing Hattie facing off with Myrna.

"Why are you attacking me?" Myrna yelled at Hattie.

Hattie scowled at the witch that had been the bane of my existence. "I'm here to have a conversation."

One of Myrna's eyebrows lifted to her hairline. "Really? You barge into my house, causing my wards to explode. The only reason they would do that is if you meant me harm."

"I don't have a knife in my hand. Unlike the lackey, you hired to stab me. What I don't get is why you would do that. You know full well that if I had died without an heir, the world wouldn't have survived the vacuum created by my power." Hattie stalked further inside the entryway. The front door was lying in the yard several feet behind Hattie.

Myrna gasped, her eyes flying wide. "I don't know who told you I hired someone to hurt you, but I would never do that. I've spent the last two weeks trying to help you."

Hattie's head snapped up, and her mouth opened a fraction. "How about Layla and Tsekani. Are they here of their own free will?"

Myrna glared at the two of us before her expression softened. "Of course, they are. I took them in after they'd been abandoned by their parents."

Hattie pursed her lips. "That's odd behavior for shifters, especially dragons. They guard their young more fiercely than the wolves. It doesn't fit. I never thought about it before. There's an easy way to clear this up. Let's ask them."

Myrna sighed and rolled her eyes as she gestured to us. "Be my guest."

Pain lanced through my skull, reminding me that I couldn't answer freely. Hattie approached us and grabbed Layla's hands. "Do you want to be here anymore?"

Layla shook her head from side to side then cried out. Myrna acted so fast I hardly saw her move. Before I could blink, a ball of light shot from her hands and struck Hattie in the back. She went flying, but I caught her before she could slam into the wall.

An invisible explosion blasted the two of us apart. Hattie grunted as she hit the doorjamb. She shouted something, and Myrna stiffened, her eyes going wide. Hattie brushed off her shirt and approached Myrna. "You might not have been behind my attack, but I know Layla and Tsekani aren't here of their own volition. I also know that two infants went missing from the hospital around the time they would have been born."

Myrna jerked, and I noticed her fingers twitching on her right hand. I wanted to laugh. She couldn't move and was going to get what was coming to her. "It wasn't them. They're shifters, not mundanes."

Hattie inclined her head. "Yet, somehow, they used to be mundies. There aren't many Japanese families in the state of Maine. The newborn of the only couple that used to live in Camden went missing at the same time you found two abandoned shifters. I know you did something, and I am going to find out."

Hattie turned to me and held my hand. *"Open your mind to Hattie. She is going to search your memories."* My racing heart slowed a fraction when Tarja's voice entered my head. I took a deep breath and did as she instructed.

Hattie's expression hardened at the same time pain exploded through my brain. It felt like a wolf was clawing it to pieces. I doubled over, balancing with my hands on my knees.

The pressure and pain eased, and Hattie put her hand on my shoulder. "I feel the spell binding you. I can lift it but it's going to hurt like hell. It's in there deeper than anything I've ever experienced before."

Myrna jerked against the spell holding her in place. "No! They're mine. You can't touch them. They belong to me."

Hattie got in Myrna's face. "News flash. People aren't objects to be owned. I am going to free Layla and Tsekani then they can tell me how they feel."

"I found them and have raised them. They belong with me," Myrna objected.

Hattie ignored Myrna, and her focus shifted to Layla and me. *"Libero!"*

I sucked in a breath and dropped to my knees. Whatever she did turned my brain to boiling liquid. I was dimly aware of Layla crying out, but I'd lost all ability to move, think or breathe. Sweat dripped from every pore of my body while my muscles cramped.

After what seemed like forever, the pain eased and I sat up. Hattie was crouched next to us with a sorrowful expression on her face. "I'm sorry about that. Now, I need you both to tell me if you'd like to stay here or leave with me."

"Leave with you," Layla and I blurted at the same time.

Hattie smiled then reached out to Layla and me. She helped us up then glared at Myrna. "You're not going to interfere with them packing up and moving out."

Myrna smirked at Hattie. The sight told me we wouldn't get out of this so easily. I didn't stop to think as I ran down the stairs and grabbed the duffle bag I kept packed at the foot of my bed. I wouldn't bring anything if I could get away with it.

"Can you believe we're getting out of here?" Layla asked as she came running out of her room.

"It seems like a dream," I admitted.

Hattie frowned when Layla and I returned with one bag each. "Is that all you have?"

"We've never been able to buy much. I'd leave this behind but I need them to get a job. Mundies don't like nudity." My face heated as I admitted how little my life amounted to. I had no skills or job prospects but I didn't care. I was getting out of there.

"I've got a job for both of you, if you're interested," Hattie replied. "We can discuss it at my house."

Layla wrapped her arm through mine as we headed to the door. I lifted a foot and froze. That familiar control made my foot fall back to the ground. My head dropped to my chest as despair washed over me. Layla sent pleading eyes to Hattie, who growled and clenched her hands into fists at her sides. "You will regret ever treating these two like slaves. You will not keep them under your thumb a second longer. *Libero!*"

Hattie's voice echoed through every cell in my body. Her power was warm as it seeped into me. My blood turned to lava and burned through the darkness I'd always felt in the shadows of my mind. It happened so fast I didn't have time to do more than blink.

I looked at Layla then Hattie. Hattie smiled and gestured outside. "You're free. You can leave."

"No! They belong to me. Do not take one step out that door," Myrna shouted at the same time Layla and I walked out of the house. Tears flowed down my face as I hugged Layla to me. Letting go of Layla, I grabbed Hattie and hugged her close. Layla added her arms to the mix.

The three of us hugged and cried in the middle of Myrna's lawn while she screamed about owning us in the background.

Layla smiled through her tears as she looked up at me. "Where do we go from here?"

"You're free to do as you please. I will help you both get on your feet wherever you'd like to settle. And I will support you until you get on your feet. I failed you both by not seeing what she was doing sooner," Hattie told us.

I wrapped an arm around her waist and led her to the parked vehicle along the curb. "I can't speak for Layla, but I feel like I didn't do enough to save you from harm, and I want to be by your side, protecting you. Myrna will never give up on getting your power. I have to be the one to stop her."

Layla wiped her eyes. "I want to be there, too. We don't have anywhere to go, but we can make a home in the woods around your house if you allow. That way, we will always be close in the event she makes another move."

Hattie's eyes went wide as she hugged us both close again. "I can look out for myself. I learned my lesson about letting my guard down, but I would love for you both to move in with me at least until you figure something else out. When my business takes off and makes money, we can build you small homes on the property. There's enough space."

I was free. No longer would Myrna control my every move. I could do whatever I wanted. Date whomever I wanted.

Murtagh's image flashed into my mind. He would be a great place to start my foray into dating. There was something about him that drew me to him. I could find him once I got settled. I had time and opportunity now.

I smiled so big that my cheeks hurt. Layla and I finally had our freedom. We would never be forced to do Myrna's evil bidding again. I owed my life to Hattie Silva. In spite of the fact that we had failed her, she wanted us to be a part of protecting her. I would dedicate my life to ensuring she was safe, happy, and successful.

The End.

ABOUT THE AUTHOR

Reviews are like hugs. Sometimes awkward. Always welcome! It would mean the world to me if you can take five minutes and let others know how much you enjoyed my work.

Don't forget to sign up for her newsletter Website of Brenda Trim! which is jam-packed with exciting news and monthly giveaways. Go to www.BrendaTrim.com

Author Brenda Trim | Facebook

Never allow waiting to become a habit. Live your dreams and take risks. Life is happening now.

DREAM BIG!

XOXO,

Brenda

ALSO BY BRENDA TRIM

www.BrendaTrim.com

Dark Warriors' Alliance 1-24

Midlife Witchery 1-10

Mystical Midlife in Maine 1-8

Twisted Sisters Midlife Maelstrom 1-2

Hollow Rock Shifters 1-7

Brambles Edge Academy 1-3

Midnight Doms Series 1-3

SAVAGE VALLEY
SHIFTERS

WILD

NEW YORK TIMES BESTSELLING AUTHOR
MARGO BOND COLLINS

BLURB

Rejected. Unwanted. Unloved.

As her clan alpha's daughter, Macy Martin is destined to be mated to the son of a rival clan's alpha. Together, they will form a new leap, binding their clans and ending generations of inter-leap rivalry. All her life, she has wanted nothing more than to take her rightful place, to do her duty.

But when her promised mate violently rejects her during the public mating ceremony, she is humiliated and faces death.

Macy is left with two options—stay and accept her fate, or run to Savage Valley, where only the most brutal of shifters survive.

But now that she's free of her clan, she's becoming something new.

Something feral.

Wild.

Enter the world of the Savage Valley Shifters. Fans of G. Bailey, G.K. DeRosa, Jen L. Grey, Kelly St. Claire, Annette Marie, Shannon Mayer, Leia Stone, Jaymin Eve, and Linsey Hall will adore this dark, rejected mate paranormal romance.

CHAPTER 1

Macy

A shiver of anticipation ran down Macy Martin's back as she smoothed her hands over her hips, the satin of her mating-day dress shimmering in the lamplight.

"You look beautiful," her mother murmured, peering over Macy's shoulder into the full-length mirror against the wall.

Macy had to agree. The dark green of the dress might not fit any human ideas about the appropriate color for a wedding dress, but it brought out the deep green of Macy's catlike eyes and turned her pale skin to a gorgeous ivory color in a way no white dress ever could have done.

Besides, the dress was only meant to last through the first half of the ceremony. In the second half, her new mate, Vance Felton, would shred the dress with his shifted claws, freeing her to take her leopard form in reality and, at the same time, symbolically freeing her to take her place in the leopard clans' hierarchy as second-in-command to her father, just as Vance would become second-in-command to his father.

Their union had been planned since Macy's birth, an agreement designed to bring the two leopard-shifter groups together, ending generations of warfare between them.

Even before their mating ceremony, it had worked. Ever since their betrothal ceremony, in fact, the two clans had refrained from attacking one another.

Eighteen years of peace.

Now that Macy had turned nineteen, that peace would become permanent.

And once Macy had her first kits, the two clans would become one leap—the biggest collective of leopard shifters in the entire world.

"Do you think Vance will like the dress?" Macy asked nervously.

Her mother laughed and turned Macy around to embrace her. "Of course, he will, sweetheart. It's beautiful. And so are you."

Macy returned her mother's hug, drawing in Layla Martin's comforting scent. A few moments later, she pulled away, straightened her shoulders, and checked herself in the mirror one last time, smoothing down her long, chestnut-colored hair. "Okay. I'm ready."

They made their way out of the rental cabin, the largest one in the compound reserved for the ceremony. The leopard clans' alphas had agreed it would be best to hold the ceremony on neutral ground, far from their home territories, even though those territories bordered one another and would soon be joined.

Soon, we won't need those kinds of negotiations any longer, Macy thought as she fought to keep her steps steady and her heartbeat calm.

As Layla and Macy made their way down the path toward the portion of the campground that had been converted into a small, circular arena, a slight chill blew through the air, catching Macy by surprise.

Instinctively, she glanced up at the small mountain range nearby.

On the other side of that range, she knew, lay Savage Valley—the reason this particular campground did not belong to anyone shifter clan's territory.

No one dared lay claim to any land so close to the feral shifters who ruled Savage Valley.

The sooner we complete the ceremony and get out of here, the better.

Not that the feral shifters were likely to attack from so far away—not when it was understood that anyone renting the campground was merely a temporary resident.

Still, the touch of frost in the air this early in the season felt more worrisome than it should have been, and Macy had to wonder if she was sensing something more than just the end of summer.

As she and her mother came around a turn in the path, she caught sight of her father waiting for her.

"My beautiful daughter," he called out, opening his arms.

Pulling away from her mother, Macy ran to him, burying herself in his warm hug.

"Are you ready for this?" he asked.

"I am." A slight quiver in her voice betrayed her anxiety, though.

John Martin slid his hands down the backs of Macy's arms to take her hands in his. "I'm proud of you, sweetheart," he murmured. "You are the most wonderful daughter any parents could ever wish for, and I am grateful to you for taking your place in the clans this way."

It wasn't anything he hadn't said to her before, but Macy appreciated hearing it again. "Our clan is important to me," she assured him for at least the thousandth time. "I will always do whatever is necessary to keep our people safe."

"I know you will." John planted a kiss on Macy's forehead. "Are you ready to meet your mate?"

She nodded, trying to force her eagerness to outweigh her anxiety. "Yes."

Not that Macy had never met Vance before—but it had been over six years since she had last seen him, back when he was barely eighteen, and headed away to a human college to complete his education.

At barely thirteen, Macy had been far too shy to make much of an impression on him, she feared.

Of course, after tonight, we will have all the time in the world to get to know each other.

Starting with a ceremonial hunt after the wedding, the first time, the members of the two clans would run together as one leap.

"I'm ready," she announced. Taking each of her parents' hands in hers, she turned to face her future. "Let's go join our clans to one another."

CHAPTER 2

Colin

Colin Stalker peered over the ridge and down into the campground below.

His brother Gavin had been right—there really were other shifters down there. Other leopards, from the scents he had picked up as he prowled the edges of the campground earlier.

Colin had even taken the risk of stepping into the crowd a couple of times, slipping along the edges as if he belonged.

Everyone there had been discussing an upcoming mating and the joining of the clans.

But soon enough, he had melted back into the shadows of the surrounding foliage, as his presence made other shifters, shifters from outside Savage Valley, nervous—even when he didn't speak, when he was simply a passerby, it was as if they sensed something about him—before they caught his scent, before their conscious brains had time to process what they were seeing. It was as if he exuded *otherness*.

Wildness, his mother had called it. Unlike Colin and his brothers and unlike their father, Colin's mother had been born into a leap of leopards outside Savage Valley. One with many more clan members.

His mother had even known full humans—the same kind of humans sometimes rented the campground near the Valley, who hiked through its wilderness, never knowing how close they stepped to a brutal death full of sharp claws and hungry teeth.

He turned his attention back to the campground. He had never seen a formal mating ceremony before, though he had heard of them from his mother.

The whole idea seemed vaguely preposterous to him—that two clans could be joined simply because of a mating.

In Savage Valley, clans were too small to split into separate units, and any change in leadership came through battle.

Which was the way things ought to be, Colin reflected. Only the strongest could survive in the Valley, so it made sense that the very strongest should be the ones to lead the clans.

And although he had never told anyone, he had plans to become the clan alpha of the leopards someday, just as his father had been before him.

Not yet, of course. His father was still a strong, competent leader.

But the day would come when that was no longer true. And on that day, Colin would step in as his father's champion and successor. Through a fight to the death with any challengers, he would ensure his father's right to live out his days in comfort while Colin took over clan leadership.

But being a strong leader meant knowing as much about the world around them as possible—not merely Savage Valley but also the clans beyond and the shifters who sometimes made their way to the Valley, those with no other choice but to join the Valley clans.

He needed to know as much as possible about the clans that sent their exiled, unwanted members to Savage Valley.

And right now, that meant settling in and observing what was happening below.

As he prepared to drop down to the ground to watch the ceremony, he considered whether to do so in his human form or his leopard shape.

In general, he preferred his leopard form. And that would allow him to hear what was going on better. His human shape, on the other hand, would allow him to see what was going on. Like most cats, his leopard shape had comparatively poor eyesight but excellent hearing, and his two-legged body had much better sight.

He peered down at the small crowd below him. He had been able to drift in and out of the group as a human because none of them were in their animal forms.

That suggested that something about the ceremony might be important, able to be stated only in words, and that probably meant he should be able to hear them.

Besides, I have already seen everything I need to see.

Just as the thought crossed his mind, a woman stepped into the clearing with two older shifter adults, one on either side.

Even from this distance, she took his breath away.

She was tall for a leopard shifter, and the long sweep of her green skirt only served to emphasize her height.

She turned to speak to the male by her side and reached up on tiptoes to kiss him on the cheek.

A possessive growl rumbled in Colin's chest.

Mine, his inner beast insisted.

Colin shook his head. What an insane thought. Still, his beast scratched to be let out, and he could almost feel its tail twitching.

That decided it. Whatever was going on below, he needed to hear what was being said, even if it meant reducing his vision of the scene below blurry figures moving about.

She was the only one he cared about, anyway, and that distinctive green dress would make her visible, even from this distance.

Closing his eyes, he relaxed his shoulders, dropping into that inner space where his beast always waited, ready to come out at a moment's notice.

His bones cracked, the pain of them breaking and changing excruciating but temporary, passing almost as quickly as it appeared.

And although his human voice begged to cry out, he felt his inner cat place a restraining paw on his inner human, reminding him that showing weakness was dangerous in Savage Valley.

He dropped to his knees, and by the time his hands hit the dirt, they had become paws, tipped with claws that could wound and shred an enemy.

His tail twitched, and he chuffed out a quick laugh of joy, delighted to again be in the form that felt most natural to him, the shape that allowed him to fully relax into the forest of Savage Valley.

He crouched down in his spot on the ridge, his tail curling around his haunches, the tip of it twitching back and forth eagerly. He tilted his ears forward as he concentrated on catching every word the human-shaped shifters said below.

As he had predicted, their figures were now merely blurry shapes, the colors faded to almost black and white.

But the green dress stood out.

He would learn everything he could from watching. And then, somehow, though he did not know exactly how, he would find a way to make the woman in the green dress his.

Forever.

CHAPTER 3

Macy

Macy stepped out into the circle of light cast by the torches and candles scattered throughout the clearing. A ring of chairs surrounded the outer edge of the clearing, providing seating for the few elderly shifters who had chosen to attend.

Most of the leopards, however, stood in their human forms on either side of a fabric runner leading to a traditional human wedding arch decorated with late summer flowers.

John Martin stepped forward to join Vance's father, Brady Felton, under the arch. The two alphas would officiate the ceremony, which had become a tradition among the clans. They had also both arranged to be ordained online so that any shifter marriages they performed would be legal in the human world, as well.

Excitement curled in Macy's stomach, and she found herself grinning uncontrollably as she glanced at her mother, who would accompany her down the aisle.

As she stood waiting, Vance Felton stepped up to join the two alphas.

An inscrutable glance passed between him and his father, and a thread of worry began worming its way through Macy's excitement.

"What was that look about?" her mother murmured under her breath.

But then both Felton males glanced up, focusing their gazes on Macy, their expressions clear.

Vance was every bit as beautiful as Macy remembered, with dark golden hair and eyes almost the same color, light brown with flecks of gold shimmering through them.

But for the first time in her memory, something about him set her teeth on edge.

As it was, the expression she had seen flicker across his face when he looked at his father bothered her. Or maybe it was the sharpness of his smile—too many teeth showing, something closer to a snarl than a sign of true happiness.

He's just nervous, she told herself as the music started.

She had chosen traditional classical music, not necessarily songs common in a human wedding, but music that suited her, nonetheless.

As she moved down the aisle to the strains of Brahms's String Sextet No. 1, shifters on both sides of the white satin runner handed her seasonal flowers picked from the nearby forest—probably again some conservation rules, but in keeping with the shifters' tradition of blending with nature whenever possible.

By the time she reached the two alphas and her intended, Macy had a complete bouquet. Layla Martin tied a ribbon around the stems to hold them together, finishing it off with a bow. Then she kissed her daughter on the cheek and stepped back to join the rest of her pack members on the bride's side.

Bride's side and groom's side—another tradition taken from the humans. In a shifter wedding within the clan, there would be no separate sides. But today's festivities called for such a division, at least until the ceremony was over.

Brand-new wildflower bouquet in hand, Macy turned to face Vance, who took her empty hand in his and then wrapped his fingers around the hand holding the bouquet until he had her firmly in his grip.

Macy fought the urge to shake away the thought—why would she consider him holding her hands being 'in his grip'?

She shoved the thought down, promising herself that she would examine it later when the ceremony was over.

We will have our entire lives to work out our relationship, she promised herself. She forced herself to pay attention as her father began to speak.

"Today," John Martin said, "We come together not merely to join this man and this woman in human marriage, but to join our clans through this mating, this connection of our two groups, our two peoples."

Murmurs of agreement rose from the gathered crowd.

"I believe the bride and groom have each prepared a few words," he continued, gesturing to the couple before him. "I present to you Vance Felton and his bride-to-be, my beautiful daughter, Macy Martin."

As they had discussed, Macy went first. There had been no rehearsal, but Macy had been practicing her words for as long as she could remember.

"I stand before you today in joy," she said, "not only to be joined with my lifelong betrothed, by to speak the promise in my heart both to him and to you that I will always represent our joined clans as if they are one—because they will be—and to let you know that as clan alpha, I will share the duties of governance with my mate with no preference for my clan for his clan, but always with the goal of representing *our* clan."

"Hear, hear!" someone from Macy's side of the audience shouted.

She turned her gaze to Vance, ready for him to take his turn.

His golden eyes glittered almost feverishly, and his lips turned up once again in that sharp, wicked smile that had so disturbed her before.

His hands tightened around hers, and he began to speak, his voice carrying over the crowd. "Well said, Macy Martin." His tone took on a strangely sardonic edge. "I, too, stand before you today to proclaim that there are not two leopard shifter clans, but only one."

Something pricked the back of her hand, and Macy glanced down to see that Vance's hand had partially shifted so that sharp claws protruded from his fingertips.

What the—

"But not one clan as Macy envisions it. No—only one *surviving* clan." He paused dramatically. "My clan. *Mine.*"

Before his full meaning could even sink in, a roar erupted from the groom's side of the clearing, and all the members of the Feltons' clan surged toward the Martins' clan, already in various stages of shifting.

Just as Macy figured out what was going on, Brady Felton lashed out with one hand, raking his claws across John Martin's throat.

At the same moment, Vance's mother, Heather, almost fully shifted, and landed atop Layla Martin, sinking her teeth into Macy's mother's throat and flinging her head skyward in a spray of Layla's arterial blood.

As if in slow motion, Macy heard a scream, then realized it came from her own throat.

She tried to pull away from Vance, but his grip was like iron, even when he transferred her hands to one of his, freeing the other to slash away her beautiful green gown.

As her wedding dress shredded into ribbons, revealing her soft, human skin beneath, he hauled her up against him. "Don't worry, little kitten," he hissed. "We will still be together." He chuckled, a sound that promised violence. "But not as equals. You belong to me now."

His gaze raked down Macy's body hungrily, and no matter how hard she fought to break his grip, she could not pull away from him.

All around her, hisses, growls and yowling screeches erupted as Macy's people fought and died. Her parents bled out before her eyes, their lifeblood soaking into the dirt at her feet, pooling until the satin runner began to soak it up, turning the white fabric a dark crimson.

I have only one chance to fight for my people, she realized.

She forced herself to relax, to go limp in Vance's grip as if she were giving in.

And then she allowed herself to shift.

CHAPTER 4

Colin

The moment he realized the mating ceremony below involved the woman in the green dress, Colin leaped up and began loping down the long path from the top of the ridge to the clearing, a single litany repeating in his mind.

She is mine.

By the time he reached the bottom of the path, the cheers he'd heard at the beginning had turned to screams—and then to the sounds of battle.

And not the carefully moderated fights that allowed the shifters of the Valley to transfer power from one alpha to the next, but an all-out war.

At the edge of the clearing, he skidded to a halt, reminding himself that he needed to take stock of the situation before leaping into the fray.

That resolution lasted exactly as long as it took for him to catch sight of the male holding Colin's mate flush against his body, whispering in her ear.

My mate? His inner human repeated in tones of shock.

But Colin was already moving, darting around opponents locked in bloody combat as he made his way toward the flower-covered arch at the end of a now gore-soaked satin runner.

He was still several yards away when his mate twisted in her captor's grasp and dropped to the ground, her ripped green dress fluttering down around her as she shifted into her leopard form.

The male who had been holding her started to follow her down to the ground, his shape shifting into his own leopard form.

Colin let out a growling screech and leaped over two intervening fighting leopard pairs just in time to bat the male away from his mate.

Colin's claws were fully extended, and he caught the skin of the other male's face before it had finished sprouting fur. Long scratches opened on the half-shifted male's face, and blood began streaming out.

He let out a scream somewhere between a cat's yowl and a human's shout.

The female came to her feet behind Colin, screaming her rage so loudly that it echoed through the clearing. Colin was certain even the elders in the Valley had heard her.

But the male had turned his focus to Colin, apparently realizing he was facing a challenger he did not know.

And there's no way he's prepared for me.

No soft shifter from outside the Valley could ever hope to defeat Colin, who had spent his entire life preparing to become alpha of his leap.

He darted in under the other male's guard, batting his opponent's head again, claws still fully extended. He didn't open up any serious wounds this time—the male had finished shifting and was protected by his fur—but Colin did manage to rip a notch in the delicate skin of the outsider's ear.

Serves you right.

Colin backed away slowly, looking for another opening.

But all around them, the sounds of battling shifters began to fall away, and the remaining shifters started to draw closer, encircling the female, Colin, and the other male.

If he allowed them to completely enclose them in their circle, there was no way Colin could win, he realized. Facing one soft male was one thing, but if that soft male had backup, Colin would be in more trouble.

Even if the female joined in the fight on his side.

At almost the very moment Colin decided to make a run for it, the other male shifter jumped toward him—and to Colin's surprise, went sailing over him, landing atop the female and grabbing her by the scruff of the neck as if she were a kitten.

Colin's beast roared a challenge.

She is mine.

Even without words, the meaning was clear. The other male ignored him, though, and bore down on the female, pushing her to the ground with his superior weight and strength.

She fought back, but the male had surprised her, and no matter how hard she thrashed, she couldn't get away.

But Colin could play by the same rules. In one swift move, he slipped in beside the other male, grabbing the intruder by the scruff of the neck. Rolling onto his back, Colin dragged the other male with him and began scrabbling at his opponent with his strong back legs, raking his claws down the other male's spine.

The male refused to release the female, but he was no longer in a position to use his weight against her, and she wrenched her neck out of his mouth, leaving him with a mouth full of fur, skin, and blood.

As soon as she was free, Colin shoved the other male away and flipped onto his feet. Blood dripped from his teeth as he snarled a warning at all the leopards in the clearing. The shifters surrounding them began to pull back, moving to form a half-circle behind the injured male.

As if unconcerned by their presence, Colin turned his back on them and began strolling away, pausing to nudge the female to join him.

She continued facing the male, snarling a promise that didn't need words to be translated.

I am not through with you.

She backed away from her attackers, still growling.

Colin made sure to stay between the female and the other leopards as the two of them moved toward the edge of the clearing.

The female was leaving a trail of blood that the other shifters could track easily—but that was a problem for later. Right now, they needed to get as far away from this campsite as possible, preferably all the way into Savage Valley, where Colin's knowledge of the terrain and his clan's strength would give them the advantage.

By the time they reached the top of the ridge, however, Colin could already hear the other shifters following them, and the female was weaving on her feet.

She put on a burst of speed, and for an instant, he thought they might actually make it to safety.

He paused at his earlier vantage point to look back at the clearing below them.

Bodies, both human and leopard, lay scattered in the circular space.

All the living shifters had disappeared, presumably following Colin and the female.

From behind him came a slight thud. He spun around, half expecting to discover his opponent had caught up with them.

Instead, he found his mate had collapsed.

As he watched, her form shimmered between leopard and human, finally solidifying as a human woman lying naked and unconscious on the ground.

I do not have time for this.

But if she was injured badly enough to pass out, he needed even more desperately to get her to safety.

He forced himself through a rapid shift, enduring the extra pain so that he could quickly scoop her unconscious body into his strong human arms.

She was covered in blood.

No wonder she lost consciousness.

"I'll get you to the healer," he promised her in a whisper and set out at a jog back toward Savage Valley.

Chapter 5

Macy

Sharp pain flashed through Macy's body, starting at the back of her neck, and she fought to swim up through the darkness toward consciousness.

But something was waiting there for her—something horrible.

I don't want to wake up.

The thought was her own, but it almost seemed to come from somewhere else.

Another sharp pain stabbed at her, and she tried to struggle against it.

"I'm almost finished here," a deep voice echoed through the darkness. "But I need you to be still for just another few moments."

This time, she recognized the feeling of a needle.

Why would somebody be giving her a shot in the back of her neck?

Tears slipped out from behind her closed eyelids.

Why am I crying?

The answer waited for her somewhere out there, and she knew without examining it too closely that she did not want to know.

Where am I?

Suddenly, she didn't want the answer to that either.

Her memory began returning in bits and pieces.

She had been in the clearing, about to complete the mating ceremony with Vance Felton.

And...

Oh, God. My parents.

A sob escaped her before she could clamp down on her emotions.

"I think she's awake," the same deep voice said.

"Can you open your eyes?" a different deep voice asked. This one, gentler and slightly raspy, spoke from somewhere near her face.

A painful tugging at the back of her neck caused her to whimper and squeeze her eyes shut even more tightly.

"There you go. All stitched up." A rustling behind her accompanied that first voice. "Let me know if you need me to talk to her," whoever was speaking continued, this time apparently not to her. "Otherwise, I'll be back in a few hours to check in."

A door shut, and she was left alone in the room with the second speaker.

Slowly, she forced herself to open her eyes, terrified of who she would see when she did.

Had Vance found her? Was she truly his captive now?

But it wasn't Vance. A young man, probably in his mid-to-late twenties, crouched next to the bed she rested on so that his face was almost even with hers.

With a gasp, she sat up straight, pulling away from the stranger—and almost immediately, she wished she hadn't.

Every muscle in her body ached, and the back of her neck burned.

Carefully, she reached up to feel the wound, finally remembering that Vance had held her down, trying to force her to accept his will.

But not until after he and his clan had murdered her parents—and if she remembered correctly, all the other shifters who had accompanied them to what was supposed to be a joyous occasion.

"Where am I?" she asked, her voice coming out scratchy and harsh.

"You're in the leopard alpha's cabin in Savage Valley," the man replied, standing up and moving to a nearby chair, where he sat, his legs sprawled out before him. His pose was lazy, unconcerned—but his sharp gaze never stopped following Macy.

She didn't buy his negligent act. Not one little bit.

"You forced Vance off me back there," she said, watching the stranger's response.

He dipped his head once in acknowledgment. "You looked like you could use some help."

"I'm Macy Martin," she finally said. "My father is—" She broke off, then tried again. "My father *was* the alpha of our clan." Her voice dropped to a whisper. "I guess that means I'm the alpha now...of whoever is left."

"That was supposed to be a mating ceremony, yes?" the stranger asked.

"Yes. I've been promised to Vance since I was born."

The stranger's gaze narrowed, danger emanating off him in waves. Macy shrank away from him, and he instantly tamped down his manifest anger. "I'm Colin Stalker."

Macy blinked in confusion. "Stalker?"

He laughed, instantly dissipating the last of his rage, and the amused sound sent shivers from Macy's neck down to her toes. "It's a real family name, from Scotland originally, though I suspect it's connected to our hunting ability in our leopard forms."

She moved to sit cross-legged, forcing herself to ignore the way his laugh made her feel—like nothing she had ever experienced before.

Besides, she had more important things to consider right now.

"They killed my parents." Her voice came out flat, all the emotion she felt, all the rage and pain, so deep and dark that it leached everything out of her voice, leaving nothing but the bare facts.

"They did," Colin agreed, matching her tone. "Were those your parents standing with you?"

"Yes," Macy replied with a sob. "I saw them do it, saw Vance Felton and his father murder my parents. And the Feltons are still alive."

Colin tilted his head, his eyes narrowing. "And you want to make sure they don't get away with it."

Fierce determination welled up inside her, a kind of stone-cold resolve she had never felt before. "That's exactly what I want."

"Then we will make sure they get what they deserve."

His easy willingness to help her sent competing emotions rolling through her body. On the one hand, she was grateful she wouldn't have to do this alone. On the other hand, though, she had to wonder what, precisely, this stranger thought he could gain from helping her.

She had never been cynical before, but recent events had changed that.

Macy had spent her whole life as a political pawn. She knew it—had known it for a long time—but she had accepted it as her duty, the one way she knew to help keep her clan safe.

I will never allow that to happen again, she vowed. *I will never again be someone's pawn.*

"Why are you so willing to help?" she asked bluntly.

A flush crawled up Colin's neck, staining his cheeks a dark crimson. "I do have selfish reasons," he acknowledged. "And I am absolutely willing to tell you about them. But I would prefer to wait until we have taken out your enemies to discuss it with you."

Macy shook her head emphatically. "I'm not going to accept your help without knowing the terms." Her voice was as hard as her determination.

"I would never ask you to pay something you're unwilling to part with," Colin promised.

Macy stared into his eyes—so similar to Vance's in some ways, with their golden flecks.

But Colin's eyes were darker, warmer.

And somehow, she believed him. Still, she needed more. "What do you hold most sacred?"

Colin blinked rapidly. "You give me conversational whiplash." He essayed a grin as if checking to see how Macy would respond.

"Not really. I want you to swear on whatever you hold most dear that you will never request that I do, be, participate in, or part with, anything unless I want to."

The smile dropped from Colin's face, and he nodded. "I swear on the lives of my clan here in Savage Valley that after I help you, you will owe me nothing. Anything you choose to do in return will be entirely of your own free will."

His vow carried the ring of truth, and Macy nodded once, firmly, "Then I agree—I'll accept your help."

"Good. We need to move fast. We should plan our attack before your erstwhile mate, and his clan leave the area."

CHAPTER 6

Colin

Macy closed her eyes and nodded, almost unconsciously squaring her shoulders. Despite all her outward calm, anger and grief poured off his mate, and Colin longed to sweep in and wrap her in his arms, comforting her for her losses.

But that would never work—she was in too much pain right now. Colin understood without her having to say so that even the slightest touch might shatter her delicate control.

No—tenderness was best reserved for later. Right now, what his mate needed more than anything was the kind of retribution that Savage Valley shifters were expert at doling out.

"The man who was going to become your mate—" he began.

"Vance Felton. He and his father were the ones who instigated the attack."

"The Feltons, then."

Macy nodded and gestured for him to continue.

"They and their clan followed us as far as the ridge above the human campground. Once you shifted, it healed you enough to stop the bleeding, so they couldn't track us as easily. I lost them once I carried you into the forest that covers most of the Valley."

With one hand, Macy reached up and felt the stitches in the back of her neck.

"The healer said those were mostly a precaution. They'll dissolve once you shift again."

Macy gave a brisk nod and uncurled her legs as if she were planning to stand up.

"The healer also said you needed to rest and eat before you tried shifting again."

"I don't have time to rest. Not if we're going to get those bastards before they leave."

"My brother Gavin is watching them. He caught their trail and sent our youngest brother Errol back to report."

"Are they in Savage Valley?"

"No. They made their way back to the campsite to clean it up. Apparently, they have the good sense to recognize that a massacre like that would draw attention to them—both from the human authorities and from the Savage Valley shifters."

Macy's face paled at his use of the word *massacre*, and Colin cursed himself silently for forgetting for a moment to keep her recent loss at the forefront of his mind.

A knock on the door gave him a little sigh of relief. "Hamish, our healer, said he was sending someone with food for you."

"I'm not hungry." Macy placed one soft hand on her abdomen as if attempting to physically hold down the contents of her stomach.

"You should at least try." Colin paused for a moment, then added, "You'll need the energy if you're going to take your revenge."

With that, he stood and made his way to the door. When he opened it, Nancy, a clan elder and one of the very few females in

Savage Valley, bustled in with two fragrant bowls of stew, already speaking to Macy. "I didn't know if you would prefer raw meat or more human-style food, but I thought this would be a good place to start."

Nancy handed the two bowls to Colin. "Hold these." Then she moved back out to the hallway and brought in two wooden trays on stands, setting them up efficiently in front of Colin's chair and Macy's spot on the bed.

With one more trip out into the hallway, she also delivered two large glasses of hibiscus tea. "I added lots of sugar to these," she told the two of them.

Colin's nose wrinkled at the mention of sugar, and Nancy gave him a stern look. "If you're going to be shifting as much as I suspect you will in the next day or two, you're going to need the extra energy." She raised her eyebrows at Colin until he nodded. "And I'm going to stand here until you take at least one bite," she said, turning to Macy. "I know you may not want to—it might seem like the last thing that matters right now is food." Her voice dropped into a kindlier register, something Colin had rarely heard from the woman who had been considered the den mother ever since his own mother had died.

Reluctantly, Macy picked up the spoon Nancy placed on the tray and scooped up a small bite of the stew. Dutifully, she chewed and swallowed.

With a satisfied nod, Nancy left the room.

As if on autopilot, Macy continued eating.

Colin picked up his bowl of stew and finished it in record time, setting his empty dish down before Macy had eaten even half of hers.

"Nancy's right about the tea," he said, taking a large gulp, even though his face screwed up at the overly sweet taste. "We'll be doing a lot of shifting over the next few days. The more energy we can store up for it, the better."

He waited until Macy had followed his example and taken a sip of her drink. Holding his breath, he chugged the rest of the sickly-sweet tea down, then sat silently until Macy had finished her meal.

"I do feel better," she admitted as she set her glass down next to the empty bowl on her tray.

"Enough better to make a plan?"

Her gaze hardened. "I plan to kill them all."

Colin nodded. "I agree—and it's my plan, too. But I think we should go in with some kind of strategy. Otherwise, we're liable to get ourselves killed in the process."

"I don't care," Macy snarled.

"I don't blame you. If I were in your position, I wouldn't care about my own life, either. But the longer you stay alive, the more certain you will be to take your revenge on everyone who participated in that travesty of a mating ceremony."

Macy's jaw tightened, but she nodded. "You know the terrain. What's our best bet?"

"I'll send Errol to check in with Gavin. If we can take the Feltons unaware, we can wipe them out while they're still dealing with the campground."

"And if we can't take them by surprise?"

Now Colin's gaze turned cold. "Then we will lure them into Savage Valley, onto our territory, where we can pick them off one by one."

"I like that idea." Macy's expression tightened. "The longer we can make them suffer, the more afraid we can make them, the better it'll be." She flashed a glance at Colin. "But I want to be the one to deal the deathblows to both the Feltons. They led their people to wipe out almost my entire clan. This is my revenge, and I want to take it."

For all that he realized her ferocity came out of grief, Colin was glad to see her taking the initiative against the Feltons.

The beautiful, soft woman he had seen under the wedding arch would not have responded the way she was reacting now.

This was good.

To survive in Savage Valley, she will have to grow harder.

Fiercer.

Wilder.

CHAPTER 7

Macy

Serena's tears dripped onto the paper, causing the ink to bleed. The words swirled together in a black river, rolling down the page. Her doctor had given her the prognosis in person, but it wasn't real until she read the words.

Less than three hours later, Macy was stretched out on her stomach, peering over the ridge that looked down on the campsite where her parents had been slaughtered.

She'd shifted twice from human to leopard and back again, and true to Colin's word, the stitches in her neck had dissolved, leaving only a slight scar where Vance had slashed her skin open.

Colin was with her on the ridge, along with his brothers, Gavin and Errol, and a tall, olive-skinned, taciturn man Colin had introduced as Lorenzo, the mage of Savage Valley.

"Mage?" Macy had asked. "As in magic?"

"Apparently, there are very few of his kind left in the world," Colin replied. "We're lucky to have him here—and lucky that he's willing to work with all the Savage Valley clans."

Macy surveyed the site below them. Her stomach curdled watching Vance and his clan drag the lifeless bodies of her people to one side, dropping them in an undignified heap.

Macy gave a little whimper, and Colin drew back from the edge of the ridge, motioning for everyone to follow him. They retreated to a slight distance, far enough away that their soft voices wouldn't carry to the clearing below.

"So, what's our plan?" Gavin asked. Colin's brother looked quite a bit like him, with dark hair and eyes and pale skin, but his features were heavier and rougher, and although Colin had mentioned that Gavin was younger, Macy would have taken him as the eldest of three.

"We need to take them out before they finish cleaning up the campsite." Colin glanced around to make sure everyone agreed. "And the best time to attack is while they're distracted."

"We'll need to take them by surprise," Errol said.

Colin glanced at his youngest brother. "I'd prefer you weren't involved at all," he said mildly.

Errol scowled at him. "I am eighteen years old and have had all the same training you have," he argued. "I'm as capable of protecting the Valley as you and Gavin are."

Colin tilted his head and gave a slight nod—not a ringing endorsement of his brother's argument, but an acknowledgment that he wouldn't try to stop the boy from participating.

"I can help you take them by surprise," the mage said.

Together, the five of them mapped out their plan.

When they were ready, Colin pulled Macy aside. "I don't like your part in this," he said.

Knowing that he worried about her sent a ribbon of warmth curling through her chest. But his concern would never be enough to stop her. "It's my clan," she said simply.

"I know, and I won't try to stop you. I will have your back, no matter what."

The ribbon of warmth unfurled, flowering into an emotion she had never felt before—not even with her parents, the people she loved most in the world.

"Thank you." She wanted to add more but couldn't think of the right words.

But Colin reached out and took her hands in his, giving them a comforting squeeze, and somehow, she knew that even if she didn't have a way to say the words aloud, Colin understood what she meant.

"Let's do this," he said, then pulled away and stripped out of his clothes, folding and leaving them in a stack under a nearby shrub to pick up later on their way back to Savage Valley.

Assuming we survive, Macy thought.

All the shifters followed suit and then began to shift.

The five of them—four shifters in leopard form and one human mage—made their way down toward the clearing, splitting up and moving around to approach from different angles.

Macy crouched in the camouflaging foliage, downwind from the Felton leopard clan, certain they couldn't scent her out.

She could smell them, though, and every wafting breeze left her seething with anger. She wanted nothing more than to destroy them, rip them to shreds.

And Colin had done nothing to try to dissuade her from the plan. In fact, he had encouraged it. If anyone had told her three days ago that she would be preparing to slaughter as many members of the Felton clan as possible, she would have laughed, called them crazy.

Because she had fully believed that shifters no longer needed to follow their baser instincts.

We have evolved from that, she would have said. That was what she'd been taught—that she was more human than animal, able to control her killing instincts even when she wore her leopard form.

Her leopard purred at the thought of decimating the Felton clan.

Savage Valley had taken its name from an early settler, but its reputation stemmed from the violence of its residents. According to the rumors, Savage Valley shifters were feral, barbarous.

Wild.

And now, Macy was embracing that side of herself, as well.

I am wild.

She waited for the mage to cast his spell, she hugged that realization to herself.

Lorenzo's signal came exactly as the mage had told them it would: a loud noise, like a clap of thunder, the Savage Valley shifters' cue to close their eyes.

The noise was followed by a flash of light so bright it penetrated through Macy's squeezed-shut eyes. She counted to three in her mind, then raced into the clearing, where the Felton shifters stood, all but frozen.

"I won't be able to stop them from moving altogether," Lorenzo had warned, "but the spell will slow them down. They'll react much more slowly than they might otherwise. It probably won't last more than about five minutes, not with that many shifters, and it might not affect all of them equally, so watch each other's backs. I'll come in after you to try to slow down anyone still up and moving, but the initial spell will take a lot of power, so I might not have much left."

She saw what he'd meant as she dashed into the clearing. The Feltons, who were still in human form, were trying to shift, but their bodies weren't responding particularly well.

Colin and his brothers had each jumped to attack the first Felton shifter they encountered as they entered the clearing and were shredding their opponents.

Macy turned around in a slow circle, searching for her two targets.

There was one. Brady Felton, Vance's father. He was still in his human shape and had slowly turned around to face her.

With a screech that she recognized instinctively as her leopard's battle cry, Macy leaped for his throat.

Her human self whimpered in the back of her mind, but Macy batted down that conscience with a single thought, allowing her most vicious instincts to rise to the surface.

When Macy hit him, the elder Felton went down instantly, landing in the dirt next to the ruined satin runner that Macy had walked down so proudly just a few hours before. She landed atop him and sank her sharp fangs into his throat on either side of the jugular.

Hot blood flooded her mouth with the taste of iron, and she ripped the skin away with a single toss of her head. Blood spurted out, drenching her fur with its wet heat, and she roared her triumph to the sky, holding him down with all her weight as he writhed feebly, his motions slowing and finally stopping.

Now for Vance Felton.

But just as she stepped off Brady's body, a figure came flying from behind her, bowling her over and scrabbling at her with teeth and claws.

Vance Felton, in his leopard form.

And before she could gain her feet again, he had pinned her to the ground with a threatening hiss.

CHAPTER 8

Colin

From across the clearing, Colin saw one of the shifters from the Felton clan attack Macy. Several other Feltons in various stages of shifting stood between him and the one who had jumped Macy.

But it didn't matter. Colin let out a screech that drew his brothers' attention to him and then began racing toward Macy, dodging all potential opponents in his way, trusting his brothers to keep them from attacking from behind after he passed.

By the time he reached Macy and her opponent, they were locked in fierce combat, rolling in the dirt and clawing at each other.

Despite his urge to join the fray and save his mate, Colin forced himself to hang back long enough to choose his moment.

As soon as the Felton shifter once again landed atop Macy, attempting to pin her down long enough to deal a killing blow, Colin moved, coming in from the side to shove Macy's attacker off her.

Colin raised his paw, prepared to rip out the other shifter's throat with his claws, when a warning growl gave him pause.

Macy had stood, shaking the dirt out of her fur, and prowled across the intervening distance, the low, rumbling growl emanating from her throat letting Colin know he needed to stop what he was doing.

This must be one of the ones she wanted to kill herself, he realized.

Dipping his head in acknowledgment, he dropped his raised paw, using it to hold the Felton shifter on the ground.

Macy gave a happy chuff, the feline equivalent of laughter, and leaned in over the other shifter to peer into his eyes as if willing him to understand what was happening.

The Felton shifter began to thrash, but Colin was more muscular, stronger, and heavier, and the other shifter couldn't get away.

Then Gavin and Errol joined them and helped Colin hold the Felton shifter still.

Macy lifted her paw over the Felton shifter's face, claws extended. He turned his face away, but he had nowhere to go. At the last moment, he squeezed his eyes shut as Macy dug the claws of both front paws into the middle of his throat and then pulled them out in opposite directions, slicing him open.

Colin expected her to let the other shifter bleed out, but instead, she ripped into his belly, tearing his body open with a ferocity that Colin couldn't help but admire.

When it was done and the Felton shifter's body lay cooling in the night air, Macy stepped away and shifted into her human form. Colin and his brothers moved to encircle her, facing outward.

Once she was fully human again, Macy spoke aloud to all the Felton shifters who remained alive. "Your leaders are dead," she said flatly. "If you wish to stay and fight, you will die too." She glanced around at the few shifters still standing. "Or you can leave now. Go home to your families—what's left of them—and never again attempt to destroy another clan. All the leopard shifters in the world except for you are now under the protection of the Savage Valley leopard clan." She glanced down at Colin, who nodded in agreement, before continuing, "If we ever hear of another Felton attack, we will hunt you down, and nothing will save you or your clan. Make your decision now."

The remaining Felton clan shifters glanced at each other nervously and then began shuffling for the edges of the clearing, fighting off the last of Lorenzo's spell in their haste to retreat.

Macy stood in her circle of Savage Valley shifters, her chin held high, her naked body streaked with the blood of her enemies.

I've never seen anything so amazing, so beautiful, in my entire life, Colin thought.

Macy waited until they could no longer hear even a hint of the retreating Feltons.

And then she collapsed to the ground with a sob.

Colin carried Macy back to the alpha's cabin as his brothers and Lorenzo stayed behind to gather the bodies and arrange to transport them back to Savage Valley, ultimately using a pickup truck with the keys still in the ignition that had belonged to one of the dead or scattered shifters.

It took until late in the morning of the next day to erase all signs that anyone had even been at the campsite—much less died there in bloody battle.

In the meantime, Colin watched over Macy as she slept, determined not to leave her alone for a single moment, and Gavin oversaw other members of the stalker clan as they dug graves for the Martins and the Feltons alike.

When all was readied for a funeral service, Colin woke Macy. "My father, the Stalker clan alpha, is going to say a few words if it's okay with you," he murmured after she had showered and put on the jeans and T-shirt Nancy had thought to have retrieved from the cabin she had been staying at the campsite.

Macy nodded, her face drawn and pale. "I would like that."

Colin wanted more than anything to claim her as his own in front of his family, to pronounce to the entire world—or at least all of Savage Valley—that she was his mate.

He wanted to protect her from the pain he knew she was feeling. But now wasn't the right time.

Later, he promised himself. *When she is ready.*

"Then let's go bury your family," he said gently, taking her hand in his and drawing her toward their family cemetery.

CHAPTER 9

Macy

Macy stood dry-eyed over her family's graves, barely hearing the words Colin's father spoke as he gave a short eulogy about clan loyalty and family love and the value of retribution when one's clan was dishonored.

Then the Stalker clan alpha moved to Macy and embraced her. "You're welcome to stay with us as long as you like," he murmured.

"Thank you." She swallowed, uncertain what to say next. But she was saved from having to continue speaking by Nancy, who pressed a bouquet of autumn flowers into her hand. "For the graves."

Macy glanced down at the flowers, so similar to the ones she'd carried for what was supposed to have been her mating ceremony.

Her stomach hurt as she moved to drop flowers into each of the graves—even the Feltons', whose gravesites have been dug on the opposite side of the cemetery from her family members' graves.

They were loved by someone, too, she reasoned.

Then she stood over her parents' grave—she had requested that they be buried together, and now she watched as Colin's brothers began filling the hole that held her whole life, her whole world until now, with dirt.

Burying my past.

A sob escaped her throat, and Colin spun around, gathering her in his arms. "It's over now, sweetheart," he murmured, his breath ruffling her hair.

She nodded, a tear slipping out of the corner of her eye. "I know. But now, I don't know what to do next. Everything in me—my entire heart and soul—was focused on revenge.

Honestly, I didn't expect it to happen that fast."

"Come with me." Colin threaded his fingers through hers and led her away from the gravesite.

"Where are we going?" she asked, anxiety coiling in her gut.

"My cabin. You don't need to be alone tonight."

Macy didn't answer him, but another feeling began to intertwine with the grief, something akin to what she had felt when Colin had promised her earlier that he would have her back.

His cabin was small, a building that would be called a 'tiny home' in human culture. It had a galley kitchen opening to a living room and stairs that led to a loft bedroom. Everything was neat, carefully put away.

"I like it," Macy said as she glanced around. "It reminds me of a ship."

The cabin even had round porthole-style windows.

Colin grinned. "That's the idea." He gave her an odd, searching glance. "And I designed it so it could be expanded later if I needed more room."

A tiny thrill shivered through Macy's entire body, but she didn't respond.

Colin led her upstairs, where the room was almost entirely taken up with a king-size bed, leaving just enough space on either side for a small bedside table and a path to walk. Sliding doors led to a closet on one side and a tiny bathroom on the other.

Drawing Macy over to sit on the bed next to him, Colin reached up to wipe away the tears she hadn't even realized were still falling. "I lost my mother when I was fifteen," he began.

"Oh, no. I am so sorry."

"I told you that just so you'll know that I really do understand what you're going through. And I promise, your grief will lessen. It'll never go away, not entirely—but someday, maybe even sooner than you expect, you'll be able to remember your parents in the good times, in times other than this. And you'll always love them, so part of them will live on in you."

Macy dropped her face against his chest. "Thank you," she murmured. "I needed to hear that right now."

"I thought maybe you did." With one finger, he tilted her chin up, his gaze searching hers. Slowly, so slowly that she could pull away easily if she wanted to, he lowered his mouth to hers.

His lips were soft and gentle, as searching as his gaze had been. The scent of him surrounded her, holding her safe, just as his arms did.

Suddenly, though, it wasn't enough.

Macy twined her arms around his neck, grabbing the back of his head with her hands, threading her fingers through the short hair at the nape of his neck. She pulled him in closer, tighter, deepening their kiss.

Their tongues tangled, and Macy moaned deep in her throat.

With a strangled noise, she slid her mouth down to his chest, shivering at the feel of the hair on his chest.

He groaned deep in his throat and inhaled as if he couldn't get enough of the scent of her.

Just as I couldn't get enough of his scent, she realized.

She reveled in the feel of her mouth against his skin until he gently pulled her up to his mouth again, his tongue dancing with hers as his hands drew her shirt up over her head and tossed it on the floor. Then he pushed her back to lie on the bed and kissed his way down her torso, stopping to claim first one nipple and then the other with his mouth, his tongue teasing them into hard peaks, kneading each breast lightly even as he licked and sucked at it.

Macy moaned at the sensations sliding through her entire body.

By the time his mouth trailed down her stomach to the top of her jeans, Macy trembled all over. A hot throb of desire flashed through her, settling in her core, at the very deepest part of her.

With a deft motion, Colin unbuttoned her pants, sliding them down her hips and dropping them on the floor with her shirt.

Then he stood and stripped off his clothes, as well.

She had seen him naked before, watched him shift into his leopard form after removing his clothes. But now, she stared in awe, wanting to touch him all over, explore every part of him.

When he stretched out beside her, she trailed her fingertips from his shoulders down to his waist, then beyond. She slowly caressed the tip of his cock, running her hands over it and sliding her finger across the slight wetness there, circling the head.

His cock jumped as if it was all he could do to keep from spilling. When Macy leaned down and gave it a small kiss, he groaned and pulled her back up until he could kiss her again, his hands roaming up and down her back, his touch both strong and gentle.

"Please," she whispered, her desire finally making its way into words.

Colin paused, staring deep into her eyes. "I was going to wait," he said. "But you should know before we go any further...." He paused, seemingly at a loss for words.

"Tell me," she whispered, even though she was pretty sure she knew what he was going to say.

He inhaled deeply, as if nervous. "From the moment I saw you," he finally said, "I have known that you are my fated mate."

She laughed aloud, a sound of pure joy. "I thought you might say something like that."

"And?" He gave her a long, questioning look.

"And...I'm not sure how I know, but I think you're right."

With a smile that could have lit up the entire Valley, he pushed her back, his palms spreading her knees apart until he could taste her. With long, sure strokes, he licked and sucked her pussy until she writhed beneath him. The feel of his mouth against her left Macy wet and panting, aching for more.

"Please," she begged again.

He paused, hovering over her, holding her gaze.

"Say it again," he demanded. "Say we're mates." His voice was scratchy with need.

Images of him from the past two days flashed through Macy's mind. Colin saving her, caring for her, fighting with her.

"Colin," she breathed. "I don't know how I know, but I am certain that we're fated mates."

At Macy's words, Colin slid into her with a groan. Macy met his thrust, pushing until he touched that innermost part of her.

They moved together, spiraling toward ecstasy until first Macy and then Colin tumbled over the edge, crying out their joy and sealing their bond of words with their bodies.

Epilogue

Colin

One of the things that Colin had always loved best about winter in Savage Valley was his clan's run in the first snow of the season.

And this year, it would be better than ever because Macy would be with him.

Six weeks. That's how long they had been together. And it had been the best six weeks of his life.

She was still grieving, of course, and she would be for quite some time. But he hoped—believed, even—that being with him had alleviated some of the pain she felt.

As had the fact that, after she had reached out to the few remaining members of her family's clan, several of them had chosen to join her in Savage Valley.

And there had been no word from the Feltons. Lucky for them, since Colin fully intended to destroy anyone who dared cross his mate ever again.

Tonight, though, he was determined to focus on nothing but the joy of the run.

Macy stopped him inside the door of their now-shared cabin before they headed out to shift and take off coursing through the forest.

"Wait," she said, taking both his hands in hers. "I want to make sure you know just how much I love you. And no matter how hard it was to get to this point, I wouldn't change any of it, because it brought us together."

Colin frowned. "You're not planning on taking off in the middle of the night without telling me, are you? Because that sounded a lot like a goodbye speech."

Macy laughed aloud. "Absolutely not. I will never leave you." She stepped in close and planted a kiss on his mouth.

"It would destroy me if you left. I can't imagine my life without you in it."

"Perfect," Macy said. "I don't plan to leave Savage Valley. Not ever. Now, let's go meet the others. I'm ready for this fabled snow-run you keep going on about."

They stepped outside and shifted, and then hit the woods running. The nighttime wind blew through Colin's fur, bringing with it the scent of his mate. The yips and yowls coming from the forest around him drew his attention, along with the snow sparkling in the moonlight.

Then his mate pounced on him from behind, yipping playfully and bowling him over into the snow, and the two of them joined their clan for the first truly wild run of the winter.

The End.

Enjoy this novella? Be sure to leave a review for the set!

Want to read the first full-length book in the series? Preorder today! Look for details in Also by Margo.

ABOUT THE AUTHOR

USA Today, *Wall Street Journal*, and *New York Times* bestselling author Margo Bond Collins is a former college English professor who, tired of explaining the difference between "hanged" and "hung," turned to writing romance novels instead. (Sometimes, her heroines kill monsters, too.)

Want to hang out with the author, win book prizes, see the cool covers first, and support Margo's books on social media? Join The
Vampirarchy, Margo's street team on Facebook!

Join Margo Online

www.MargoBondCollins.net

Bookbub

Facebook

Twitter

Instagram

ALSO BY MARGO BOND COLLINS

www.MargoBondCollins.net

Urban Fantasy and Paranormal Romance

Midlife Monsters Series

Lindi Parker, Shifter Shield Series

Ilsa Deverell, Midnight Assassin Series

Tessa Fury, Accidental Bounty Hunter

Savage Valley Shifters Rejected Mates

Science Fiction Romance

Khanavai Warriors Alien Bride Games Series

Interstellar Shifters Series

Galactic Gladiator Games Series (cowritten with Sasha Caine)

Preorder Unbroken today!

A Rejected Mate Wolf Shifter Romance: A Savage Valley Shifters Novel

Welcome to Savage Valley. Your hell away from home.

As much as wolf shifter Roxie Rose hates the idea of an arranged marriage with Leopold, the alpha of the country's strongest pack, she's willing to do whatever it takes to secure her pack's place in the North American hierarchy.

During their mating ceremony, though, Leopold offers only brutal rejection, announcing his desire to offer his new mate to the Luna Goddess to secure his own pack's rank.

Now Roxie's pack must choose between protecting her honor by declaring a blood feud or saving themselves by allowing Leopold to sacrifice her.

Roxie, however, has a plan of her own.

In the shadow of the Dark Moon, she flees to Savage Valley, home to the world's most dangerous shifters, where she hopes to find sanctuary among the feral monsters all other shifters fear.

But Savage Valley is every bit as ruthless as the world she fled, and this time, there may not be any escaping the alphas who claim her.

Can Roxie remain forever Unbroken?

Enter the world of the Savage Valley Shifters. Fans of G. Bailey, G.K. DeRosa, Jen L. Grey, Kelly St. Claire, Annette Marie, Shannon Mayer, Leia Stone, Jaymin Eve, and Linsey Hall will adore this dark, rejected mate paranormal romance.

Preorder Unbroken today!

DRAGON AWAKENED

BESTSELLING AUTHOR
MARIA VICKERS

BLURB

Aarik had everything taken from him. His home, his life, his parents...

Dragons were worshipped as gods, but jealousy burns brightly, and the other gods force the dragons to earth, forever banished from the home they loved. Aarik must
lead the few dragons who remain, but how? He isn't ready, and he doesn't know if he can trust the alluring Sevina.

Sevina feels guilty, and she will do anything she can to right the wrong done to the dragons she has always loved. Especially Aarik. If she could, she would take his pain for him.

Both will need to open their hearts and their minds if they want to survive and forge a new path together, but that might be too much to ask.

CHAPTER 1

Aarik

It wasn't supposed to be this way. They were gods, ruling both heaven and earth with the other gods. But even gods succumbed to the beast known as jealousy.

Aarik looked around him. Dust hovered in the air, and they were surrounded on all sides by a large mountain range. It was either that or when they were kicked out of heaven, they created a crater so deep that the mountains were formed. Bodies surrounded him, some moaning while others lay still, and the only sign they lived was their blinking eyes.

"What happened? Why do we look like this?" Eamon, his brother, asked.

Shaking his head, Aarik scanned the area again. Only ten of them had survived the battle. "I don't know." He tried to get up on shaky legs and fell. They were dragons. Great beings of magic and might who were worshipped by everyone, and they had been banished. One minute, they were feasting, celebrating the birth of a new star, and the next, they were being driven out of their home, forced to flee. They fought, burning what they could, slashing anyone who came near them, but soon, they were overpowered and backed to the very edge of heaven. A hundred against thousands...they lost.

A drop fell on his head, followed by another, pulling him out of his dark thoughts.

"The other gods may have been jealous, but heaven itself weeps for us," Ossenia declared. Aarik's sister had always believed that heaven was as much alive as the gods who inhabited it. She was wrong, though. If it lived and breathed and wept for them, why didn't it save them the humiliation and pain of being banished?

They were mighty dragons! Yet now, they sat in a hole on earth as humans.

"You may look human, but I can promise, you are anything but human, Aarik, son of Honrue, leader of the dragons. Put these on."

Aarik swiftly got to his feet and stumbled, but he refused to fall again. A large pack appeared at his feet, and he kicked it, ready for something, anything, to happen. He would protect his remaining clan.

"Tis nothing but garments. The rain is coming. It will make the air colder."

"Who are you?" Aarik bellowed.

"You do not need to fear me," the voice called out again.

He scanned the area, searching all around him for the person who dared address him, a god. Ulrik, the youngest of his clan, opened the pack before Aarik could stop him, and inside were various garments. "Ulrik, don't." The youngling didn't heed his warning, though, and had pulled on a pair of breeches that covered his bottom half. "Ulrik," he groaned. The young one had always been precocious and too trusting, and it had gotten him into more trouble than Aarik ever wanted to think about.

"I promise, they are nothing more than something to clothe yourself with," the voice called out.

Brown wool hit him in the face, and releasing a frustrated sigh, he reluctantly put them on. "Where are you?" Aarik hated feeling like someone had the upper hand, and after what they had just experienced, he was not too keen on someone speaking to him from the shadows.

"Up here." The feminine voice had a teasing lilt to it. "Or maybe here."

Suddenly, a woman covered from head to toe in a heavy woolen cloak that had been dyed a deep purple appeared in front of him, startling Aarik. He curled his fingers in as if they were claws, ready to swipe at her. He would protect his people, even if he had to die doing it.

"Peace, Aarik. I am not here to harm you."

"And why are you here?" Drawing his hand back, he waited, and if her answer displeased him, he would rip her apart. He may not have his claws any longer, but he would find a way.

"To help. I am Sevina."

"So, you can help us return home?" Ossenia asked excitedly.

Sevina's expression made her look as if she was about to weep, and she dropped her head. "I am sorry, but that can never happen. You are forever forbidden from entering heaven again."

"Why would that be?" Aarik couldn't get a read on her. He had always been able to look into the heart of man and woman and see the truth. No one could keep a secret from him, but she was different.

"If you would allow, I could take you to a place that is warmer and much dryer."

"We go nowhere with you until you tell us who you are and what you mean!"

"Brother—" Eamon began but held his tongue when Aarik glared at him.

His father gone, his mother destroyed, most of his kind disappearing forever into the nether realm... The battle lasted mere minutes, but they should have been strong enough to hold everyone back. They had power, size, and might. How had they been overwhelmed so quickly? It did not make sense. And now this woman appeared in front of him. Aarik would not allow the rest of his clan to be destroyed. He would protect them, and if it meant standing in the cold rain, he would do it.

Turning back to the woman in front of him, he narrowed his eyes, still trying to read her, and found nothing. It wasn't that she had nothing. It was more that the power he had before, the gifts he possessed were gone. "Speak, but I warn you, I have no qualms about killing a human woman."

She smirked but dipped her head. "My temple and people have always worshipped dragons. We've called on their power enough, and they have protected us. We aren't the only ones. All throughout the land, dragons have been revered for their abilities and their power. The gods became jealous. Some here on this plane wanted to capture a dragon and do what they must to gain their abilities for themselves. My brother, Keldar, was one of those people. Unlike others, he had the ability to do what he wanted. He was the bastard child of a goddess and a high priest. Once born, the child was given to my father to raise. However, he has yet to capture a dragon. He has done something else, though."

"Are you not the same?"

Shaking her head, she released a deep sigh. "I am not. After Keldar was born, my father married another in the coven and had me. But because my father found favor with the goddess, she enhanced my powers while I was still in the womb. My gifts and abilities could never reach the level my brother has achieved."

"Continue," Aarik ordered. Something about this woman beckoned to him, something about her words that had him believing her, but he could not allow himself to be swayed.

"Dragons have been guardians and gods of the heavens for as long as light has existed. Few gods could claim they have been around longer. Most were born after your creation. People have worshipped you since the beginning, but more and more have become dependent on you and your favors over any other god. Temples and shrines of lesser gods were demolished because they were no longer favored amongst the people. Dragons, though, were different. You fought for us, protected us, and even though you couldn't answer all of our prayers, we felt safe because we knew you were out there. Unlike the other gods."

"How did we not know about that?" Hend, one of Aarik's clan, asked, confused.

"Honrue protected many of you from what was happening," Sevina responded and swallowed hard. "The gods were jealous. With each person who called out to a dragon, the envy and hatred grew. Your fires became more powerful, and the gods wanted to put an end to you. Keldar hated the dragons even though our coven had a pact with Honrue. Maybe it was not hate but jealousy like the others. When his mother called upon him to assist the gods, he eagerly followed. If there were no dragons, he could claim he was greater than them. His magic is like nothing I have ever seen before. He found a way to prevent you from ever returning. The taller mountains behind you are pieces of heaven that were broken off when you were banished. They merged with the earth. You were stripped of your godhood, but that does not mean you are not dragons."

"What do you mean?" Aarik was trying to wrap his mind around everything she said, but the betrayal stung, and it was hard to understand when and how everything had fallen apart.

"As soon as I discovered my brother's duplicity, I crafted my own spell. I could not save you from your fate, for I am not powerful enough to defeat my brother and the gods, but you can still transform into your beast form."

"Still transform?" Ossenia scoffed.

Sevina lifted her chin and declared, "I happen to know your father transformed into a human and walked amongst the people many times over the course of his life."

"That is true, but not many know," Aarik said cautiously. "How do you?"

She appeared anxious as she shifted from foot to foot and clasped her hands together, catching a handful of her cloak, her finger turning white from the pressure. "I..." She cleared her throat and licked her lips. "He was my teacher for a time."

"Did you perchance fancy yourself in love with him?" Aarik laughed, but he did not relax his stance. He was prepared for anything.

"No!" Her denial came too quickly, and her cheeks reddened.

"I can smell your lie." He took a step closer and growled, "My father would never have lowered himself to sleep with a mere human. He loved my mother, and unlike other gods, he was faithful."

"I know," Sevina stated simply and lowered her gaze, suddenly finding interest in the mud on the ground. The rain began to fall faster and harder. "May we move this to another location? I can tend to the wounded and—"

"Can you bring back our dead?" Hend demanded.

Aarik did not know if he heard her sniffle and weep or if it was the wind. "No one can bring back the dead. Not even the gods who thought themselves all-powerful."

She shook her head slowly, never raising her head. "I am sorry. I cannot. I wish that I could."

Looking around, the remaining dragons surrounded him, creating a semi-circle around her. If she tried to leave, they would stop her. Or they would try. Given she appeared out of thin air in front of him, he was not sure they could. "Why should we believe you?"

"You have no reason to believe me, but I offer this." She held out a red cloth that was wrapped around something.

Hesitantly, Aarik took it and opened the wrapping, sucking in a sharp breath when he revealed the contents. Wrapped in the finest cloth, trimmed with gold, sat his father's dagger. The one he said he'd given to someone special. At the time, Aarik thought it was a servant or another god who found favor with the dragon.

To find out that it was this woman set him on edge, and he didn't know why.

"Your father said if something should happen, I was to do what I could and meet you here. I believe he knew the other gods were getting restless. To know exactly where I should attend you, though, was a surprise."

"He had the gift of foresight," Ossenia mumbled as she reached a finger out and touched the dagger's hilt.

Aarik stared at it. While not needed in dragon form, he remembered his father carrying it with him on the rare occasions he transformed into a human. His father, Honrue, believed that the gods were the servants of the people, created to help them. Yes, they were above the humans and could do what they wanted, but the humans were more than their toys. They had expectations, and it was up to the gods to help if possible—a rare idea amongst the holy beings who inhabited the realm above. To most, humans were there for enjoyment, and if the human pleased the god or goddess, they might receive a small heavenly token that would fade quickly enough. It was a vicious cycle for the humans. Pray, make offerings, plead, get favor or nothing, and repeat over and over again. It was no wonder some gods were losing favor with the humans.

Honrue had taken Aarik down to the earthly plane many times, saying it was part of his son's education. There, they spoke to humans, ate with them, and pretended to be something they were not. The joke was on his father because now they were human, banished forever for merely existing.

"I am unable to change your fate, but I was able to alter some of my brother's...intent," Sevina said.

"What do you mean by that?"

"Keldar fully intended for you to become human. He would then seek you out and kill all of you. His mother did not want any dragon to survive."

Aarik needed to know. She had spoken of the goddess but had yet to give them a name. Who was the goddess who wished harm to his clan? "Who is his mother?"

She shifted again and took a small step backward. "The goddess, Ane."

This couldn't be. Aarik felt lightheaded and pinched the bridge of his nose.

"Lies!" Hend seethed.

"And yet, look at what has happened? We were attacked by the very gods we once lived in harmony with. We were sent to cower on a small piece of heaven, and that was severed along with our powers. Look around you, Hend. Heaven and earth have melded together to become one," Aarik snapped and pointed behind him. He didn't want to believe it, but it all made sense. Lesser gods wouldn't have been able to go after his family, but a powerful one, one with a demigod for a son, had been able to devastate them.

"She wouldn't!"

Bowing his head, Aarik squeezed his eyes shut. The betrayal was sharp and made him feel as if his blood spilled out of him, the flow unable to be stopped. Ane was his mother's half-sister. When Cellie's mother disappeared, her father found someone else to occupy his bed, not that most gods and goddesses practiced monogamy, and Ane was conceived as well as several others. Altogether, there were fifteen princes and princesses. His mother was married off to the dragons so that her father would have more favor with both heaven and earth. No one expected the eldest princess to find love with the dragon.

CHAPTER 2

Sevina

He didn't remember her. Sevina wasn't sure why she thought he might, but her hopes were dashed when he looked as if he might rip her heart out instead of embracing an old friend. When she was a child, Honrue brought Aarik to the temple where her coven met. They played and fought, and she even gave him a black eye. Quite by accident, of course. Was it her fault his face got too close to her elbow when he tried to take her fruit?

Aarik's father knew something was coming, something bad, but she did not believe even he could have foreseen this. When she was eleven summers, Aarik stopped coming with his father, and she never understood why. Sevina later found out that he was sent to court to learn the ways of the upper echelon of the gods. The dragons belonged there, but they preferred their own parcel of heaven to playing politics or bowing to others. It was probably another reason they were so hated.

Honrue soon stopped coming down to teach her, yet he surprised her with a visit a year ago. He gave her the dagger and told her to keep it safe, that she would need it one day soon. Things were shifting in heaven, and he wanted to make sure his clan was safe. Looking at the handful of dragons, she inwardly wept. There had once been so many, and now there were so few—ten, including Aarik.

Her brother did this and stripped them of their heavenly gifts, but she had made sure they were not all human. Not as powerful and lacking in many aspects, she did what she could and would have done more if she had the ability.

"I am unable to change your fate, but I was able to alter some of my brother's...intent," she said.

Aarik's head snapped up, and he glared at her. "What do you mean by that?"

"Keldar fully intended for you to become human. He would then seek you out and kill all of you. His mother did not want any dragon to survive."

"Who is his mother?"

She swallowed hard, her mouth parched. "The goddess, Ane."

A sharp intake of breath could be heard over the patter of rain. "Lies!" Hend snapped.

"And yet, look at what has happened? We were attacked by the very gods we once lived in harmony with. We were sent to cower on a small piece of heaven, and that was severed along with our powers. Look around you, Hend. Heaven and earth have melded together to become one," Aarik snapped and pointed to the tallest mountain behind him.

"She wouldn't!"

Aarik bowed his head, his body shaking. "She has! You think she is righteous and good, but you have never seen how she manipulates people, the way she uses them to get what she wants. Even her father has become nothing more than a figurehead. She—"

"Lies! You spout nothing but lies! I was to—"

"The betrothal? Hend, open your eyes. If Ane gave her blessing, why are we here?" Ossenia argued.

Nodding, Eamon ran his hand down his face, looking frustrated and angry. "Yes, and then within the hour, our clan was attacked." He swayed and bent forward, placing his hands on his knees as he sucked in deep breaths of air. "We were betrayed by our own."

"No, not our own. If they were, they would not have turned on us the way they did," Aarik stated. He lifted his gaze and met Sevina's. "We will come with you."

"Aarik—"

"Hend, you need to decide your own future. You cannot get back into heaven, but you can come with us, and together, we can seek revenge on those who have wronged us, or you can move into the future alone. But know, if you choose to move on without us, you are always welcome in my home."

Hend glared at Sevina, the fire in his eyes menacing and full of blame. "You did this! And I will rip you—"

"Enough!" Aarik shouted, and he whirled around to catch Hend before the other man could touch Sevina. Only, it wasn't a hand that held his friend back. It was a claw. "What?"

"Tis as I said. You are not fully human, and you have not lost all of your abilities."

He turned to Hend again. "Come with us. She can help us."

"Or bespell you." Hend spat at the ground at Sevina's feet before running toward the closest mountain.

Everyone watched until he disappeared.

Slowly, Aarik turned and faced Sevina again. She could see the hesitation and the fact he didn't trust her on his face, but she also saw the resignation that he had no other choice. "If you betray us in any way, my father's dagger will find its way into your heart." He pointed it at her, his hand once again that of a human.

"I understand." She swallowed hard. The threat was real, and the blade was sharp.

"Is there anyone else who wishes to leave us and follow Hend?" He spun in a circle, meeting each of his people's gazes. All shook their heads. Once again, he faced her. "We will follow you if for nothing else than to learn why my hand transformed, what we are now without our godly mantle."

Sevina almost sagged with relief. She could never right the wrongs of her brother, but she would do what she could for the dragons.

Throwing her cape behind her shoulders, she lifted her arms, showing off runes and markings that had been inked into her skin. They almost glowed with the power they harnessed for her. The wind carried her whispered words, and as she spread her hands out to her sides, a loud rumbling shook the ground where they stood. Next, a blinding light surrounded them, and when it disappeared, and they could see again, they stood in the middle of a great stone room that was covered with dust.

"Where have you brought us?" Aarik demanded.

"A nearby temple that is no longer used," Sevina answered, lifting her chin, daring them to argue with her. It was the safest place they could be...from her people and the gods. Shortly after it had been built, it was abandoned. According to stories, it angered the god it was built for—an old dragon. When everyone had fled, the dragon placed a powerful curse on it, keeping everyone out, sheltering it from anyone or anything that may try to find it.

"Is it safe?" Aarik asked as he walked around the large room. It was full of dirt and cobwebs, and his face showed his disgust. The dragon prince had known the finest things in life while he was a god, but that was no longer the case. He would have to adapt. Could he? Could the others? Sevina wasn't so sure, but they did not have much of a choice.

"Very. It was built for your grandfather but never used."

"Why not?" Ulrik asked.

Sevina sighed and bit her lip. Everything was a mess, and what she said next would make her sound as if she was mad.

"According to Honrue, your grandfather wanted a place where his clan would be safe when the need arose. He chased everyone out of the temple, erecting a large barrier. If someone tried to find it, they never would. Many disappeared, never to return. Those stories fed the legend, and soon people were terrified to try and locate the secret dragon temple. Many have forgotten that it exists or think it only a legend."

"Our grandfather?" Ossenia questioned.

Nodding, Sevina looked around her. "Yes. His name is inscribed on the wall." She pointed toward the wall on her left.

"Explain," Aarik said, his arms crossed over his chest. She swallowed hard at the sight. He was stunning to look at. His chest was on display, and the tanned muscles that had a few scars also showed his strength. He'd battled lesser gods when they tried to usurp the power of the highest, and he'd punished humans who tried to destroy his followers. He was not some weakling, and his prowess had been talked about by many.

"I can share what I know, but that is all. Many moons ago, before even my father cried out on this earth, this temple was constructed for your grandfather. It used to be in the valley where you landed, but when the land was raised with your entrance, the temple was as well. Your grandfather, upon seeing it, knew this place would serve a different purpose and made sure no one used it or knew of its existence. He put a barrier over it to ensure no one could find it or come upon it by chance. I cannot tell you why he did this or what he saw; I only know that it has remained abandoned and protected. I have been told that not even the gods above can see this temple."

"The gods can see everything. Who told you otherwise?" Aarik demanded.

"Your father." Sevina waited for a reaction, someone to lash out, but there was nothing. Not even the sound of their breathing could be heard, and their faces were devoid of all expression.

Several long moments later, Aarik blinked and tilted his head to the side, studying her. "What exactly did he say?"

"Your grandfather had power that no other god possessed. He could have ruled over everyone if he had wanted, but he chose not to do that. He chose to live in peace and help those below. Many worshipped him and asked for his help. He destroyed many armies and decimated whole kingdoms. It was said that the Creator gifted his own powers to your grandfather, or that your grandfather was the Creator himself."

"Yes, there are many stories about him," Aarik hesitantly said, his eyes narrowed.

"This temple was his. I did not know of its existence until your father told me about it."

"How is it you are able to travel here, you were able to find it, if no one else can?"

She swallowed hard and reached into the sash tied around her waist. "A gift from your father. He said I would need it to find my way here and to help you." Releasing a breath, she pulled out a large black scale. A dragon scale.

Aarik moved quickly and grabbed her arm, squeezing it. "Where did you get this, human?"

"I do not lie. It was given to me by your father, Honrue." She bit her lip and refused to cry out. This man and his followers had their whole world upended. They lost their home, their loved ones...everything. And now, she was sharing a tale that was hard to believe. If she were them, she would have a hard time accepting it as well. "He..." Pausing, she sucked in a breath and swallowed hard. "He told me to tell you *veritas*. He said you would understand."

Aarik released her quickly and backed away, the suddenness of his actions making her fall to the dirt-covered floor. "Forgive me." He reached down and pulled her to her feet, and she gasped when his hand wrapped around hers. It was like fire and ice at the same time, and it sent her pulse racing.

Stepping away from him, she tried to release him, but he held tight, forcing her to yank her hand back, which had her stumbling slightly. Thankfully, she maintained her dignity and remained on her feet this time. "You understand?" Sevina was a little surprised because she had been skeptical when Honrue had told her to use it to gain Aarik's trust. One simple word and he believed her? Was it truly that easy?

"I do." Aarik nodded.

Ossenia placed her hand on her brother's shoulder. "Our father told us only an ally would know the word. We will trust you."

"But—" Eamon tried to interject, but Aarik cut him off.

"Enough! Ossenia speaks the truth. We will listen to what you have to say, but be aware, if you try to cross us, I will kill you with my bare hands. My grandfather and father were not the only ones with a reputation."

"I am fully aware of your reputation," Sevina stated before she spun on her heel and walked toward the innermost wall. Pressing a hidden panel, the stone slid open and revealed another chamber. She stepped into the doorway and called, "Come. I have everything you will need to begin your new life."

"Tell us what you meant about not being fully human," Ulrik questioned, standing the furthest away from her.

Nodding, she sighed. She was weary and felt as if several bags of sand sat on her shoulders. Why hadn't Honrue prepared his people for this? He had known what the future held, yet they had known nothing of what was coming for them. They had not known how jealous and vindictive the other gods truly were. They were banished for no other reason than existing and doing what the people wanted. "Come. I have food and drink. I will tell all."

CHAPTER 3

Aarik

There was something about this Sevina that pulled at him. Something familiar. But how could that be? Before today, he had never seen her before. He was certain of that. Wasn't he?

The moment she spoke that word, one simple word that meant truth, he knew his father had sent her to them. Her. A female. A woman. Not a warrior. This was a battle between the dragons and the whole of heaven, but his father had sent a female to assist them. Why her? Why had this happened to them? The gods had always been petty and vain, but to take it this far did not make sense to him.

Glancing around the room, his gaze finally settled on her once again. She looked uncertain, scared, tired, and a little hurt. Was it because of his distrust of her? That had to be expected since she was a complete stranger to him. That niggle of something pulled at him again. What was it about her?

"Why must we go in there? Why not here?" Eamon questioned. Aarik could see the distrust still present in his brother's eyes, and he did not blame him. They had trusted others in heaven and were betrayed. No one came to help. They battled on their own and lost too many that they mourned.

"This room was intended for storage. Maybe a treasury. There is no air, and soon it will feel stifling. If you follow me, I will lead you to a room where we can be comfortable and breathe."

Ossenia tilted her head, her brow furrowing. "Why bring us to this room then?"

Sevina signed and appeared defeated. "I was not sure how many dragons would be here. I needed a large open space. This was the best solution. It is at the heart of the temple and can easily fit two hundred men."

The pang of loss hit Aarik in the chest. If only he could have done more, fought harder. Swallowing past the lump in his throat, he nodded. "It could. Lead us to the other room. We will follow."

"This way," she said and stepped into the darkened chamber on the other side of the door.

Before he stepped across the threshold, the space lit up with the fire of torches on the wall. It was a smaller chamber, about half the size, but it had slits for windows, and a cool breeze flowed through, bringing in fresh air. Tables lined one side of the room, laden with food and drink. On the other, blankets and pillows were lined up and piled to the ceiling, waiting for anyone to use them. Against the far wall, where another door could be seen, was a multitude of tall clay jars. Most of the room was taken up with various items. "How long have you been preparing? Why not use the other room for storage?"

He shifted his gaze to the makeshift windows. The sky was dark, and the slits let in what little light there was, so the flames made the room glow and come alive. There was something about the shape of the window, an arrow pointing up. It was almost as if he had been here before, but that was not possible. He had hardly ever left heaven except...

Aarik gasped and spun to stare at her. "The girl! My father met with a priest, and there was a girl. You were her." It was her eyes. When he was a child, he remembered playing with another whose eyes were the color of storm clouds. She had changed much since the imp he knew. Her lips were full and her eyes, once so full of merriment, held pain and sorrow. She was taller, too. "You have changed."

"As have you. We have both reached adulthood. It happens to all living things." She quirked a brow and bit her bottom lip.

"That it does," he smirked.

"This is her? I thought you said her name was Serpent or something."

Shrugging, he released a long breath. Aarik did not know if he could trust her, but knowing they had met before, eased him some because he could remember one incident very well. A little boy was picking on another, and Aarik was amused watching the two. One was a bully, and the other needed to get stronger. Back then, he didn't like meddling in the affairs of man, or in that case, children. Sevina pushed him to the side and then jumped into the middle of the fray, pummeling the bully, who then got a stern lecture by someone half his size. Aarik had been impressed. She fought for those who needed help and could not fight for themselves. Or at least she had as a child. Did it still hold true today? "'Twas a brief encounter."

"Serpent? You told them I was a snake?" Her cheeks glowed a fiery red.

"I do not remember what I told them. It was a long time ago."

"Yes, twenty summers."

Shaking her head, Ossenia rolled her eyes. "Ignore him. He only remembers his name because our father and mother..." she paused and swallowed before continuing, "were always yelling at him."

Aarik approached his sister and pulled her into his arms. Now was not the time for tears. The sorrow could wait until they got their bearings and knew what their future held. "Sevina, tell us what you meant earlier." If he could distract his sister, he hoped the tears would stop. He could feel his own eyes burning, and until he got his revenge, he would not allow a single tear to fall.

"You have told us that we can still transform, but how? Tell us about your brother as well."

Her head dropped, and she stared at her feet. Even when she offered them all food and drink, she did not lift her gaze. When everyone was settled, she began to speak, "Keldar was a troublesome child. He liked to attack others or torture them. My father would either turn a blind eye to it, or he would talk to Keldar. The talks never worked. Father kept Honrue's identity a secret from him. I think he was afraid of what Keldar would do since his hatred for the dragons began at an early age. None of us understood why until Ane called for him. She had been visiting him, teaching him, filling his heart with hatred and lies. When she demanded his service, he willingly went. I do not know what he did or how, but it gave the gods an edge and banished you. You are no longer gods and can no longer return to your home in the skies. I could not reverse what he did, but I was able to protect you some. Your dragons are still alive and well within you. You can do almost anything you could as a god. However, you are no longer invincible. You can die and be injured. If it is not grave, a wound could be healed by shifting. You also cannot bestow any favors amongst the humans. All of your power is now centered upon you. You cannot share it. Heaven is on another plane, and you will never be able to reach it again. This is now your home."

She never looked up, never moved from where she stood in the middle of the room. This bothered Aarik. He remembered a vibrancy and raw power within her. She fought the challenges head-on. He didn't like seeing her like this.

"So, it is done," Ossenia said softly.

"I am sorry," Sevina whispered, her voice catching.

Eamon stood abruptly, his wine goblet falling to the ground, spilling its red contents on the floor. "That's it? How do we seek retribution for the things they have done? We are supposed to accept our fate and bow down to them? They took our home! Our clan! Our parents! Ane murdered her own sister to cut out the threat our clan posed. We supported them, but because they hated how people worshipped us, they sought to destroy us!"

"No, we bow to no one," Aarik growled. "We are worshipped and revered. Not them. We may be forced to live amongst the humans, but that does not mean we are meek and will subjugate ourselves. They are too proud and will believe they have brought us to our knees. When they come here, and they will, we will prove to them why we were the mightiest in the heavens."

CHAPTER 4

Aarik

A week flowed slower on earth than it did in heaven. At least that was the way it felt. Aarik's clan drank, ate, and mourned the loss of their people and their home. None had attempted to shift, not even him. There was fear and pain. What if they couldn't shift? What if their dragons were forever dormant because the spell did not work, or Sevina wasn't as powerful as she thought she was. Aarik would admit that she had abilities, but until one of them attempted to shift, they would not know how successful Sevina's countermeasures were.

Standing on a balcony of the large temple, Aarik looked around him. In the middle of the valley, surrounded by mountains, water had begun to fill the crater where they had landed on their descent. Soon, it would resemble a lake instead of a hole in the ground. The rain had been non-stop since they were banished, and he thought maybe heaven itself cried for them.

Did he dare risk disappointment and transform? What if he could not shift? What if he failed?

What if he succeeded?

"Are you well?" Sevina appeared at his right, her cloak wrapped closely around her shoulders. The first time she shirked the bulky garment that kept her warm, Aarik sucked in a silent breath. Her dress clung to her curves, accentuating everything. He had to keep reminding himself not to stare, which he failed at many times.

Sevina was beautiful. Her ivory skin looked as if it almost glowed, and her long black hair held a hint of a wave. He wanted to wrap his hand in the strands and pull her to him.

"What are you thinking about, Aarik?"

He shook his head and stared at the horizon. "Tis nothing."

"You have been out here since dawn. It is midday now."

Smiling, he chuckled. "It is." Whenever she was near, his blood boiled, and lightning hit him. It was wrong. She was there to help them, and he wasn't completely certain he could trust her.

"When I met you as a young girl, I thought you a fool. How could you allow one person to attack another?"

"It is the way of humans."

She nodded. "It is. Yet sometimes, we all need to know someone will be there to help us when we need it. We need to know that we are not alone. The gods were wrong to do what they did, and I wish I could return to you everything that was lost."

"You did your best."

"If so, why do you not shift?"

Why indeed? He was terrified it did not work. "Perhaps, I wanted to mourn with my people." It was an excuse and sounded hollow to his own ears.

"It has been seven moons. Do you not want to feel the wind under your wings again?"

"How do you know I have wings? Not all do."

"I was with an envoy that was attacked two summers prior. You arrived and saved us. You were only there a moment before you took to the air again. Your scales reminded me of snow, and when the sun shone down upon you, there were many more colors to be seen."

Aarik remembered the event. She said envoy, but there were several women who had been captured and forcibly taken. One of the priests his father served prayed for help and offered both food and gold. At the time, he thought it was merely a distraction, but now, he was relieved he had stepped in to save them all. "Envoy," he snorted derisively.

She hummed but remained silent beside him.

Closing his eyes, he focused on the way it felt to glide through the sky, the way the fire burned within him, ready to be released, and how his scales felt so natural. His dragon was a part of him.

He inhaled deeply, searching for the fire and the sleeping giant. He could see him, feel him. When he heard a gasp from Sevina, he opened his eyes and looked down at her, way down. He was no longer human. He was a dragon. The magic had worked.

With wings spread wide, he stepped off the large open balcony and took flight. It had been only a week, and he had missed this. Missed the way it felt to soar high above. Missed how freeing it was. This was where he belonged.

CHAPTER 5

Sevina

Sevina had begun to wonder if she would ever see Aarik's dragon again. He had been majestic and beautiful when he swooped in to save her.

It had been her own fault that she had been taken. Her father warned her to stay in the temple that day, but she did not heed his warning because people needed her. Returning to the temple after tending to a sick woman who had birthed her first child days before, someone grabbed her from behind and covered her mouth. Before she knew it, she was bound and gagged and thrown into the back of a wagon with three other girls.

A commotion had her peeking through a hole in the material covering the wagon, hiding her and the others. There, she saw him. Something told her it was the boy she had played with who had become a man through the years, and when he shifted to untie her, she knew it was. She kept her head down and her hair covering her face, too embarrassed to speak up. She only nodded when he asked if she could steer the wagon.

And now, he stood next to her in his glorious dragon form. He was tall, dwarfing her and making her appear as a speck on the balcony. His mass took up most of the space, and she gasped when she almost fell attempting to move out of his way. Her breath caught, and her heart stopped when he plunged over the edge, but she should not have feared for him because he took flight and lifted higher and higher into the sky, the rain no match for him.

He was truly beautiful and something to behold.

And the rain stopped.

"It worked?" Eamon asked, a smile on his face.

"It did." She was too scared to admit it, but she worried that they could not transform and that she had failed them. It had worked. Her spell had worked, and she released the breath she had been holding.

"My turn," Eamon announced, and before long, a giant black dragon was taking to the air.

"Me too," Ossenia said, glee in her voice.

One by one, the dragons transformed and took to the air. Like Aarik, Ossenia was almost white, but where Aarik almost glowed with various colors in the sun, Ossenia had shades of light gray like a cloud. There was only one wingless dragon. Ulrik's long serpent body danced in the air like a leaf picked up by the wind.

Sevina fell to her knees, tears streaming down her face. She had done it. The dragons lived.

CHAPTER 6

Sevina

Shoving her spare cloak into a satchel, Sevina closed it and squeezed her eyes closed, forcing the tears away. The dragons were thriving. Every day they took to the air, flying further than the day before. They didn't need her any longer, and it was time she returned to the temple. Her father was probably worried about her. She had left by the light of the moon, leaving only a note behind informing her father that she would return one day. No one could know of her true purpose because she didn't know who she could trust. Her father was weak, and Keldar was too strong for her to risk exposing Aarik and the others.

"Do you leave us?" a voice asked behind her.

Sevina whirled around and clutched her chest. "Aarik!" she whispered, although she didn't know if she was relieved or not. Over the past month, she watched him with his people and as a dragon. And every day, her feelings for him grew. She could no longer stay here. Soon, it would hurt too much to be beside him.

She wasn't daft. She had noticed one of the females who had landed with him trying to push her out of the way, attempting to be beside Aarik day and night. Sevina was a mere mortal. Aarik was a god—or former god—and it was his turn to rule over the dragons like his father and grandfather before him.

"Where are you going?" He stared at her pack and then the heavy cloak she wore. The nights were chilly, and she would need it to stave off the cold air in the valley. She could transverse great distances, moving large groups if need be, but she had never mastered long-distance travel. She could move short distances, but if she did it too often, it wore her out. Her journey home would take at least two days. If only she had learned how to focus her energy for greater distances. If only she had the ability when she had been kidnapped, maybe then, her fascination with Aarik would have never begun. No, that wasn't true. He intrigued her as a child, too.

"Home. My duty to you is finished. I must return to my own people. You will fare well without me. This temple is your home and will always be protected. If you do not want to remain, go out into the world. I believe it could still use the dragons to save it."

"What do you mean?" He stepped toward her, lifting his hand, only to drop it again.

"Men fight men. It is the way of the world. It is corrupt and fraught with war. Nothing has changed since you arrived. You could pick a side and help win a war."

"I could, but that is not what I meant. Why are you leaving us?"

"What do you mean? I was sent to help you, and I have done that. You no longer need me. I think Vesdm would prefer it if she had you all to herself and did not need to share you with me." That came out a lot more bitter than she had intended.

"What does this have to do with her?"

"You are both dragons. She is your intended."

"She is one of my clan, as you say, a dragon, but she is not my betrothed."

"But—"

Shaking his head, Aarik took one of her hands in his. "My parents had an arranged marriage. The first time my father saw my mother, he loved her. My mother was unsure of him but fell for him soon after they were wed. Most gods don't marry, or if they do, they have lovers on the side. It is more of a political arrangement. My grandfather thought he was doing the same. And he was. My father was loyal to my grandfather and to Ane, or so I thought. When I think about it now, when both of my grandfathers disappeared, something shifted. I wish I had asked. Maybe he would have prepared me more. We lost many that day."

"I am sorry—" He pressed a finger to her lips.

"It is not your fault. The blame lies at the feet of the gods." He stepped closer. "My father and mother chose to allow their children to pick their own mates. They refused to use us for political gain or allow us to be a pawn in the games of others." His hand slid across her cheek and behind her neck. "Sevina, I choose you," he whispered a moment before he captured her lips in a heated kiss.

Gasping, Sevina opened her mouth and squeaked when Aarik's tongue brushed against hers. The only kisses she shared with men were from her father. One person tried to kiss her when she was only thirteen summers, but she punched them and pushed them to the ground. When and if she kissed a man, it would be her choice.

Her eyes closed, and she gripped his tunic, holding him close. She chose to allow it this time.

CHAPTER 7

Aarik

She had been trying to escape, to leave under cover of darkness. Did she think he would not notice? Aarik had felt anxious all day and could not sleep. Finally, unable to ease the growing panic, he left his bed, allowing his dragon, or maybe it was his heart, to guide him. They brought him to the room Sevina had taken for her own.

Seeing her packed and ready to leave physically hurt him. She had become more to him than a savior. She was his friend and his chosen one. His father had always said when Aarik found the right person, he would know. And once he stopped questioning everything and listened, he found her. She was a beacon to him, and he would always find her.

Vesdm had tried to warm his bed on more than one occasion, and he had been tempted. It had been too long since he'd had a warm body lying beside him, too long since he sank into the heat of another. Unlike before, when finding a willing woman did not bother him, he couldn't go through with it this time. Sevina had changed everything, and if he tried to replace her with someone else, the dragon within him raged.

Hearing her squeak and moan as he kissed her soothed something within him. The panic that had plagued him all day subsided. She was the balm, the only one who could calm the beast within.

But even as his dragon settled, no longer pushing him, another flame was ignited. One touch, one kiss made him want more, made him desire everything with this woman. No one else compared or would ever compare. It was hard to believe that a mere month ago, she showed up out of nowhere ready to help his clan, even while he distrusted her, preparing to rip her apart should she blink wrong. Had it only been a short time? She had gained his trust, his loyalty, and his heart—something few outside of his family ever did.

Pulling back, he stared down at the woman who had saved him and what was left of his people. Her lips were red and swollen, her cheeks flushed, and she gulped in air as if she couldn't get enough of it. It filled him with pride seeing her like this, knowing he did this to her. No other man. Him.

"Why were you leaving me?" He hadn't meant to add "me," yet he could no more stop it than he could bring back his parents and other loved ones.

"It is time." She lowered her gaze and would not look at him.

Aarik also noticed that she said it *is* time, telling him that his kiss, his declaration changed nothing. "Then we go together."

Gasping, she opened her eyes, met his, and shook her head. "No. Your people need you."

"Why do you think that?"

"Because you are family!"

He couldn't help it; he laughed. It had been a long time since he had found enough cause to laugh. "We are."

"And you need to be together."

The mirth stopped, but Aarik continued to smile. "What do you know of dragons?"

"They were gods and lived in the heavens. They often served as enforcers to the royal family, and they helped many people here."

"What else?"

"I do not understand what you ask," she huffed, wrenching herself out of his embrace to step away from him.

He let her go and crossed his arms over his chest. He did not miss the way her eyes roamed over him, down, and then back up again. "When we were gods, we had a large parcel of land. In heaven, the amount of space cannot equal that of this world. It is vast yet small. Thinking about a place and willing yourself there could move you in an instant. Short distances, long...it did not matter. Nothing equated to a long journey. It was much like how you moved us from the valley below to this temple. Blink, and you were there. Dragons had much land. For the most part, we are solitary creatures. We gather around each other for festivals, if the need arises, or if we are mated to another, but it is not a habit. More often than not, when we reach maturity, we leave home and find our own corner of our land. Eventually, when those who have survived find a place they want to claim, they will leave here."

She stood there for a minute, her brow furrowed. "Why were you together?"

"Pardon?"

"When you were attacked, why were you together?"

"We were celebrating the betrothal of Hend to...one of...Ane's daughters." Aarik felt sick. "It was a trap to get us gathered together." He swallowed hard. "It had been a lie from the beginning."

"Do you think Hend knew?"

Anger strangled him. "No!" It couldn't be. Hend had been banished with them. He was not sure why he had made that sudden assumption. If anything, Hend had been betrayed, too. He thought he had found his mate, and then it had been ripped away. Aarik could understand why Hend had gotten angry and stormed off. They had not seen nor heard from him since that day, and he wondered how his friend fared. Dragons may have been solitary creatures, but they still were tied together. Hend's bond had been broken. When Hend disappeared into the hills, leaving behind his clan and friends, it was as if he had vanished.

Aarik could feel the others, like a small flame within him, but not Hend. His flame had been vanquished. He hadn't thought much about it or tried to find it before now. It was not there. Had he survived? Did something happen to his old friend? He scratched at his chest, feeling the loss.

This was supposed to be a happy time. He had declared his intentions to his mate, and now they discussed betrayal and entrapment. And he could not forget that Sevina still planned to leave him. Glaring at her, he snarled, "I will remind you that he was banished with us. His own godhood stolen. His powers ripped away. His family murdered."

"I apologize. You are right. They would have known about the festivities because Ane and her people would have been invited."

"All of heaven received an official invitation."

"All?" She looked shocked, her eyes wider than he had ever seen them.

"We were gods. The ways of mortals are not the same." Sometimes it was still hard to believe it had all been stolen from him.

"Of course. Now, if you will excuse me..." She tried to step around him, but he blocked her, refusing to let her leave.

She narrowed her eyes, clutched her satchel even harder, and disappeared in the blink of an eye.

"What?" Reaching out to make sure he was not seeing things, he felt nothing except air and smirked.

Aarik ran out of the room and onto the balcony where he and the other dragons took flight. She stood on the edge, her body stiff. He was a little surprised she had not completely left the temple. She could have. The valley was a greater distance than her room to the balcony.

He would not allow her to get away from him. If she left, he would follow. He knew where she called home, and he would find her. "Sevina, come back."

She didn't move, and when he looked more closely, he could see that her body trembled. "Sevina?"

"She is unable to do as you ask," Hend sneered when he stepped out of the shadows into the bright moonlight. "Her life is in my hands. With a snap of my fingers, I can force her to walk over the edge to her doom. Her body will be lifeless and broken on the cliffs below."

"Hend? Explain yourself," Aarik demanded. It was as if their words from moments ago conjured his old friend, but there was something different about him. The glint in his eyes terrified Aarik, and the smile upon his face was pure evil.

"Making demands? Need I remind you that this is not heaven, and you are not lord and master of me or the others."

"Hend, what has happened? Tell me, and I can help you." Aarik felt desperate. Sevina stood inches from the edge of the balcony. One step, and she would be gone forever.

"Help me? You cannot help me. You are nothing! And because of you, neither am I."

"I do not understand what you speak of."

Throwing his hands up in the air, Hend spun around in a circle, screaming at the sky. It was guttural and held no words, but Aarik could feel the pain and anger, even if he still could not feel Hend.

His friend clutched his head and fell to his knees, pulling on the long brown strands. "You were supposed to die. We were all supposed to die. No one was supposed to survive. And now, we have nothing."

Shaking his head slowly, Aarik moved a couple of paces closer to insert himself between the madman and Sevina. "We lived. Our destiny was to live and prove to the gods that they could not best us. We can still transform and make a home here."

Hend laughed, long and loud, an eerie and maniacal sound. "She has the once-great Aarik doing her bidding? Are you her slave? Has she bent you to her will?"

"No one has or will ever command me," Aarik growled. Once he reached adulthood, his father stopped trying. Aarik always did what was expected, followed through with his duties, and made sure he showed up to all festivities when his presence was needed. Most of the time, he had no issues with his life, but occasionally, he wanted to shirk his responsibilities and...live as a human. Maybe his whimsical sometimes wishes were the reason they had been banished and why his people were suffering right now. "Why have you come back? How did you find this place?"

"She hasn't told you?"

"Told me what? Stop speaking in riddles before I rip your throat out!" Aarik sucked in a breath, scarcely believing those words had come from his own mouth.

Hend threw his head back and laughed again. "She needed a dragon scale to get here. Did she not?"

Narrowing his eyes, Aarik nodded, ready to strike down the dragon he once thought of as a brother. "She did."

"Dragons can find it without that scale. We are covered with them. This was created to be a safe haven for any dragon when the time came. Your grandfather and your father prepared for this eventuality because they could see it coming. But not the mighty Aarik. I was supposed to be their champion, the next to rule the dragons. They promised me!"

"Who promised? What did they promise?"

"It was so perfect. They would get rid of you and your father, and then I would marry Agafya. With her by my side, I would rule the dragons into the future. But they ruined it. Your father fought. Your grandfather, who has been missing for eons, appeared, and your mother got in the way."

Aarik's head was spinning. Hend knew they were going to be attacked? "You helped to slaughter our own? What about your parents? Your sister?"

"They weren't supposed to die! Only you and yours!" Hend snapped.

"What are you doing here?" Aarik had to remain calm. Sevina's life and those of his clan depended on it. Everything he did had to be calculated, and he had to find an opening. Right now, Hend was too unpredictable. "You were free of us. Why come back?"

"Did you know I prayed to Ane? I begged her and Agafya to take me back. To make me a god again. I was not supposed to fall with you. I didn't fight at your side. No, I slit your mother's throat with the weapon Ane gave me. Not even gods can survive the blade."

Clenching his hands into fists, sheer willpower was the only thing that kept Aarik rooted to his spot. He wanted to reach in and rip the heart out of this madman. This is not the Hend he grew up with, the one he confided in and loved as a brother. "My mother?" he choked out.

"It was so easy. She fought beside your father but was knocked to the ground. In the chaos and confusion, I pressed the blade to her throat and dragged it across her skin. Her silver blood poured out, and then she disappeared," Hend cackled. "Maybe they did favor me some because I can still make that woman suffer for your crimes."

With speed he didn't know he possessed, Aarik was on him, and before Hend realized what was happening, Aarik pressed his claws into Hend's chest, crushing bones as he went, and squeezed. The lunatic's mouth dropped open, and the light in his eyes faded. He was dead.

Pulling his hand out, it was covered with the silver blood of the gods with flecks of red mixed in. "They didn't abandon you completely, but you stopped believing in them, yourself, and your clan. I hope you find peace, my friend."

A sound somewhere between a moan and a cry caught Aarik's attention, and he spun around, searching for the next threat. He found nothing. Only Sevina. She had fallen to her knees and wrapped her arms around herself, clutching her own shoulders. The small distance between them did nothing to hide how her body shook.

He ran to her and pulled her into his arms. "It is over. He can no longer hurt you."

"I...I couldn't leave you. I tried."

"It will be all right." He hoped she meant she was unable to leave him because she felt the same way he did, instead of whatever tricks Hend used to hold her body captive mere moments ago.

She lifted her head and met his gaze, her body shuddering with a sob. "Why do you not hate me?"

Aarik smiled and brushed away the tears that fell from her eyes. "Because I care too much about you to hate you. Did you not hear me earlier? I chose you for my mate. You *are* my mate. I can love no other. It now must be your decision. But know this, I will protect you and keep you from harm until my last breath." He meant every word. Seeing her standing there, on the edge of the balcony, and knowing Hend had done something to her, had twisted his guts. He would have given his own life to save hers.

CHAPTER 8

Sevina

It had been Sevina's intent to leave the temple the moment she left Aarik's side, and as soon as she did, her heart cried out at the loss. She loved Aarik, but he was destined for so much more. Another dragon would make a better mate. One of his own kind. Everything within her told her that was wrong. Instead of disappearing completely, she found herself standing on the balcony, on the precipice of a monumental decision.

Something happened. It was like she was cold and frozen, unable to move, but it was more than that. Whatever held her felt like it was draining her and squeezing the very life from her. She would not last long and wondered if this was it. If her choice had been decided for her, her life forfeit because she dared leave her dragon.

The moment she heard his voice, she knew everything would be all right. Aarik would save her and break whatever sorcery held her prisoner. Hend's voice had sent ice through her veins.

Sniffling, she shook her head and once again dropped her gaze, refusing to look at him. "I intended to leave you here, but instead of going home, I stopped on the balcony, afraid to go further. I was there but a moment when Hend cursed me. I could not move. Could not do anything. I was so scared." She lifted her gaze to his, a small smile pulling at her lips. "But when you spoke, calling my name, I knew all would be well." Aarik blocked her view, but still, she tried to see beyond him, both afraid and curious about what she would find.

"He is no longer of this realm."

"What do you mean?"

"His spirit has moved on."

She had known that, known his body lay lifeless just beyond Aarik, yet hearing that brought a conflict of emotion. She was relieved and happy that he could not hurt her or anyone else, but at the same time, her heart hurt for Aarik and the others. This was one of their brethren, someone they loved. And now they had lost him a second time.

"He brought this on himself," Aarik stated with so much power and conviction in his voice she tilted her head back and met his gaze, studying his eyes. There was a fire and determination that had been lost when she had met them in the valley below.

"What—" Ossenia began but stopped and hissed. When Sevina looked at her, Ossenia was staring at the lifeless body of Hend. "Oh, Hend, what did you do?" She sank to her knees, her shoulders slumping and strands of her long blonde hair blowing in the breeze.

"He believed he was forsaken. His rage and bitterness blinded him. Maybe 'tis what the gods wanted," Aarik spoke before Sevina could. "Call the others. They must know what happened."

"Can't we just take him away?" Ossenia asked, her sad eyes searching his.

Shaking his head, Aarik said, "No. I will not keep secrets from them. There have been enough secrets and pain to last several lifetimes."

"There are only nine of us now," Ossenia whispered as she got up and stumbled a little. Aarik reached out for her, but she righted herself before he could stand. "Nine dragons in existence. We were once many, but now we are few."

"We will flourish again," Aarik declared, staring into Sevina's eyes.

Sevina could not hold his heated gaze for more than a second or two and dropped her head to look at his chest. Her blush burned her skin from the top of her head to the toes on her feet. Nothing escaped, but it wasn't only from embarrassment. It was something deeper, more exciting. It made her pulse quicken, and her heart beat furiously. It made her gulp in air and rub her thighs together. A fire had been stoked in her stomach, and she had never experienced anything like this before. A dead man lay feet from her, and all she could think about was the kiss in her bedroom.

Ossenia's words broke through her haze, "Congratulations, brother. I believe you are right." When Sevina glanced at her, she could see a sad smile gracing the other woman's lips.

In the hours that followed, calamity reined. Sevina and Aarik were not together more than a few moments at a time. The others were shocked, some outraged that Hend lay dead on the balcony, but once Aarik explained what happened, they calmed down and accepted it. Still, they were not happy because they had lost one of their own.

The body was wrapped in blankets and linens, and then one by one, the dragons took flight, Aarik lifting and taking the body with them, leaving Sevina at the temple alone. She knew he feared she would not be there when he returned, and she was tempted to leave again, but she could not. Leaving him would be a knife to her heart.

Hours later, as the sun crested over the mountains, lighting up the valley, the dragons returned quietly, the body of their comrade no longer with them. From the time they left until they landed on the balcony, she waited for them, sitting with her back against one of the walls close to the temple entrance. Ulrik landed first, shifted, and dressed before he trudged into the temple, not saying a word, merely nodding when he passed.

One by one, they landed, transformed, and moved inside, only acknowledging her with a tilt of their head. Nothing more.

Aarik landed last, dressed, and walked over to her on bare feet. She had long ago gotten used to seeing their naked flesh, even if her face still burned with embarrassment. "Are you all right?" she asked softly.

He sighed, releasing a long, loud breath. "We are."

"Where...?" She didn't know how to finish her question. She was curious about what they did with Hend's body yet did not want to intrude. Growing up in a temple, there were always rituals and words that needed to be spoken when a human died. Was it the same for dragons? Or were they at a loss because they were no longer in the place they called home?

Aarik pulled her into his warm body and wrapped his arms around her, breathing in her scent. "As gods, we could die, but it was hard to kill us. Many would choose when to...disappear. My grandfather was one. I do not know what happened when someone disappeared. I thought they died too, but my grandfather was there the day the others came for us. I would like to believe it is another place, better than heaven."

"That is a nice thought." She hugged him back, trying to give him all the comfort she could.

"We took him to a place I knew about. My father used to say it was one of the places on earth closest to heaven. We stood over him as dragons and lit him on fire. I hope he finds his way home and some peace."

"He was not always like this. He used to laugh and wanted nothing more than to help those around him. Maybe not humans, but other dragons. He was close with this family, with my siblings and me."

"Love does things to men."

"It does. I would fight anyone, friend or foe, to protect you."

Happiness and sadness warred within her. She felt guilty that he had to kill one of his own to save her because she knew Hend would not have stopped until he had thrown her over the edge to her death. "Aarik—"

He stopped her by placing a finger against her lips. "You are my mate, even if you never accept me. I will do anything to ensure your safety. Never feel guilty or upset by that. It is my decision and my decision alone."

"I do accept you, Aarik. I do not understand why you chose me, but I cannot deny my heart any more than I can my gifts."

Holding her even more tightly against him, he grabbed her hair with one hand and pulled, tilting her head back. He plundered her mouth, his tongue wrapping with hers as she thrust her hips against his thigh. She could not get enough, and the longer he touched her, the hotter she got, her body seeking something but not understanding what that could be.

"Come." He took her hand and dragged her into the temple to her room, the furthest from the others, not that it would stop anyone from hearing. Dragons could hear better than the dogs her father had.

Together, they went and shut the rest of the world out as they completed their bond and sealed their promises of forever. Her dragon had fallen from heaven, afraid, hurt, and angry, but through his hardships, the dragon inside had awakened and, with her love, made him whole again.

The End.

About the Author

Maria Vickers is a bestselling author of both gay and straight romance and currently resides in St. Louis, MO, with her pug, Hunny. She has always had a passion for writing, and after she became disabled in 2010, she decided to use writing as her escape. She firmly believes that life is about what you make of it, you have to live it to the fullest no matter the circumstances. Getting sick may have changed her life forever, but it also opened doors she thought would always be out of reach.

Follow her here: AuthorMariaVickers.blogspot.com

Website:

Newsletter

Join her reader group,
Maria's Love Seekers

ALSO BY MARIA VICKERS

www.AuthorMariaVickers.blogspot.com

MF Novels

Exposed: Book One of the Love Seekers

Desperate Desires

Flirtatious Flyboy

Rock the Boat

MM Novels

By the Book

Off-Campus Setup

Unbreak Me

Somebody 2 Love

AFTERWORD

The Shifting Magic authors trust you enjoyed reading our collection of short stories. Please consider telling a friend, sharing on social media, or posting a review.

I love reading all types of fiction. Cross-pollinating Shifter & Mages, Sci-Fi Fantasy, and Paranormal Romance under the anthology umbrella allow readers to experience new work in our writer showcase. Most readers may prefer one genre over the other, but avid readers of romance will venture out to experience different writing styles.

Our heroines and heroes are often fraught with twists, turns, and harrowing experiences, but in the end, our readers crave the *Happily Ever After* ending.

I thank our authors for writing unique, original, and creative stories. Don't forget to register for the authors' newsletter to keep abreast of new releases, special pricing, freebies, and giveaways.

May love light the way!

D. L. Jones
AUTHOR